BAR-HOPPING

The first jump had been to London, and we'd stayed there about five months, during the war. That was when Fred had started letting us live right in Feng's. Then we'd been hit again and found ourselves on a lunar colony that hadn't existed when we were hit—we'd gone about six years into the future and landed in the middle of another atomic war. We were only there a few days, three, I think, before we were hit, and we found ourselves twenty years in the future, on Mars, and there was a nuclear alert in the city . . .

Two days later, *ker-blam*.

"Steven Brust isn't afraid to stretch the boundaries of contemporary fantasy."
—**Newsday**

Ace Books by Steven Brust

STEVEN BRUST, PJF

COWBOY FENG'S SPACE BAR AND GRILLE

ACE BOOKS, NEW YORK

This book is an Ace original edition,
and has never been previously published.

COWBOY FENG'S SPACE BAR AND GRILLE

An Ace Book / published by arrangement with
the author

PRINTING HISTORY
Ace edition / January 1990

ISBN: 0-441-11816-X

Ace Books are published by The Berkley Publishing Group,
200 Madison Avenue, New York, New York 10016.
The name "ACE" and the "A" logo are trademarks
belonging to Charter Communications, Inc.

PRINTED IN THE UNITED STATES OF AMERICA

10 9 8 7 6 5 4 3 2 1

This book is dedicated to my children:
Corwin, Aliera, Carolyn;
and to Toni, who doesn't have one yet.

ACKNOWLEDGMENTS

My sincere thanks to Emma Bull, Kara Dalkey, Pamela Dean, Will Shetterly, and Terri Windling, who helped with the manuscript in its various stages.

My thanks also to David Dyer-Bennet for assistance with firearms information, and to Beth Friedman and Betsy Pucci for medical information.

Finally, for the music, a few of those to whom I am indebted are: Bedlam Rose, Boiled In Lead, The Clancy Brothers & Tommy Makem, Gallowglass, Fred Haskell, Raven's Tir, Mark Soderstrom, Dave Van Ronk, and The Weavers.

CHAPTER
1

I've been a wild rover
For many a year.
**"The Wild Rover,"
Traditional**

Cowboy Feng's Space Bar and Grille has the best matzo ball soup in the galaxy. Lots of garlic, matzo balls with just the right consistency to absorb the flavor, big chunks of chicken, and the whole of it seasoned to a biting perfection. One bowl, along with maybe a couple of tamales, will usually do for a meal.

As for entertainment, Feng gets some of the best Irish musicians you'll ever hear—good instrumental backing, fine singing, some stupendous fiddle playing, and driving energy. Hell, some of the songs are actually Irish.

I was there that Thursday, sitting in my favorite booth—back middle, just under the picture of the big, grinning Chinese fellow with the mustache and the cowboy hat—while I waited for the rest of my band, the Jig-Makers, to finish tuning. It's my favorite booth because you can see the whole dining room to your right and most of the taproom to your left, and you get a great view of the stage.

We weren't playing tonight, but Fred, the manager, let us use the stage to practice. The place used to have live music every Wednesday and Thursday, as well as on the weekends, but it didn't pay, so Fred canceled it. He was the practical sort; not me, I'm sentimental. This has caused me any number of difficulties, but there it is. My other problem is that I'm easily distracted. Sorry about that. Where was I? Oh, yeah. Thursday. Which reminds me: Did you hear the one about how, after the nuclear attack, the town of Sanctuary, Venus, had to change its name? To Sanctuary, Jupiter? Anyway, Thursday was the day someone lobbed an atomic warhead at Jerrysport, Mars, and reduced it to rubble.

It was damned uncomfortable when the bomb hit; we must have been within a mile or so of ground zero. If we'd been much closer that would have been it for us, and I might never have found out what goats are really useful for, but it wasn't, so I did and maybe I'll tell you. In any case, I was knocked to the floor, and then I rolled and something fell on me and I blacked out for a while. It hurt to wake up again, but I didn't mind too much, since I was having a confused dream about Irish ghosts and they all looked like geeks.

Fully conscious, I decided I wasn't injured, since a headache doesn't count as an injury. Diffuse, pale light came in through the frosted windows high on what had been the west wall when the place was built and the north wall in Ibrium City and the south wall in London and Jerrysport. The room contained vast quantities of ambient dust. I thought about my band over in the taproom, but they were safer there than I was here, as long as the pool tables didn't start flying around. I was pleased I remembered them; one effect the jump has, we've learned, is disorientation, to a greater or lesser degree. I'm not sure why. After the first one, it took me a few days to remember even the most basic things, and a month later there were still bits and pieces coming back. And with the jostling we'd gotten lately, it was bound to be pretty bad.

I pulled myself up to a sitting position and looked around. Fortunately or unfortunately, there had been no customers in the place, but that wasn't surprising, as I've found that business always slacks off when there's a nuclear alert in a city.

Someone said, "You all right, Billy?"

Billy? I blinked twice. Yeah, that was me. I looked for the voice, and spotted a likely-looking pile of debris—likely-looking mostly because it was moving. I stood up, decided I weighed more than I should, and sat down. I tried again, took a couple of deep breaths, and helped remove a table, tablecloth, and part of a booth from Rich Vonderick, who had a neatly trimmed beard, a bear-like build, and the personality of a rabid crocodile on Valium.

"I'm fine," I told him. "You look a bit dusty, though."

"Yeah?" he said. "What could have caused that?" This was irony.

"Something about an atomic warhead, I think." So was this.

"Yeah," he said. Then, suddenly, "Eve!"

"She's in back," I said quickly. "I saw her just a minute or two before it hit."

"Oh." He relaxed. "Okay."

See that? I had trouble remembering who I was, but had no trouble remembering who Eve was, or where I'd just seen her. Fascinating thing, the mind. I said, "Glad you were here."

"You, too."

I snorted. "I'm not going to get left behind; I have too much to do."

"Like what?"

"Uhh . . . ask me tomorrow."

"Right." He looked like he might be about to argue, but instead said, "Where are we?" as if I'd know.

"We'll find out," I told him. "When the place opens for business. Got your tool kit?"

"Always," he said, glancing around and spotting it. "Why?"

"It'll probably be useful in getting the lights working."

He nodded. "Any idea who else made it through?" There was a certain amount of tension in his voice; we've both known people who happened not to be in the restaurant at the right time.

I said, "I'm pretty sure everyone did."

"Good," said Rich. "In that case, how about if we ask Libby for a drink?"

"Drink?" said someone behind me. I turned around in time to see a short, pretty, dark-haired woman walking in from the taproom.

"Hey, sis," I said. "How is everything?" A moment later it occurred to me that she wasn't really my sister; I just called her that.

"Hi, Rose," said Rich. "How do you feel?" Rose. That was it.

"I need whiskey," she said.

"How's the band?" said Rich.

"Jamie broke a D-string and the bridge on my fiddle collapsed and Tommy lost his last pick and we can't find the tipper for the bodhran and I need whiskey." She blinked twice by way of punctuation.

I said, "But all the instruments are okay, right?"

She cocked her head to the side and said, "If the instruments weren't okay d'you suppose I'd be so calm?"

"Damn," said Rich, who only pretended not to like our music. I think.

I said to Rose, "You aren't scared or anything, are you?"

"Noooo," she said patiently. "I just need whiskey." Then she frowned. "I couldn't hear at first, though, and that scared me. And it sounds like you're talking through a tunnel, although it isn't as bad as it was a few minutes ago. And I forgot where this room was for a minute."

"It's the jump," said Rich. "My vision keeps going in and out. It probably will for a few days yet."

"Whiskey will help," said Rose confidently.

I went up to the hole in the wall where waitresses got drinks. Then I turned back and said, "Libby isn't here. She was probably in back or something when it hit. I hope she's—"

"I'll look," said Rich.

"Nothing can happen to Libby," explained Rose patiently. "She wouldn't allow it."

I tended to agree with her, though I couldn't say so. At that moment, however, I heard her in the kitchen calling to Fred to get the power switches. I felt tension go out of my shoulders. Then I wondered where the power switches were and it bothered me that I couldn't remember. I closed my eyes and saw my hand reaching to open a metal box—right. Top of the stairs, back of the kitchen. I opened my eyes.

"What is it, Billy?"

"Nothing. No need to stand on ceremony." I shuffled around to the bar and came up with a bottle of Jameson, passed it to Rosie, sat down.

"Thanks," she said, cracked it, and swallowed some, and closed her eyes. A beatific smile lit her face. Then she came up behind me, still holding the bottle, put her arms around my neck, and kissed my cheek. "We were worried about you. We didn't know where you were when the bomb hit."

"I was in here waiting for you guys to tune, as usual."

"Ohhhh," she said, and kissed me again. "You could have asked about the rest of your band."

"If anyone had been hurt, you wouldn't have been so calm."

She nodded. Then, "You know," she said in a reflective tone of voice, "getting nuked all the time is really bad for our practice schedule."

Rich held out his hand. Rosie put the bottle in it and he took a hit, passed it back, at which point Eve came in. Rich stood up and they held each other for a while. She was short, with long, straight hair that must be called "fair" rather than "blond." It was a touching sort of scene, the two of them standing there, broken by Jamie's voice from the next room, calling, "Rooose!"

She turned her head so she wasn't yelling into my ear and called back, "Yes, dairlin'?"

"I need smokes!"

"Coming, dairlin'."

She kissed my cheek again and sashayed back into the taproom. I walked over to the waitress stand and got coffee started. Rich raised his head from Eve's shoulder and said, "Want to look around outside?"

I said, "You crazy, Charlie?"

"Why not?"

"How do you know we aren't going to be hit again?"

He shrugged. "How do you know we are?"

I shrugged. "Maybe later," I said.

"Oh, c'mon. Aren't you curious about where we landed? And when?"

"Yeah. But either I'll have plenty of time to look around, or there's no point in it." He had made me curious, however, so I went over to one of the windows and pulled the heavy blinds aside. It was daylight, and we seemed to be in a light commercial district—if this time and place made those distinctions. There was a great deal of variety in style and size of structures, but, judging by a pair of preteen boys who were locking their bicycles and a middle-aged couple who were walking by, the people looked like people. This was good. I was always afraid we'd end up somewhere with one-eyed, green-scaled monsters who eat radios or something. Just people, though. Two women walked by, arm in arm. At the time and place I had left, they wouldn't have done this. In London they would have, but it wouldn't have had any significance. In Ibrium City it would have meant they were lesbians. In Jerrysport it meant even less than it had in London. What the hell.

No one was looking at Feng's, though, which was good even if expected. I'll never know how that's done, but let the record show that I'm curious. The kids finished locking their bicycles (I made a note of the fact that bicycle locks were used) and went into the building directly across the street from us. It showed every sign of being a bakery. I hoped it was a good bakery, so Feng's would carry fresh bread like we had in Ibrium City. My mouth watered as I remembered that crusty sourdough from the—

The place that was now radioactive dust. Great. Isn't it fun how you always remember the right sort of stuff?

Presently Rich stood next to me and watched for a while. I said, "I think I'll go see how my band is doing, maybe do a tune or two, then I'll worry about the outside."

"Okay." He looked down at Eve and said, "How 'bout it?"

She nodded, her head still buried in his shoulder. I wondered if she wanted to see the outside, or just didn't want to be separated from Rich. He said, "I'm glad I put the bike in the back hall this morning. Was that this morning? Never mind."

I said, "Going to get the power working first?"

"Yep."

"Good," I said, moving toward the taproom. "Have fun."

Big, blond, bearded Jamie was smoking a cigarette and holding a dustpan while Rose swept shards of glass into it. Tom, tall and very skinny with fair hair and scraggly beard, was blotting the floor with a bar towel.

My instrument was, indeed, still in its case next to the table. I sat down and hauled out banjo and tuner, plugged the one into the other, and tuned to an open G. I had a moment of panic that I'd have lost this skill, at least temporarily, but I guess only my head was affected, not my fingers.

Jamie said, "Shouldn't we help get, uh, this place in shape?"

"Feng's," said Tom.

"Yes, we should," I said. "But I'm not going to. Not until I've done a couple of tunes."

"All right," said Jamie. "What should we play?"

"Something we already know," said Rose.

"Good idea," I said, "since all of our music is probably buried under three tons of flour in the back room."

Tom said, "We could go back there and play flower music."

Jamie said, "You're so weird."

Fred came strolling through the taproom, turning off lights that didn't work, I suppose in preparation for restoring power. He said, "I trust everyone survived the experience?"

"Uh-huh," said Jamie.

I heard sounds in the next room that were probably Libby taking care of this and that.

I picked up the banjo, feeling just a bit guilty, and said, "'Beggarman.'"

Jamie said, "Right."

Tom said, "Maybe we're so far in the future they don't have beggars anymore. Then we can't play it."

Jamie said, "You're so weird."

I hitched the capo up another two frets, slipped the fifth string under the nail, checked the tuning again, adjusted it. Then I said, "One . . . two . . . one, two, three, four—" And we did it. It's our own arrangement, three times through the whole thing, bumping the speed each time, with a vocal verse the first and second. It's a good warm-up tune. I blew the first run-through of the "a" part at top speed, but that was okay. By the time we were done, we were all much calmer. Just about that moment the lights came on.

"Yea," I said.

We played about another half dozen tunes, then Tom put his mandolin down and announced, "I'm hungry," as if he were amazed that this could happen.

"So am I," said Jamie.

"I could eat," said Rose.

"Yeah," I said. "Me, too. I guess that means we ought to find out what we can do to get the kitchen working. I'll ask the Fred unit." I sighed, knowing that this meant I was about to be put to work. Nor was I wrong.

An hour of hard labor later, Fred joined us at the table, one arm protectively around Libby, who needed protecting like I needed a pet armadillo. Fred was thin, quiet, and nowhere near as dull as he looked. In addition to being cook and waiter, he was de facto manager of the place, and, according to Jamie's theory, was someone who actually spoke with the semi-mythical Feng himself. Libby was of medium height and buxom and exuberant and charming. She said, "So, what a fun place this is. Someone should find if they still have Hags disease so we'll know whether to put pancakes and flounder on the menu." Fred and I chuckled.

Jamie said, "That reminds me. I got this from, uh, I don't remember. Some guy in Jerrysport. Watch." He stood up and stomped on the floor, like, stomp stomp, wait, stomp stomp, wait. "You know what that is? CPR for a Hags victim."

Jamie thought this very funny. So did Rose. Actually Libby and Fred chuckled, too. There's no accounting for taste.

Speaking of taste, we were all eating gyros and saganaki with baby peas in vinegar when Rich and Eve came back in, wrapped around each other as usual. We turned and stared at them. Eve was smiling and Rich had that glow in his face that he gets after a wild motorcycle ride.

"Well?" I said. "What's it like?"

They sat down at the table with us, and Rich said, "What can I say? I laughed. I cried. I fell down. It changed my life. It was good. The end."

"Thanks," said Jamie.

"Does that mean we're at the end of the universe?" asked Tom.

"What's the place like?" I said.

Rich smiled happily. "I don't think we're in the same solar system anymore," he said.

There was a great deal of quiet all of a sudden. Tom said, "Well, really, what's a star or two among friends?"

I said, "Did you get funny looks, riding the bike around?"

"A few," he said. "Not many."

Jamie said, "How odd is it?"

"The bike?" said Tom.

"The sky's funny," said Rich. "It's great. You should go look at it."

Jamie gave an exaggerated shudder, which he did well. He was very big, and much too handsome for his own good.

Tom said, "What kind of movies do they have here?"

Rich ignored him. I said, "Man, you're weird."

"That's Jamie's line," said Tom.

"*Man*," said Jamie.

Rich said, "The big news is that I didn't see any signs of nuclear warnings, or alerts, or anything. We might be here for a while."

"Good," I said, and meant it. "I've been needing to be somewhere solid for more than—however long we were in Jerrysport."

"I know," said Rich and Libby together.

"About this sky," said Rose.

"Yeah," said Rich, his eyes shining. "It's like, really high, and sort of pale, and there's a kind of white-looking sun in it. It might be a white dwarf, I don't know anything about astronomy. But it makes the ground look—"

"What are the buildings like?" asked Jamie.

"Go and look," said Rich.

Eve broke her customary silence long enough to say, in an almost inaudible voice, "There's one that looks like a giant golden arch, and we were going to ask if we could get hamburgers there, but it turned out to be too far away."

Rich smiled a Mephistophelian smile within his beard and sat down at the table next to Eve. Fred went back to get him some food. Libby said, "I could see looking around myself, if you macho types aren't going to wimp out."

"Oh," said Jamie. "A challenge. I think I hear a challenge."

"A touch," said Tom. "I do confess—"

"Come on," said Rich. "Let's do some exploring."

"If we stay here, will we be *in*ploring?" asked Tom.

At which point the first customers of the new location walked in, wearing that first-time-at-a-new-restaurant look. The guy's hair was done in that puffy-in-front style that we'd just left in Jerrysport, and he had orthopedic clogs on his feet and tight straight-legged dark pants with a loose dark shirt. His companion had a miniskirt and high black boots that made me think of the Beatles. I decided I was going to like this place.

They took a corner booth. Libby got up to go back to the bar in case they ordered drinks. A few surreptitious glances at the customers told me that they weren't making surreptitious glances at us, which meant we didn't look too out of place, so that was good.

Jamie, keeping his voice low, said, "Well, Rich, did you find out the name of the city?"

"No. I get the impression that it's a colony world, though. There seems to be quite a bit of off-planet export."

"That doesn't prove anything," said Jamie. "Why didn't you get the name?"

Rich blinked. "Can you imagine walking up to someone and—"

"Yeah, I see your point. Did you find out what year it is?"

"Local year sixty-one," he said.

"Did you find out when the colony was founded?"

"No."

"Or how long the local year is?"

"No."

"Well, that's real useful," said Jamie.

Rich said something not very nice to Jamie, and I cut in before things could get worse, saying, "You didn't get any indication of when we are compared to where we were? Um, when we were. I mean, you know what I mean."

He shrugged. "Transportation technology hasn't changed much. Like I said, my bike didn't get too many stares. They do have one thing I haven't seen before, though." He got the I've-found-a-new-toy gleam in his eye, reached into his back pocket, and pulled out what looked like a socket wrench.

I sighed. "All right. Where'd you find it?"

"A sale in a hardware store. I traded the electric ratchet press for it."

"The one that got you so excited you couldn't stop talking about it?"

"I never got it to press evenly. The guy up the street likes playing with broken things even more than I do."

I sighed and nodded. "Okay." I looked at the object in his hand again. "What does it do?"

He told me.

I said, "What?"

He tried again.

I said, "Never mind. I'm sure it's important. Is it for the bike?"

"Hmmm," he said. "I hadn't thought of that. I could probably use it to—"

"I don't want to hear about it."

He sighed. "Nobody speaks electronics, nobody speaks motor-cycle."

Which reminded me of something. I said, "Do they speak English here?"

"Some. Most people speak French."

"It's Canadian French," said Eve quietly.

"Great," I said. "Do any of us speak it? Except Eve, of course."

"Fred speaks some French," said Jamie.

"Good," I said. "He can take orders, at least." I gave a listen to Fred and the couple who'd come in, and, yeah, it did seem like French. They were pointing at the menu and Fred seemed to be smiling and nodding. Maybe they thought a menu in English was an affectation.

"Should we practice?"

"Speaking French?" asked Tom.

"Sure," said Jamie, ignoring Tom.

Rose said, "I don't believe I could do that right now."

"Why not?" I asked, trying to keep irritation out of my voice.

"I don't think I feel quite like playing, just at the moment."

I caught Tom's eye. He shrugged. "All right," I said. I got up and went into the back room, opened up the case, and put my banjo into double-C tuning. While I was doing that, Tom came in and picked up Jamie's Gibson six-string. His movements were quick and precise. Tom was built tall and thin; something like Fred only more so—he always looked a bit emaciated, whereas Fred just looked skinny. Tom's hair and beard were light, whereas Fred's hair was dark, and he had the sort of fine skin that made one think he would be unable to grow a beard.

While we were checking our tunings, Tom said, "Do you know that all of our instruments are antiques now?"

"Scary," I said. " 'Arkansas Traveler'?"

"All right. Start it."

Then we were lost for a while in melody and countermelody and variations, and the sweet sound of strings. Every time we came back to the start, I moved further up the neck, and Tom made his part more Baroque, throwing in frills and rolls that ranged from old-timey to rock 'n' roll. At one point I heard someone give a "whoop" and I wondered who it was, but my eyes were closed by then and I couldn't spare the concentration to open them. I started double-thumbing and Tom starting doing tremolo like he was playing mandolin and we blew it out the top, came all the way back, and ran through it once in its simplest, most basic form, and ended together on a bluegrass lick that I don't think either of us had planned.

When I opened my eyes, Libby was there, grinning at us and practically emitting sparks. She laughed and shook her head. "You guys were really plugged."

"It felt all right," I said. God, aren't we modest?

Tom was doing his down-home hick smile.

Jamie came in and joined us, along with Rose. Apparently Jamie had spoken to her, because she picked up her fiddle, looking only a little sullen. We practiced until about three in the morning, then crashed on the floor in back, as we had every night for the past—how long? Two weeks, maybe? Several hundred years? Depends how you count it.

The first jump had been to London, and we'd stayed there about five months, during the war. That was when Fred had started letting us live right in Feng's. Then we'd been hit again and found ourselves on a lunar colony that hadn't existed when we were hit—we'd gone about six years into the future and landed in the middle of another atomic war. We were only there a few days, three, I think, before we were hit, and we found ourselves another twenty years in the future, on Mars, and there was a nuclear alert in the city. Two days later, *ker-blam,* and here we were.

Before I fell asleep, Jamie rolled over and said, "Hey, bror?"

"Yeah?"

"Do you have any idea what this is about?"

"The wars?"

"Well, no. Yes. I don't know. We walk into a restaurant, get hit by a bomb, and—"

"Get thrown through time and space?"

"Yeah."

"Don't be ridiculous. It could never happen."

"Yeah." He turned over. Tom started snoring. Rose, between Jamie and me, shifted. Jamie said, "Do you believe in God?"

"No," I said.

"I don't mean necessarily the—"

"I know what you mean," I said.

"But, look, I don't mean to sound all mystical, but why were we spared?"

"Maybe we were in the right place at the right time, is all."

"But what is it about this place—"

"Ah-ha," I said. "Now, *that* is just the question I've been trying to figure out. I do not believe that a supreme being or a primal life force or a great energy pool has singled us out to play Irish music to the cosmos. But there is *something* about this place that makes it bounce when nuclear weapons hit it."

"Yeah," said Jamie. "I want to know what it is."

"When you find out," I said, yawning, "tell me."

"I will," he said.

I wanted to ask him if he meant he'd tell me, or that he'd find out, but I don't remember doing so, so I must have fallen asleep.

Intermezzo

We're all met together here,
     To sit and to crack
With our glasses in our hands
          And our work upon our back.
**"The Work of the Weavers,"
Traditional**

"How did I end up with this job?"

"Via linguistics, same as I did. We don't need translators for any of this stuff."

"You sure about that? What, by the Grand Banana, *is* all this shit, anyway?"

"Look at it."

"I *am* looking at it. *The Godfather. Potempkin. Mutiny on the Bounty. Star Wars. Magic Incorporated. Chinatown. Butch Cassidy and the Sundance Kid. Who Framed—*"

"They're motion pictures. Entertainment. Just like—"

"I know that. But—"

"And the ones over there were reproduced from audio discs. Music that was popular at the time. Those, under the table, were from written works. Novels, newspapers, magazines, that sort of thing."

"It can't be all we have from the period."

"Not quite, but damn close."

"And we have to go through all of it?"

"There will be twelve of us by the time everyone gets here. We have to go through as much as we can in twenty hours. Then we rest for eight, and meet and try to put together a passable facade, for which we have forty hours."

"What's the hurry?"

"Got me. It's supposed to be something important, though."

"I don't believe that, in twenty hours, we can absorb enough about a vanished culture to fool those who live there."

"I'll bet we can come close, and Feng will probably be able to deal with any gaps after—"

"Why don't we just get some people to have overlays? That way—"

"Are you volunteering?"

"Umm, no—"

"Besides, it takes more than fifty hours to prepare, plus eight or nine to recover. That wouldn't give us anywhere near enough time."

"It's crazy, isn't it? Twelve of us are supposed to create a building that will pass for Old Earth of half a millennium ago, right down to pictures on the wall, construction, technology, with no anachronisms, in sixty-eight hours? We don't even know what kind of place it should be. A business? A house? What?"

"We'd better get started, hadn't we?"

"This is crazy."

"You might enjoy it. What I'm doing here is one of the best ways to learn about the culture, and I'm enjoying it."

"You would. All right. I might as well. Hit Play for me, would ya? Thanks. Hmmm. Who the hell was Clint Eastwood, anyway?"

"Got me. What's a five-letter word for 'Dr. George, or city north of Bismarck?' "

"Maps and bios are in the cupboard. Hand me some popcorn, would ya?"

CHAPTER
2

Jenny, lass, ye stole me heart.
Fol de rol the day-o.
Ye may have it, or any other part,
Fol de rol the day.

"Jenny Say You're Mine,"
William Kevely

Feng's always opened for business within a few hours, subjectively, after a bombing, and no one on the outside seemed surprised. It was as if, well, imagine that you're riding your bicycle or whatever down some street that you've been going down for years and years, and all of sudden you go, "Hey, that looks like an interesting place. I wonder why I've never noticed it before. Maybe I'll stop in and see how the food is." Well, that's what it was like, it seems, for everyone who went by. For those of us on the inside, you understand, it was a bit different. When we were in London we hired some locals to help out, but, until New Quebec, we didn't stay anywhere else long enough to do any more than minimum business; three days is insufficient to build up a base of regulars. Some of the locals were pretty decent people, too; there was a real nice guy named Willie whom we picked up in London and left in Jerrysport. This was one of the things that made me so skittish about leaving Feng's.

Electrical service was probably the trickiest part. Rich took care of that. Back in the States, we used 110/120-volt AC outlets. Then, in London, it was 220. In Ibrium City they'd gone to a reverse-ground switched-current arrangement, and in Jerrysport they used Broadcast Variable Direct from solar collectors. Our band quickly gave up trying to get any of our electronic equipment to work, but Feng's just kept right on going, with hardly a pause to get the lights on.

You want to know how it ran? Well, Fred and Eve switched off doing the cooking and waiting tables, mostly Fred. Tom and Jamie and Rose and I pitched in when and as we were needed, in exchange for our accommodations, and because Fred didn't want to hire outside help. It was a pretty small place, too, and with Libby running the bar herself, it wasn't much of a problem most of the time. In fact, by the time we had a few regulars, which took a few days, we were all into the routine pretty well. We were still short on supplies, but had begun to get ideas on where to get them. The hardest thing was adjusting to it being Monday again when we were all set for Friday. But that sort of thing, too, we were pretty used to.

"Business," Rich remarked when Friday finally rolled around, "seems pretty good."

The two of us were in the pantry cleaning up blankets and making a list of things to find a local supplier for quickly. "Good," I said. "Light bulbs. I think our fixtures will hold what they're using."

"They will; I've checked. And we should find out if humanity has yet devised a good way of cleaning a grill."

"Yep. Local whiskey, brandy, and beer."

"Not wine?"

"Have you seen the wine cellar? After the way Fred stocked up in London, we don't have room for anything else."

"Got it. I'm going to look for hard cider, though."

"That makes sense."

"You guys playing tonight?"

"If anyone shows up to listen," I said.

"Eve and I put up a bunch of posters."

"That was nice of you. In English?"

"No. We found a printer and Eve—"

"Paper towels. What did you use for currency?"

"I pawned my spare helmet."

"Well, thanks," I said. "Yeah, that could bring some people in."

"You should look around."

"I intend to. Vegetable oil."

"The name of the sun is Chaucer, by the way."

"Really?" I said. "I like that. What's the planet?"

"Laurier."

"Cool. Bean sprouts, or the local equivalent, and hot peppers. That should do it for the stuff that can't wait."

"Good. Thanks. The mysterious Mr. Feng almost certainly appreciates your help."

"The mysterious Mr. Feng can kiss my ruddy bum, as someone or other would say."

"Think you guys will do okay tonight?"

"I guess. I've got a few other things on my mind, to tell you the truth. Although don't mention that to the rest of my band."

"Don't worry. I won't."

"I think they're all pretty hot to go on. Shit, we've only been waiting to play for, what, a few hundred years, maybe? And I was always nervous about playing Irish music in London, anyway, with all the real Irish bands floating around. This'll be fun."

"I hope so."

We didn't often get called back for a second encore, so I was pretty happy when we came down off the stage. Happy, exhausted, exhilarated, all of that. It's funny how you never get used to the highs and lows of performing, no matter how much you play.

Even Rich seemed pleased, like he might almost admit we'd sounded okay if he wasn't careful. A young guy in a brown fur coat that looked too hot and his apparent girlfriend with perfect bangs had been sitting in the front row drinking in every song. They came up and pumped my hand while chattering away in French. I smiled and tried to indicate that I was glad they'd liked it, until Fred appeared to usher them out of the bar. I was pleased as well as surprised by the turnout, which was pretty spectacular considering that we hadn't even been in the solar system the week before.

Jamie had found a short, pretty woman with a whiny voice and chestnut hair—or, rather, she'd found him. I watched the courtship ritual for a while, then I shrugged and started putting my instrument away. I go through occasional fits of jealousy about the way women flock around Jamie, but I know it's stupid. This time I just shook my head and smiled while I tucked my banjo strap behind the head.

"*Man.*" It was Jamie's line, but Tom said it. I turned, saw him staring, and followed his gaze to a small, thin, blond-haired woman with big, bright blue eyes, and a very pretty, round face.

"Good luck," I told him.

"What do you mean?"

"Go for it."

"You crazy? What am I supposed to do? Walk up to her and say, 'Hi there, you're the most gorgeous woman I've ever seen'?"

"There are worse lines."

"Shit."

I shrugged and turned back to my banjo case. The flap that lets you get to the inner pocket of the thing has been broken for a few centuries now, so it takes major work to get to it. When I had the tuner stored, she was gone.

"Her friend was giving you the eye," said Tom.

"Who?"

"A redhead she was sitting with during the show."

"Hmmm. Point her out to me if they show up again."

"I will."

"You should have said hello to the blonde."

"Next time."

Rose was watching Jamie leave with his new friend. "Watching" may be too mild a word. Rose and Jamie have nothing going on between them, Rose has no shred of jealousy in her, and she isn't bothered at all by Jamie's attentions to other women; except when they do and she does and she is. I saw the look on her face and knew what came next in this script, so I went over to her to help her with the Jameson, since she was too small to be expected to finish the whole bottle herself. And besides, it was Jameson.

Presently Fred shut out the lights. Rose talked, I listened, and we drank.

I don't get hangovers.

I keep telling myself that. I figure that if I can convince myself it's true, maybe I won't feel quite so bloated, shrunk, dehydrated, sweaty, achy, numb, stretched, and tender the next morning. Tom has been growing gradually less sympathetic to the morning-after conditions of those around him. He said, "Are you going to be able to play tonight?"

I nodded, while trying to pick burrs out of my tongue with my teeth—which was hard because my teeth had turned to foam rubber during the night. "Water," I said. "Water would be a good thing. Water. Then coffee. That's what I'm going to accomplish today. Great. I have a plan. Ambition. A goal in life. Yeah. Water, then coffee. But first, the bathroom. Good. We're getting organized now." Tom smiled, hooked his hands behind his head, and leaned back in his pile of odds and ends that passed for a bed. He lit a cigarette, inhaled deeply, and let it out slow, probably to tell me how nice it felt not to have a hangover. But I was going through one of my periodic fits of not smoking, so it just made me feel superior.

I got up and stumbled to the bathroom, going through the kitchen so I didn't have to look at the breakfast crowd, whose sounds I was hearing through my fog. I tried to remember what time Feng's opened, but couldn't, and it annoyed me that I didn't know if I couldn't remember because of aftereffects of the jump or of drinking.

I made it to the bathroom, where I splashed water on my eyes, cheeks, and the back of my neck, while making sounds that were not unlike a tin can and a smoke detector achieving simultaneous orgasm.

I was about to leave, still dripping water from my face, when I heard a noise like someone was setting off a firecracker just outside the bathroom door. It was sharp, though dulled by the door, and had a particular echo that my memory must be exaggerating. Or maybe not; the echo still haunts me.

Then there was another one, and another, and I think another but I'm not certain. I started to open the door to find out what was going on when it suddenly swung open toward me, jamming my middle finger. I cursed and looked for someone to be snide to. The someone fell into me and continued on toward the floor. I caught him. His face, which I'd never seen before, was branded with shock. His mouth worked like a fish's. He was breathing in gasps. I held him for just a moment, then he got his feet under him. He pushed away from me as if panicking and crashed into the nearest sink, then turned around and faced me. My right hand felt wet and sticky, and I glanced down, and knew that it was blood and I forgot about my jammed finger.

There was a big ugly red splotch on his chest, burnt around the edges, and I could see muscle tissue and, I think, bone. Then I noticed a red stain on the stomach of the pale yellow sports shirt he wore, and two more high on the left leg of his dark knit pants. One of his leg wounds was pumping blood.

His face, which was long, mustached, and dark, had a fresh scratch along one cheek. His hair was nearly as long as mine. For a second he stood upright, leaning against the wall. He looked right at me, and said, quite clearly and distinctly, "Sugar Bear." Then he slumped to the floor and seemed to concentrate all of his energy on breathing and blinking.

I did the only thing I could, which was to stand there, unable to move or even think about anything except how ugly the guy's wounds looked, feel my heart pound, and say the words *gunshots gunshots gunshots* over and over in my mind.

Presently I realized that things were quiet, which was how I realized that I'd been hearing screams from the next room. I stood there, heroically paralyzed and staring at the guy who was probably dying or something. Then I heard Tom calling my name from the other side of the men's room door.

"I'm in here," I said. "There's someone hurt." I somehow couldn't say "shot."

When the door opened it was Libby and Fred. Libby glanced at the guy, who was still bleeding and all like that. She knelt down next to him. I said, "Is there anything I can—"

She looked at me, shook her head, and said, "Just go sit down."

"Right. Sit down," I said. "Good idea."

She said, "Fred, make sure no one comes in."

"Will do," he said, as if he'd done this sort of thing thousands of times. Then I saw that he was holding a small, flat, silvery grey automatic pistol in his hand. Something about the way he held it told me he knew how to use it. I said, "Did you—" My voice caught.

"No," he said. "I'm being careful."

I heard Libby said, "Can you hear me? I'm a paramedic. I'm going to . . ." as I walked out. I made my way through what was rapidly becoming a large group of curious people. I sat down in one of the booths and had coffee. I think Rose brought it to me, but I'm not certain. There were a lot of people gathered there, and I knew several of them, but I'm not exactly sure, in retrospect, who they were.

Someone sat down next to three or four gunshots, Mr. Kevely, kay-ee-vee-ee-ell of a way to start to get an idea of where he was standing when did you first hear you play sometime, sir, but why is it that your band lives within the township of New Quebec Municipal Police Force, Criminal Investigation Division of labor makes sense, Officer, so we work here as part-time employees when we're not playing in the band of raggle-taggle gypsies—oh, sure, I'm fine, thanks, Officer, except this is the first time I've seen or heard the phrase sugar bear sugar bear sugar bear up under this kind of questioning for three fucking hours and that is yours so those must have been his orders to investigate the shooting death of a male Caucasian height of idiocy to just let him stay here when we aren't sure if he knows more or less everything we can get from Billy take this and some water, you should lie down and rest of the time between now and then we just have to guess that should be enough help him or her is that you Libby thanks for being here or therefore I may as well sleep for a while.

My last conscious thought was, How the hell am I supposed to play tonight?

The answer was: in a fog, and I'm not sure the others were doing much better. I remember none of our usual arguing over the set list, nor do I remember any details of the performance itself, except that at one point I had trouble with my jammed finger, but I don't even know what song we were doing. I kept getting the shakes in the middle of tunes and almost losing it. I tried to lose myself in the music, but then I'd remember why I was trying to do so and I'd get the shakes again.

During the first break, Tom started talking to the woman we'd noticed the night before. During the second break, he introduced me to her and her friend. I promptly forgot both of their names, but, then, I might not have been able to come up with my own if I needed to in a hurry.

When the show was over, I noticed Tom rushing to put his instruments away, I guess to go talk to his new friend. I took some time putting mine away. I sat on the stage and took two deep breaths.

"There were police here," someone said.

"Excuse me?"

"I'm wondering why there were police here, earlier today."

A redheaded woman with bright green eyes that were probably tinted contacts sat at the table near the stage, drinking something clear out of a Tom Collins glass. There was fruit in it. After a moment, I placed her as the woman who'd arrived with Tom's friend.

I said, "Someone was shot in the bathroom this morning."

Her eyes widened. "Shot, dead?"

"Yes."

"That's pretty scary." Her English had the barest trace of French accent, but was otherwise faintly Oxford.

I said, "I was right there when it happened. Scared hell out of me."

"I would it imagine."

I realized that I wanted her to keep talking, because I liked her accent, so I contrived to do so. She gave me her name, and I forgot it, and she gave it to me again. Souci. Pronounced "Sou" as in taking someone to court, with the accent on the "cee."

I got us coffee, and we covered a variety of subjects, but always came back to the dead man.

I said, "It's one thing to know you're going to die someday. It's another to see it happen so suddenly like that. You can't help identifying with him."

"I know," she said.

"But think about it. Your whole life, all your plans, everything you're going to do tomorrow and next year, and the things you want to see, and then, *blam,* it's over."

"I know."

"It's how *fast* it happened, that's what gets to me."

"I don't think you should think about it anymore right now," she said.

"I guess." I shuddered. "Let's get some food. They'll still serve if we hurry."

"I could eat a little," she said.

Feng's always served food until at least three-thirty, and we were picking at the remains of French onion soup and Cajun blackened chicken until something like four o'clock. I learned that Souci was local, didn't really care for Irish music, but her friend, the blonde, did, and Souci allowed that we were all-right. She said she was a dancer. I raised an eyebrow, and she shook her head.

"No. I dance for clubs like Montague's," as if that should explain things. She added, "I do not strip," as if it were perfectly reasonable for me to wonder.

"Okay," I said, and we went on from there.

I can no more remember that conversation in detail than I can remember playing that evening, but it went on for a long time.

When the day finally caught up with me, and each eyelid acquired a ten-pound weight, I asked Souci if she'd like to crash in the corner of the storage area where I kept my futon. It didn't seem odd at the time, and she said yes, and I fell asleep almost at once. Souci, curled up in my arms, was soft and warm.

She was still asleep when I woke up. It was only when I saw her there, asleep, that I realized just how beautiful she was—which was odd, because I'm not normally that slow to notice, and mornings aren't kind to anyone. She had a few freckles, and her hair may have been dyed, but she had the complexion to match it. Her cheekbones were high and quite pronounced, and the line of her jaw was emphatic, almost West Indian, ending in a very strong chin. Her eyes were deeply set, the brows fine, and there was a permanent, very slight pout to her lips. Her skin looked like fine silk. Her face, taken as a whole, was almost otherworldly, with an odd sort of perfection that hit me very hard.

It was impossible to see what the rest of her looked like under the blankets, but from what I recalled from the night before she had no excess weight and all of the right curves. I wondered how in the world I'd been able to fall asleep so easily with her next to me.

She woke up and caught me staring at her. I quickly looked away and said, "Good morning. Want some coffee?"

"Ummmm." She stretched. "Cream."

"What? Oh. Uh, right."

When I went to get the coffee, I found Tom sitting in a booth with the blonde. They were on the same side of the booth, Tom was leaning forward with his hands on the table in front of him, she was leaning back, her hands folded over her stomach. I could tell right away that neither of them had had any sleep. There was a coffee decanter on the table in front of them. "Good morning, folks," I said.

"Don't say that," said Tom, screwing his face into a grimace.

"Sorry."

"This is Carrie. Carrie, that's Billy." He blinked several times, rapidly.

"Nice to meet you," I said. She nodded. Tom said, "What time is it?"

"I don't know. Do you really want me to find out?"

"Well, no," said Tom.

When I came back that way with coffee, his friend was leaning forward, her head next to his in that position that always gives me the impression that people are exchanging thoughts directly through their foreheads. I left them alone. I set the coffee down, ran off to use the men's room.

When I got back I sipped at my coffee. I told Souci, "The police markings are still on the floor in there." I licked my lips. "It was a strange thing for me."

She nodded. "I suppose you pretty much hated it."

"Yeah," I said. "Pretty much. Not half as much as he did, though. You ever been there when someone was killed?"

"No." She tilted her head to the side and pursed her lips and said, "I almost killed someone once, though."

I said, "Oh?"

"I threw a desk chair at him, down three flights of stairs."

"You're kidding."

"He was my boyfriend. We were at a party at our own house, and he was, what is the phrase? Coming on to his ex-girlfriend."

"What happened to him?"

"He stopped coming on to her."

"No, I mean—"

"Oh. It missed his head, but broke his collarbone. I used to have a nasty temper," she added judiciously.

"I guess. But now you're a pussycat, right?"

She smiled. Then she said, "You were pretty tired last night."

I nodded. "And upset."

"I could tell."

"How?" I asked, intending the question to be sarcastic.

"You didn't make a pass at me."

This took me back a bit. I wondered if it was the norm in this society to be that direct. I suspected it wasn't. I almost asked if she expected every man she hung around with to make a pass at her, but I didn't because, on reflection, it would have been a pretty stupid question. So I said, "Did you want me to?" I wanted my tone to be light and bantering, but it didn't come out that way.

"Yes," she said.

I sat there for the length of a couple of breaths while I checked with my short-term memory to make sure I'd heard that correctly, and checked with my facial expression interpreters to make sure I wasn't being laughed at. I felt my heart pounding. "You could make a pass at *me*," I heard myself saying.

"Want to make love?" she said.

"Yes." I was surprised at how even my voice was.

One nice thing about mornings is how much energy I have. Her, too.

"Hi there."
"Mmmmm."
"Move over this way just a bit."
"Mmmmm."
"I liked that."
"Mmmmm. Me, too."
"I just changed my mind about something."
"What?"
"I think I want to get an apartment, after all."
"What do you mean?"
"I'd been thinking about just staying here for a while, but—"
"Why would you do that?"
"It's cheap."
"But—all right."
"I changed my mind."
"Mmmmm."
"Do you think you might be able to help me find a place?"
"Let me go home and change first."
"I'll buy you breakfast when you get back."
"Okay."

When she came back, about an hour later, she was wearing a loose-fitting black sweater, low black boots with high heels, and baggy black pants. I almost jumped her again, but instead bought her hash brown potatoes made with green peppers, red peppers, mushrooms, and onions; a soft-boiled egg; and English muffins. I had the same except I had a bagel. We both had a great deal of Feng's Roast coffee, then we attacked the outdoors. It took me a moment to work up the courage to step outside, but I did at last—and stopped, cold.

"What is it, Billy?"
"It's just—nothing. I'm just enjoying the morning."
"Afternoon."
"Whatever."

I'd gotten a look out the window before, but I hadn't been outside. Think of a high, deep blue, the air rippling like it does off the pavement on hot days, and no clouds, and a small, pale yellow sun set in the middle of it, like it was lost. That was my first view of New Quebec on Laurier around Chaucer. Across the street, yes, it was certainly a bakery. To my left was a square little shop whose sign read, "*Salon de Coiffure Pour les Chiens.*" To my right was a very tall building that could have been a grocer or a drugstore.

Streets—at least the three I could see from the door—were wide and very clean, as if they'd been scrubbed, and buildings were widely spaced and quite varied. There was a Victorian mansion with five towers and three chimneys and a bright red door just down the way, and next to it what seemed to be an underground bunker, and what could have been a church but wasn't was to our left. What *was* a church was to our right across the street and next to it was a small storefront, looking naked with nothing touching it, and just beyond that a tall businessy-looking place with lots of reflective windows. I made a note to see what it looked like at sunset, after establishing which direction could be considered west. It was, for the record, left as we stepped outside, so the old west wall was the north wall, if you chose to look at it that way.

There were a few people on the street: one elderly couple leaving the store, a man carrying an infant across his chest, two girls looking in the bakery window. They looked like people, with nothing to distinguish them from anyone on the streets of Ibrium City or Jerrysport, and it seemed that, for how far we'd come in time and space, there should have been more.

But what really got to me was a little thing—the street signs looked just about the same as they had back home, where I call home, before London. I hadn't consciously expected anything else, I hadn't thought about it, but I was startled. We were standing on LaVelle, with Valois running just to our left.

There was a breeze from my left to my right that brought the temperature down to where I almost get goose bumps, and when the wind stilled, the back of my neck felt hot where the sun struck it. I tried to remember if people here seemed exceptionally pale or unusually tanned, but I couldn't remember so I guessed not. The breeze brought me a smell that might have been cinnamon, but might not have been.

I held out my hand and Souci took it and we walked that way and a bird made a funny low whistling sound as we crossed a wide street called LeDuc, and as we looked for apartments we didn't say much that stays in my memory, but I think we learned a great deal about each other. She found a third-floor place in a six-unit house built of grey bricks. It was right up against the street and both taller than the houses around it and set apart from them, as if it were looming over the street to pounce on pedestrians. It was only half a mile from Feng's. It was clean, affordable, and the landlord or caretaker or whatever, spoke passable English—a big plus as far as I was concerned. The apartment was much larger than I was going to need, and included a view that looked out over the Quebec, the local river.

Rent was extremely cheap, but that was usually the case with colonies—lodging and food are cheap, clothing and entertainment cost. Anyway, it turned out I could pay a month's rent (fortunately this colony didn't have such customs as forced marriages, trial by ordeal, or damage deposits) with what we'd gotten for the last two nights of playing. It left me with nothing for food, but I could pile up debts at Feng's, or, local customs permitting, earn some extra money playing in the street with Tom. I asked Souci about it, and she said that local customs would, indeed, permit, and she indicated that if I chose to do this, I should warn her in time for her to be well away from the area. I was beginning to realize that, in some ways, she was not a nice person.

I paid, got the key, and asked if it was possible to rent furniture. Well, yes, but it was expensive. I shrugged. I had my blanket and futon, and the floor of the place was carpeted. What else did I need?

Before going back to Feng's, Souci and I made love on the carpet and it was a very fine thing, indeed. We rested, then, and I wondered about many things.

Intermezzo

I am a little beggarman
    And begging I have been
For three score and more
    On this little isle of green.
        "The Beggarman,"
        Traditional

Define "center" as the place where time turns to ice. Chip chip, you go, and a chunk breaks off. You'll look at it later, and say, "That was it"; a chunk of the ice of life, so to speak. Then it will be the apex, or the center point, or the deepest part of the valley, or.however you wish to consider a series of events viewed as a two-dimensional array of the data points we call "incidents."

We're picking one, and we're calling it pivotal because, among other reasons, it is. But remember, please, that you can't have any sort of perspective about it while it's in the process of happening, and if you try you'll just confuse yourself. Perspective is for then, occurrence is for now.

Now, then:

Rich said, "What happened?"

Linda said, "None of your fucking business."

The exchange took a little less than ten seconds, and can be seen as the moment to which everything had been building, and the instant from which the change occurred.

Rich's immediate reaction was, *I wonder if it would bother me as much if she didn't seem to like it? Well, yes, but in a different way. Maybe a cleaner way.* But he shook his head at that. The last year, with his wife's succession of lovers, had taught him to view his own reactions with a little more cynicism than that.

Why am I putting up with this?

Rich had been, among other things, a crisis counselor, and was thus operating under the impression that he ought to be able to figure out what, for example, he was getting out of his relationship with his wife of five years that made it worth going through this. He was wrong, of course.

Three nights ago she'd come home with welts on her thighs and he'd been too stunned to say anything. *Maybe I'm not quite as blasé as I'd like to think,* had been his reaction then. And, over the next three days, he'd given himself hell for that reaction, and for not confronting her about it directly.

So, tonight, when she was undressing and he saw bruise marks on her breasts, he gathered his courage and asked about them directly, and been told, "None of your fucking business," which left him asking himself why he put up with any of it. For another timeless three seconds of ice he stood there, then—

"I'm going for a walk," he said suddenly. And, because he was feeling nasty, added, "I might be back."

She didn't answer, and this caught him for a moment, and that moment was filled with changes and rearrangements in thinking and feeling that wouldn't settle in fully for years. In brief: *Why is she that certain I can't be serious?* and then: *Aren't I?* He stopped, half in and half out of the door, and realized, with the feeling of a weight lifting from his shoulders and a simultaneous pang, that, in fact, he wouldn't be back.

He wondered how Linda would react. But the scary thing was that, as near as he could tell, he really, honestly, couldn't care less.

An end, a beginning, and a center point.

The door closed behind him with a hollow sound.

CHAPTER
3

As we rolled down to Fenario
Our captain fell in love
With a lady like a dove
And her name it was called pretty Peggy-O.
"Peggy-O,"
Traditional

It was early evening when I brought her to Feng's to buy her another meal by way of saying thank you for helping me find the apartment. We took a different route back, a more hilly set of streets, by way of LeDuc up to LaVelle. As we passed a low brick building with a small hand-lettered sign she said, "That's my agency."

"Do they keep you working a lot?"

"As much as I want," she said.

"That's good."

"Yes."

She held my hand. There was a glow somewhere in my middle. It frightened me. We arrived at Feng's, and I was pleased that my favorite booth, beneath the Cheerful Chinaman, was unoccupied. We sat next to each other. Souci looked into the taproom and

30

pointed at the model Colt .44 Peacemaker on the wall and said, "Is that real?"

"No," I said. "It's a replica. But that's real." I nodded toward the suit of armor in the corner. She studied it, then glanced at the painting over the stage, with the Indian shooting a machine gun from the window of an old Deusenberg at a covered wagon while the knights in the wagon threw spears back at the car.

"This is a really weird place," she said.

"Tell me about it."

We ordered, and talked more, and the food came and we ate it. She didn't like my wine choice, but agreed that the chicken in champagne sauce was pretty spectacular. I'll note in passing that the colonists on New Quebec took better care of their chickens than most places I'd been, so it did, in fact, taste even better than usual. Fred was on duty, so I introduced her to him.

When he'd left, she said, "Kind of cold, isn't he?"

I said, "Huh? Oh, just when he's working."

"Mmmmm," she said. "He tried to throw me out last night."

"When?"

"After you'd finished playing."

"I'll kill him."

She smiled. She had dimples. There was a dropping sensation in my chest. About then, Rose joined us, and I introduced them as well.

"I like your necklace," said Rose.

"It's like the one Traci Devonois wore in *Leeches*."

"I haven't seen that. Is it good?"

"Yeah. The first time Paul Languedoc came out of the lake, I screamed so loud I got a sore throat."

"That's what happened to me the first time I saw *A Nightmare on Elm Street*."

"You saw that, too?"

"Those claws."

"I know. And *Alien*, where the alien comes through—"

"Don't say it. Did you see the original *Invasion of the Body Snatchers*?"

"About ninety times," said Souci. "What about *Creep Show*?"

"Yeah. What made it so scary was how matter-of-fact it all was, you know?"

"I know. Just like *City of Terror*, where the bug-things start eating through the walls, and everyone just watches. Ish."

"I didn't see that," said Rose. "But—"

"Excuse me, sis," I said. "Do you know where Jamie is?"

Rose looked at me and blinked. "Gone," she said, which meant that he'd either stepped out for a moment or been hit by a bus, and she couldn't care less which it was, and it would be wise if I didn't bring up the subject again.

"Right," I said. "I rented an apartment, just down the road. There's room for all of us, if you guys want to help out on the rent." The band, and sometimes Rich and Eve, had lived together off and on in London and before, and we could stand it when we had to.

Rose nodded. "It sounds fine as long as that man isn't around."

"That man" is one of the ways she refers to Jamie when she isn't happy with him. "Jim" is another. Or "James." I keep track, during dull moments. This time I nodded and ignored it, since these things never make a practical difference in anything either of them does.

"Is it big?"

"Big enough," I said. "Two bedrooms and a den, and someone can sleep in the living room if—" I caught myself before saying, "if you and Jamie aren't sleeping together," and said, "if things work that way. The rent is pretty cheap."

She agreed to think about it, then she and Souci went back to discussing monsters and I concentrated on my food. Eventually I drifted off to find Tom. He was curled up in his corner of the storeroom, fully clothed, with the blonde he'd introduced as Carrie. They snored in unison. They looked very cute. I was disgusted.

When I went back to the table, Rose and Souci were gone. I felt a pang, which I shook off as stupid. Having sex isn't precisely the same as a lifetime commitment. I was annoyed at how relieved I was when they came back a few minutes later and Souci sat down next to me.

She said, "I'm dancing tonight at La Violette. Do you want to come down?" There was something guarded in her voice, as if she was trying to sound like she didn't care too much.

I said, "They have dancing on Sundays?"

"Seven days a week," she said.

"Is there a cover?"

"A what?"

"Do they charge you to get in?"

"Oh. Yes, but I'll get you on the list. And Rose, too."

"Thanks," said Rosie.

"You'll really be there?"

"With bells on."

"What?"

"Yes. Really. For sure."

"Where are you from, anyway?"

I shrugged. "Lots of places. Never mind. Should we go up to the bar and have a drink?"

"I'd like that," said Souci.

"Whiskey," agreed Rose.

I signed the check, and Souci, Rose and I moved around the corner to sit at the bar with our backs to the stage. "Hey, Libby-love, this is my friend Souci."

"How d'ya do?" said Libby.

"Hi," said Souci.

Libby wiped the bar in front of us, put a toothpick in her mouth, and said, "What would you like?"

"Do you have Juliana Dark?"

"No, but we have Dos Equis."

"What's that?"

"It's imported from—just try it. If you don't like it I'll give you something else. What about you, Billy?"

"Beer," I said.

"Right. And you want whiskey, Rose?"

"Whiskey," she agreed.

"Should I run a tab?"

"Yeah," I said.

The liquor showed up, and Souci decided the Dos Equis was good enough if one added lime. Libby polished the bar in front of me and said, "I haven't really had a chance to ask you, are you doing all right?"

"You mean from yesterday? Hell, yeah. Thanks to you."

"Right." She laughed a laugh. "I'm highly skilled. Take two of these and talk to me when you wake up."

I shrugged. "It was what I needed."

"Good."

"How about you?"

"What about me?"

"Well, losing a patient—"

"Man, you don't have to worry about me. I've lost patients before." She shrugged. "I don't like it, but if I'm going to get bummed out, I might as well give up."

Rose said, "I thought you did give up on it, which is why you're at Feng's."

"Hell, no. Feng's wanted to find someone who could tend bar and be a paramedic."

"Are you joking?" asked Rose.

"No, I'm not joking. That was what I applied for."

"Weird. Did Feng say why?"

Libby smiled. "Wouldn't you like to know?"

I said, "How's the place been going?"

"All right. There's the usual percentage of jerks. One guy wanted a Lafleur ale, and when I said we didn't have it he asked if we had anything local, like it was some big political deal or something."

"What did you say?"

She laughed. "I told him we only had imported beer to drink and local assholes to drink it. He stormed out." She polished the bar some more, still chuckling.

"How was business during the show last night?"

"Fine."

"Good. I don't ever want to know what I sounded like on stage, though."

"You were okay," said Libby. Souci was supposed to have added something similar there, but she missed her cue. Oh, well.

I stared into my glass. "It's scary, having it happen right here, where we feel so safe. And dealing with the police and everything."

"I know."

"Did you find out anything?"

"No. There was no way to get a good description of the guy; there were too many witnesses."

"I understand. None of us saw it happen?"

"No. Fred was out of the room, and I was getting the bar ready. As far as I can tell, the guy went to the bathroom, and someone followed him there and shot him four or five times as he was opening the door."

"As you said," said Souci. "You're better off than he is."

"Maybe," said Rose.

"What do you mean?" said Souci. "Billy's alive."

"There might be worse things than dying."

"Like what?" said Libby, before Souci or I could.

"I don't know. Maybe being reincarnated as something horrible."

"Oh," I said. Libby nodded thoughtfully. Souci said, "That's such shit."

"How do you know?" said Rose. "Have you ever died?"

"Have you?"

"No, but I had a friend back—a while back—who was dying of Hags disease, and he said he could feel—"

"He should have been shot," said Souci.

"You're joking," said Rose.

"No, I mean it. Anyone who has that and won't stay away from—"

"It isn't all *that* contagious," said Libby.

"I don't care. It's one hundred percent fatal, it's—"

"Let's not talk about it, all right?"

"Okay," I said. "We'll talk about something cheerful, like the guy who was shot down in front of me." I paused, considering. "I still wonder about his last words. Did it mean something, or what?"

Libby shrugged. "The cops will probably figure it out."

"He said something to you?" asked Souci.

"Nothing that makes sense," I said. "Didn't I mention that? Just as he was falling over he sort of looked at me and said, 'Sugar Bear.'"

I wasn't certain, but I had the impression that Souci started when I said that. I looked a question at her, but she looked it back. She said, "Well, it's all pretty weird."

"Yeah."

"Look, I should be blasting off."

"Oh. Already? I'll see you tonight, then."

"Yeah," and she stood up and left. When she was almost gone, I called after her, "What should I tell your friend?" I'd forgotten her name. But Souci didn't answer, she just turned the corner into the dining room, and then I heard the front door open and close. I sat there and drank my beer and wondered. Libby didn't say anything. After a moment, Rose took off to find Jamie, Libby went back to do bartender things, and I took out my banjo and sat there, noodling.

Carrie came in an hour later, along with a compact, dark-haired, well-groomed guy with narrow eyes and a pale, short-haired woman with a loping, athletic walk. I would have guessed them both to be in their mid-twenties. They looked vaguely familiar, and it took me a minute to realize that they had been with Souci and Carrie the night Souci and I met.

Carrie said, "Is Tommy around?"

"He was a couple of hours ago," I said. "I don't know where he is now."

"Okay. This is Justin, and this is Danielle. This is Billy."

I said hello and so did they, and Carrie announced that she was heading off to find "Tom-Tom."

Danielle, who seemed to have some trouble with English, said, "So, you are in a band with this Tom, yes?"

I nodded. I won't try to describe her accent.

She said, "I would like to meet him."

The guy called Justin may have silently snorted, I'm not sure. He had beady eyes and his mustache was like mine except smaller and more neat. I was running into a lot of mustaches like mine. The guy who was killed had one, too. Maybe I should shave mine off.

"Yes," I said. "Tom's a good guy." I really didn't want to start thinking about the dead man again. I remembered then that I'd dreamt about him, but I couldn't remember what the dream was. I said, "Does the phrase 'sugar bear' mean anything to either of you?"

"No. Why?"

"Just wondering."

Had they reacted? Maybe. Maybe not. Justin looked at me, then his eyes shifted away. I decided he squinted too much. I said, "What do you people do?"

"I'm a foreman for a construction company," said Justin.

Danielle said, "I take pictures. Of models, yes?"

"A photographer," I said.

"What about you?" she said.

"I just do music."

She nodded. "It is good that you can make a living at it, at doing what you want."

"I don't need much," I said.

"But still—"

"Isn't that what you're doing?"

"Yes," she said, and smiled. "I like it." Nice smile.

Justin studied his nails.

Danielle said, "How did your band start?"

I wondered if she really wanted to know, or if she was just making conversation. Hard question, in any case, but I could pretty much stick to the truth. "We met right here," I told her.

"At Cowboy Feng's?" She pronounced it "Fenges."

"Yeah."

"I thought you were from someplace different."

"We travel quite a bit."

"And you happened to—"

"Jamie and Rose came in to hear some guy, and I opened for him."

"Opened?"

"Played first."

"Ah."

"We got to talking after the show, and—" I stopped, as Jamie came walking up. "You can ask Jamie about it."

"About what? Hi, I'm Jamie."

I said, "Danielle, Justin. Danielle was asking about how we got together."

"Oh. Rose and I introduced Billy to Bushmill's Irish whiskey."

"That was it," I said.

Tom and Carrie joined us and Carrie performed introductions. She seemed excited about the whole thing, almost hyper. Her arms flailed madly about as she spoke, describing arcs and circles. I wondered if she was always like that. We brought Tom up-to-date on the conversation, and he said, "That was about the time I met Rose and Jamie, playing on the street. It was just a few days later, I think."

"Yeah," said Jamie. "Then, what, a month later, maybe, we went back to hear another band, and ran into Billy again, stayed up all night playing music, and had a band by morning."

"Feng's was the first place we played, too," said Tom, which, like the rest of the story, was true as far as it went; we still hadn't mentioned that it had been on another planet in another solar system in another time.

"And now you are back?" said Danielle. "It is wonderful. How many days will you play?"

"I don't know," I said. "This weekend for sure, after that we'll see. And speaking of performances, anyone want to go to see Souci tonight?"

The three locals said they were busy. Tom said he'd like to come along. I said, "We probably don't want to stay out too late, since I want to move tomorrow."

"Are you going to move it to yesterday, or to today?"

"*Man*," said Jamie.

"That almost isn't funny," I said.

• • •

La Violette turned out to be only a few blocks away. One thing I've noticed about colonies is that most businesses seem unwilling to pay the expense of neon. I've about come to the conclusion that this is good. The outside of the place was covered in bright fluorescent paint with scenes of people dancing, and, well, it seemed both fun and inviting. We went in.

I wonder how far back in human history the concept of "bouncer" goes, and if it has always been easy to pick them out. This one had red curly hair, a wide face with a square chin, and he wore a sleeveless grey sweatshirt. He probably took steroids. We yelled at him over the music, discovered he didn't speak English, but when I told him my name, he found it and Rose's on the pass list. After a brief discussion with Eve, the rest of our group was waved through.

It was the sort of club that seems as if it could have existed in any place at any time. Too dark, too crowded even on a Sunday night, air that was too stale and too full of smoke. The band was a five-piece called Les Sons Magiques. I couldn't hear anything except the bass drum and the electric bass, with the exception of occasional notes from a Strat copy set to armor piercing. There were two rooms full of people trying to drink enough to distract themselves from how crowded and stuffy the place was, and I was very glad we weren't there on a weekend.

"This is great," shouted Rich into my ear. There's no accounting for taste.

I shouted into his, "I'd like it more if they'd mix the vocals higher."

"Why?" he shouted back. "You don't speak French, anyway."

A point. We found a table that was big enough for two. The six of us stood around it for a moment, then Rich and Jamie wandered off, and eventually came back with three chairs each. I don't know how they do these things. By that time I'd begun to enjoy the swing quality to the beat and to appreciate some of the honky-tonk piano licks the keyboard player was throwing in. From the lead guitarist's expression, he wasn't taking things too seriously, which I liked as well. After watching him for a while, I decided he was sharing some sort of inside joke with the keyboard player; at least, they'd look at each other and laugh whenever they played a C-major seventh. I still wished I could hear the vocals.

Rich and Jamie set off once more, this time on a quest for drinks. By the time they returned, the band had taken a break, and there was canned music coming over the PA at just about the same volume. I didn't recognize any of it—which was interesting. We'd left behind most of what was popular when we left London and arrived at Ibrium City—but then there'd been a whole style of music influenced by the bop of the 1950s that had followed us as far as Jerrysport, and it seemed we'd finally left it behind in exchange for an approach based on Classical European harmonies, Baroque melody lines, and Middle Eastern rhythms, the whole overlaid with some of the twisted minor-key changes I recognized from French Canadian fiddle tunes.

The vocals were still mixed too low.

Souci came on at the beginning of the next set, and, yeah, she was a good dancer. She and another were positioned at either side of the stage, and they got a high proportion of the total lighting in the room, and, from what I could see, the attention of the assembled hordes. She was wearing all black, and either makeup or the lighting was making her face even more pale than I'd remembered it. Someone, I don't remember who, told me redheads aren't supposed to wear black. Whoever said it was nuts.

It looked like we made eye contact and there was a flicker of recognition on her face, but I might have imagined that. I went back to watching the show. The other girl danced all right, but seemed a bit lackluster. The dancing involved wandering around the stage in a kind of shuffling walk, all but ignoring the music, then, at irregular intervals that must have had their own internal logic, they would break into hyperactive ballet movements. It really did fit quite well. The dancing taking place on the floor involved keeping one's feet motionless, or else moving very little, while undulating one's shoulders and neck. It looked unhealthy. Eventually Jamie and Rose got up and danced, and then I danced with Rose. They said it was more fun than it looked. We all drank some more. Tom drank nonalcoholic beer. I didn't smoke. There you have it.

When the set ended, I had the bouncer send a message to Souci that we were here. She didn't appear right away, but I bought a drink for the lead guitarist, who was a pleasant fellow with very long brown hair and a shaggy beard. His name was Christian, and it turned out he spoke English and had a collection of old discs that included the Neville Brothers, Merle Travis, and B.B. King, as well as some that I probably should have known but didn't. I drank some more and Tom started making jokes but Christian didn't seem too put off.

Then there was another set, which was much like the first, then the night was over. Christian stopped over to say good-bye, and we suggested he swing by Feng's next weekend, and he said he might. I had another gin and tonic while we waited for Souci, and I decided that I wouldn't ask her whether I'd imagined her jumping at "sugar bear" yesterday; she could tell me or not. I also decided that I didn't really want to let her know how hard I seemed to be falling for her; I had the impression that knowing about it might frighten her.

After about half an hour I asked about her and was told that she'd left for the night. Then we went home.

The next day we moved into the apartment that what's-her-name had helped me find. It was a much smaller production that you might think. We brought Rose's fiddle, my banjo, Tom's mandolin, and Jamie's six-string, one bundle of bedding each, a coffee maker, coffee, and cocoa powder. Tom's new friend Carrie came along, and whenever nothing else was happening they were looking soulfully into each other's eyes. It was to fwow up.

We sat on the floor and did a few tunes and drank coffee. I was feeling a sort of pleasant melancholy, and it was one of those rare, wonderful evenings where everyone is glowing with each other's company, and you're not talking about anything important, except that you are, and we didn't laugh much, but smiled a great deal.

Later Jamie and Rose and I drifted back to Feng's and I had spaghetti with white wine sauce which Rose refused to touch because it had mushrooms in it and Jamie pretended to be surprised about because it wasn't spicy and he thinks I can't eat anything that isn't spicy. Rose went off to practice her scales, and Jamie said, "What's the plan for tomorrow?"

"Nothing in particular," I said. "You?"

He dropped his voice and leaned toward me, conspiratorially. "I'm going to start trying to figure out about this place."

It was a moment before I realized that he wasn't joking, then I remembered what he'd said before. "How are you going to do that?"

"I don't know. I was hoping you might have some ideas."

"Exactly what are you trying to find out?"

"Why it is that we keep landing places that are about to have nuclear weapons dropped on them, and why we keep bouncing out of them. Haven't you ever wondered?" I think this last was irony.

I said, "There hasn't been much chance to wonder since we,

um, departed London. And when we arrived there, I think we were all pretty much in shock."

"That's true. Do you see any reason not to try to find out what I can?"

"Not offhand."

"Okay. Any ideas on how to go about it?"

"I don't know. Start with asking Fred and Libby. Maybe they'd know something."

"Good idea. Want to help?"

"No, I'm going to find a library. I want to find out what's happened in the universe since we've been away. For all I know, we've jumped a few hundred years."

"I doubt it," said Jamie. He looked around. "I haven't seen anything really, you know, futuristic."

"Sorry to disappoint you."

"Shut up, asshole."

After my morning coffee with cocoa I set out to find a local library. It was an interesting experience, which led to three different bookstores in three different parts of town before I figured out that "librairie" in French meant bookstore, and library was "bibliothèque." After that I found a pretty big one, and I sat down and began digging, and kept digging until I lost track of time.

My diligence was rewarded. First of all, I discovered, in the English-language section, that New Quebec had been founded in what could be considered Earth year 2306. Then I turned to the section on galactic history, wondering how long there had actually been a need for such a section. It took a while, but I found out what I'd wanted to know.

I sat there until a librarian came along and threw me out. I'm not sure how I managed to find my way back to Feng's, but I did, and I sat at the bar staring off into space. Libby wiped the bar in front of me and said, "What's wrong, Billy?"

I shook my head.

She said, "Is it that redhead who was in here?"

I shook my head again.

She stared at me for a while, then said, "Is there something I can get for you?"

I thought about that, and its ramifications in a number of ways, and said, "Laphroaig." She poured me a tumbler and gave me a glass of water along with it. The whisky didn't go down smooth;

it never does. But the taste is strong, and to me it tastes more like scotch than any other. A bagpiper I knew in London insisted that it tasted like bagpipes. In point of fact, it tastes like I would imagine a peat bog to taste. I guess that was why I wanted it, just then. I enjoyed it not only for its flavor, and for its rarity on this planet, but for the fact that it was, essentially, irreplaceable, as was everything else produced on the radioactive ball that used to be the Earth.

Intermezzo

She looked so neat with her two bare feet
And the sheen of her nut-brown hair.
**"Star of the County Down,"
Traditional**

Once upon a time there was a girl who lived in a house called fear.
Every window was a place where strangers could look in, every
door a means whereby they could enter. She stayed in her house
as long as she could, and she kept the windows shut and the doors
locked and only snuck a hand out every Tuesday and Thursday,
early in the morning, to bring in the mail.

But she was not a foolish girl. In fact, she was very smart, and
especially wise in the ways of the house of fear. While she knew
that leaving the house was to invite strangers to poke and pry at
her, and to Find Out about her, she also knew that she couldn't
stay there forever.

She made herself go out of the house. She never liked it, but she
did it. She made herself act as comfortable as she could on the
streets, because if she looked as frightened as she felt, it would
attract the strangers.

Soon, she became skilled in blending into almost any crowd, any environment. She learned to speak foreign languages, and she made herself visit foreign countries, because she was frightened to. Each of her fears, in turn, she faced, and faced down, and defeated, because she knew that it was the only way she would be able to find someone strong enough to guard and protect her, so she could safely go back, and never emerge again from the house called fear.

CHAPTER
4

"Oh, bedamned then," said Jack,
"This is quare bungle rye raddy rye."
"Bungle Rye,"
Traditional

I finally told Libby, of course. I had to. Oh, I briefly entertained thoughts of keeping it to myself, but she'd have found out, anyway, and I make a lousy martyr. So after my first glass, I took a deep breath and said, "I've just learned what the current condition of the Earth is."

"Oh," she said. "Yes. I know about it. Maybe I should have told you before." She appeared unconcerned by the whole thing, except that she was wiping down an already clean bar, and pressing the cloth into the bar as if she wanted to take the polish off.

I accepted a second tumbler. "Do any of the others know?"

"Fred does."

"How'd he take it?"

"Fred doesn't worry about things he can't help."

"Yeah, I guess he doesn't." I took another sip. "I do."

45

"I know. Pinhead."

I was beginning to feel a bit woozy. I've always been a cheap drunk. I finished the scotch, which burned nicely all the way down, and Libby gave me another glass. I started to take an inventory of things that were forever gone from the universe, and I felt my eyes begin to fill with tears before I reached the third item.

"I'm getting maudlin, Libby. Distract me."

"All right," she said. "Want to go into the back room and screw?"

"Anytime."

She laughed and so did I. I always wondered if she meant it. I had a little theory that she wondered, as well. I'd been tempted more than once to see what would happen if I called her bluff.

Libby said, "I want to buy some lights for this place."

"Lights?"

"For the stage. Real lighting. Psychedelic stuff."

"That'd be fun. Are you going to?"

"I'm thinking about it."

"Go ahead and do it."

She nodded, poured me another glass, focused on something behind me, and moved down to the other end of the bar.

I said, "Hi, Souci."

She said, "Hi."

There were several things I wanted to say to her, and several more things I wanted to ask her, but what came out was, "I'm drunk."

"I can tell." She sat down next to me and sipped some of my drink. She made a face.

"It's a single malt whisky," I said. "It's an acquired taste."

"Why did you want to acquire it?"

I laughed, probably more than it deserved. Her eyes were either naturally narrowed or she kept them that way to make her look more feline. It was very effective, in any case. I leaned my head on her shoulder. She tensed, then relaxed. I touched her hair. I always think of red hair as being thin and stringy, but hers was not. It might have been whatever she used on it. Or maybe it was dyed. I rubbed it with my fingers and said, "Wanna take me home?"

"Okay," she said, and helped me stand up.

On the stumble back to my apartment, I said, "Why didn't you come out and see me, at the club?"

"Let's not talk about it."

"All right."

There was silence, and I badly wished my head would clear, at least a little. I wanted to tell her about finding out that my home was destroyed, but I didn't dare, because I didn't want people knowing about Feng's, and because, well, Souci didn't seem like the sort of person you dump your troubles on.

We were at the apartment. Climbing the stairs was a lot harder than it should have been, and getting my key in the lock took all the concentration I had to spare. But we were finally inside, and I led the way to my room and collapsed on my futon, noted thankfully that the room wasn't spinning, and stared up at Souci, who shook her head sadly.

"I'm drunk," I explained again.

"I know," she said. She sat down next to me and stroked my forehead. In my drunken stupor, it seemed like an uncharacteristically, I don't know, *tender* gesture. I almost said Those Three Words, but retained enough rationality to know that would be a bad idea. Besides, what does it mean, coming from a drunk?

And, as we sat there, the thought came to me, *When did you start thinking you knew her so well that you can make all of these deductions about what she's like?* I kept looking at her. The voice inside of my head whispered to me once more, in case I'd forgotten: *You've got it bad, son.*

She kissed me on the cheek, and I almost choked up. I stroked her hair and kissed her clumsily. I was too drunk to make love, but she kissed me back, and then she was lying across me, then I rolled over, and I heard myself make little whimpering sounds. Her skin was so soft.

I'm usually no good for sex when I'm wasted, but I guess there are exceptions to everything. We made love three times that night. At one point she said, "Are you always so horny?"

"No," I said. In retrospect, I think that was the right answer.

Along toward morning, when the liquor had mostly been worked out of my body, I said, "That was pretty fine, Cupcake."

"Cupcake?"

"You called me Pumpkin."

"Cupcake sounds like something you'd name a horse."

"I like horses."

"Are there things you haven't told me? Hmmmm?"

I said, "Anyway, Cupcake—"

"I could kill you in your sleep."

"Probably. Just don't wake me up, okay? Ouch."

Sometime later I said, "Hey, babe?"

"Hmmmm?"

"I don't think we ought to be serious about it. I mean, I like hanging around you—"

She smiled. "Uh-huh."

"I just don't think we should let it get serious."

"I agree."

I sighed. "I mean, I don't know what my plans are for the future."

"Me neither."

"I'm not at a point where I can really make commitments."

"Neither am I."

"As long as we're clear that, well—"

"We don't owe each other anything, honey."

I said, "Good. And Cuddles—"

"Hmmm?"

"Never leave me."

"I won't."

I woke to Jamie's blessed face. I say blessed because in his hands were two cups of coffee.

"You," I told him, "are a saint."

"Thank you, suh," he said, doing his English butler. "Will that be all?"

"Yes. Thank you, James."

I blew on my coffee and tasted it. Sugar, heavy cream, cinnamon, and cocoa. If you're going to wake up at all after drinking heavily the night before, this is the way to do it.

Souci pulled the covers up around her chin and opened one eye. It was true; I only noticed her freckles in the morning. She sat up when I gave her her coffee, and she sipped at it, very delicately. My heart did a thing. Jamie left and I finished my coffee and crawled to the bathroom, which was mercifully not in use. I spent a good ten minutes brushing my teeth, then I showered and shaved. Souci used the bathroom after me, and when she came back she shut the door and starting kissing me.

At one point she said, "I love how horny you are in the morning." I was going to make the same comment to her, but I got distracted.

When we finally dressed and walked out into the living room, Tom was sitting there with Rose and Jamie. "Morning," I said.

Tom said, "Did you know that Chico Marx learned all of those accents so he could go anywhere in New York without getting beat up?"

"Is that true?" I said.

"Yep."

"Cool. Did you know that you look funny sitting there without Carrie?"

"Already? That's scary."

"No, she isn't here."

"What?" Then he hit his forehead with his hand. "You're doing it to me now."

"I'm becoming infected."

"What is this about?" asked Souci.

I said, "Tom is always making stupid puns, and—"

"No, about Carrie."

"Oh. Right. Carrie and Tom have been being cute together."

"Really?" she said. "Aren't you a little old for her?"

Tom stared at her like she was a dead fish he'd just found in his bathwater. She didn't seem to notice. "I have to go talk to my agent," she said. "Are you going to be around for a while?"

"Yeah," I said. "At least a few hours."

"It won't be more than two."

"I'll wait for you."

She nodded and headed out the door.

When she was gone, Tom didn't say anything, which I thought was nice of him. I had the impression that he and Souci weren't going to be best of friends.

Jamie said, "Should we practice?"

"I'm supposed to work today," said Tom.

"Wait a while," I said, "I have some news."

"Oh?"

I licked my lips. "I learned something yesterday."

They all stared at me, waiting. I took a deep breath and told them.

Jamie just stared straight ahead. Rose cuddled up with him. Tom sat there shaking his head. I said, "Maybe I shouldn't have told you."

"No," said Jamie. "We'd have found out."

Then we sat in silence for a while longer. Tom reached for his mandolin and started noodling. Pretty soon Jamie got out his guitar and I borrowed his twelve-string, since this was not a banjo sort of mood. We were all pretty much in tune, and none of us cared about the difference right then. Eventually Rose joined us, and we went into a long, slow version of "I Know You Rider."

Maybe that was a mistake, but I really don't think anything we did would have been any different. Irish music (or, as it was called on Old Earth, folk music) is, by its nature, filled with *place*. Sure, the best songs transcend their time and place of origin—that's why they keep being rewritten—but I sang the verse about the "sun gonna shine," and thought about how I wouldn't see it anymore, and tears started. Singing about "cool Colorado rain" was no better.

Stan Roger's "Giant" was, if anything, worse, and "Jack Stewart" was maybe worst of all—we were all in tears by the time we were halfway through it. I kept wanting to break into something cheerful like "Darlin' Corey," but I couldn't. We played nonstop for an hour and a half, and were just winding down when I noticed Jamie hammering on a slow finger-picked D minor, which could only mean one thing. I caught Tom's eye and he nodded. Rose was already making banshee sounds from her fiddle.

We played "Tom O'Bedlam" as we'd never played it before. Every verse was a nail in the coffins of our private memories, a teardrop in our personal wake for a lost world. Where each of us went to find our grief doesn't matter, it was there in Jamie's voice and Rose's fiddle and Tommy's mandolin. My thoughts will remain my own, as the music remained within those walls on that world, so far in time and space from where we had come, and even further yet from where we were going, together or apart, as may be.

When Souci came back I asked her if she was hungry, and she was, and she didn't mind eating at Feng's since they had a pretty good variety, so we walked down there along some tree-lined side street that ran parallel to LeDuc, slow and quiet, and I was glad we were together. We didn't say a word as we walked; she seemed to sense that I had a lot on my mind. Tell me this, my friend: Was what I was feeling at that moment real? Or was I just working very hard not to think about the Earth, and all the things I might have to do but didn't want to, and investing all of that emotion into her just because she happened to be there and willing? And, for a chance at the big deal of the day, does it matter?

Rich was in the taproom, and was just finishing drinking something clear and bubbly. I said, "Sissy water?"

"Sissy water."

"The local stuff?"

"Yeah."

"How is it?"

He shrugged. "What can I say? I laughed. I cried. I fell down. It changed my life. It was good. The end. Yeah, it's pretty good."

"Right. Rich, this is Souci. Souci, Rich."

"How do you do?"

"Hi."

"So, Rich, you finished the pipes?"

"Yep."

"Good. Where's Eve?"

"The library."

"Oh?"

"Libby was talking to us about what you learned yesterday."

"Oh."

Souci glanced at me, but Libby called for Fred from the back room just then.

I yelled back, "He just went into the men's room. What is it?"

"Delivery."

"I'll get it," I said.

"Want help?" asked Rich.

I shrugged, not knowing how big a delivery it was likely to be. Souci sat down to wait while Rich and I went back to the rear entrance. There was a neat stack of a dozen boxes just inside the door, each box about two feet by one by one. I hefted one and it weighed about fifteen pounds, which wasn't bad. I looked at the label and smiled. "The local whiskey, I think."

"We should sample it," said Rich.

"After we move it in."

"Like Jamie says, you're no fun, you're no fun, you're no fun at all."

"Right."

We had about half of them moved, when Rich suddenly said, "That's funny."

"What?"

"The seal on this one."

I looked. "I don't see any difference."

"The tape isn't even."

I looked again. "It probably came open, so some guy had to do it instead of a machine."

He nodded, picked it up, stopped, and his brows knitted. He set it down again. "Look at this."

"What?"

He pointed. There was the tiniest lump at one end of the box, near the seal. I said, "Don't ask me. Open it up, if you're that curious."

"I think I will," he said. "Have a knife on you?"

"No. Where's your tool kit?"

"The other room. I'll get it."

I moved another box while he went for his tool kit. I saw him poised there for a moment, about to break the seal, then he stopped again. "Billy, does this look funny to you?"

"What now?"

He pointed again to the strip of tape sealing it shut. I looked closely. I said, "Yeah. It's like there's a wire or something below the tape."

He nodded.

I shrugged. "If you stare at anything long enough it'll look funny," I said, but there was no conviction in my voice. My mouth felt dry, although, really, I hadn't consciously thought of anything it could mean by that time. Rich's movements suddenly became much more fluid, and, simultaneously, sharper, more precise. He kept his eyes on the box while his hand found something in his tool kit, which he switched on and pointed at various parts of the box. It beeped twice in different tones at different places.

He found something else, held it only a bit away from the top of the box, and pressed a stud, studied the display on the top. He did this again, then said, "Billy, get everyone out of the place."

I said, "Is it—"

"Do it now," he said.

"Right."

I spoke to Fred first. "We need to clear the building."

He didn't even bat an eyelash; he just said, "You take the dining room, I'll take the taproom and the kitchen area. What about Rich?"

"He's staying, for the moment," I said, and was suddenly very happy that Eve wasn't around.

I went into the restaurant and found that the only customer in the place was Souci. I said, "Let's go outside." Her eyes widened, and she didn't move or say anything, she just waited. I said, "There's something going on. I can't explain right now. We have to wait outside."

"All right," she said, and we headed out. Libby was standing on the other side of LaVelle looking at loaves of bread and talking to Fred and Tom, who'd been washing dishes. Libby said, "What is it?"

I shook my head. "I'll tell you later," I said, and walked back into the building and back to where Rich was—and if you think that was easy to do, you don't know me. Rich had his whole tool kit laid out, and the box still wasn't open. He seemed quite calm, and was making notes in a small notebook from the reading of various instruments. Without looking up, he said, "Is everyone out?"

"Yes. Can I help?"

"Not as much as you'll distract me because I'll be worrying about you."

"Are you sure?"

"Yeah. Thanks. This thing is set to go off in about ten minutes, as near as I can tell. I'm pretty sure I can disarm it in less than that. Get at least as far as the other side of the street, and make sure everyone else is, too."

"Pretty sure?" I echoed. "Can't we just call the police or something?"

"Not before it goes off."

"Maybe if we just get it out of here—"

"And put it where? Who would you like to blow up? And I can't even be sure that too much motion won't set it off."

"But what if you—"

"And we're running out of time. Get going, Billy."

"All right."

"I'll see you later."

"You damn well better."

And I made a special effort to walk, not run, out of the place and across the street. My legs were shaking. Everyone sort of gathered around me, and I said, "Rich found a bomb. He's disarming it." I didn't say, "He's trying to disarm it," which would have been more accurate. "It should only be about ten minutes."

Souci's eyes grew very wide. "Are you going to call the police?"

"There isn't time," I said. "If we're going to save the building—"

"That's crazy. Your friend is going to blow himself up. The police know how—"

"So does Rich," I said hopefully.

It was right then that Jamie and Rose showed up, and asked why we were standing on the street, so the whole thing had to be explained to them. Rose, I think, was beyond shock. Tom, who finally learned what was going on, screwed his face up, like he only does when he's really angry, and turned his back on us. His fists were clenched and there was tension in his bony back. I made a note to be careful around him; when he's mad, he's just mad, and he'll sometimes take it out on whoever has the bad luck to cross him first. Jamie was angry as I'd rarely seen him angry. He stared at Feng's like he could see right through it to whoever had sent the bomb. I could almost hear his teeth grinding. He started across the street.

"Jamie—" I said, knowing I couldn't stop him, but just then Rich emerged, smiling and holding the box. He met Jamie in the middle of the street. They walked back together, and Rich set the box down. It was mostly packing material and wires, with a few electrical doodads, as well as whiskey bottles so it would weigh the same as the other boxes.

"A good job," said Rich, holding out a lump of what looked like Silly Putty. "Enough to wreck the place and kill everyone in it, and not do much else, as far as I can tell. If we'd opened it, it would have gone."

I started shaking again. I'd say I had every excuse. If I'd been the one to pick up that box . . . no, I did not really want to think about that. Jamie hugged Rich. I said, "Good work."

"It wasn't that hard," he said.

I said, "I want to go in and sit down."

Jamie said, "I want to find out who sent that thing."

Souci didn't say a word, she just walked into Feng's next to me. We all sat down at the big corner table in the restaurant part. I asked Libby, "Going to close up for the day?"

"Hell no," she said. "We'll be getting busy in an hour."

Fred said to Tom, "You don't have to stick around." Tom glared at him, like he'd just been insulted.

Jamie said, "We've got to do something about this."

"For starters," said Rich, "I'm going to check the rest of the boxes."

I added, "And anything that ever gets delivered, here or to any of us, as long as we all shall live, amen."

Fred said, "Should we go to the police?"

"Maybe," said Rich. "Will it do any good?"

"Who knows?"

Souci said, "What are you talking about? Of course you should call the police. Someone tried to blow you up. Are you foolish?"

"Who the fuck asked you?" said Tom.

She started to flare at him, then stopped and just shrugged. The rest of us didn't say anything. The silence grew more and more uncomfortable. I said, "Cupcake, can we get out of here?"

"Sure."

Jamie said, "Wait, I thought we were going to decide—"

"To decide what? Whether to call the police in? Shit, I don't know. Whatever you do is fine by me. How to find out who put the bomb in the place? Let me know when you have an answer, and I'll help. But this place is giving me the creeps right now, okay?"

Jamie had nothing to say to that. Souci and I walked out onto the street. We stood in front of Feng's for a moment, then I said, "Show me the city."

"All right," she said. My palm felt sweaty and I was shaking, but she made no comment as she took my hand. It was what I needed just then, and that is a thing I remember.

She led me off down the street.

Intermezzo

I was feeling very thirsty
After eating salty grub
When lady luck directed me
To Mrs. Rockett's pub.
"Mrs. Rockett's Pub,"
words by Tommy Makem,
music Traditional

"Good afternoon, Mr. Feng."

"Hmmph."

"I've completed work on the Unit. How goes the, uh, that is, are you—"

"The overlay hasn't been done yet, so you can relax. Tomorrow. What about the Unit?"

"I've tested all the mechanical functions. I'm leaving a set of repair assemblers in a floater in the basement. They will keep the equipment running as long as the integrity of the floater is—"

"I've studied elementary biology. What else?"

"The various nexus points are programmed into the DNA of the assemblers, and hence into the Unit itself. The power for each shift, of course—"

"I know. What about the rest of it?"

"Rest of it?"

"What does the Unit look like, idiot?"

"Oh. Ummm, as you know, we have—"

"Don't tell me what I know. What does it look like?"

"We used a bar and restaurant motif."

"That sounds good."

"We've used all the information about Earth that you supplied us with. It was quite extensive. I think the restaurant will blend in nicely."

"Good. How will it determine location?"

"Huh? As I said, the nexus—"

"No, precise location. Blending in, and—"

"Oh. Between departure and arrival, we have enough local time—between one point six four and two point zero nine seconds—for the squirmware to analyze local parameters to—"

"Will you shut up?"

"Huh? But you asked—"

"I know all that. I want the algorithm."

"Oh. Sorry. I don't know it. You'll have to find someone who works with the—"

"Never mind. I'll find out later. I take it you're going to decorate it."

"Yes. Period, of course."

"I hope."

"We'll do our best. Ummm, we're putting a plastic banana over the door to the outside, and a 'Do the Job' sign in the kitchen, if that's all right."

"That doesn't sound like it's pushing believability too much."

"I hope not, sir."

"Don't call me sir."

"Sorry, Mr. Feng. Is there anything else we can do for you?"

"No. If the Unit will blend in, and the assemblers will keep it working, I'll find someone to verify the squirmware, and the rest is just luck."

"And skill, Mr. Feng."

"Heh. Care for a fortune cookie?"

"A what, Mr. Feng?"

"Never mind. Do the Job."

"Do the Job, Mr. Feng."

CHAPTER
5

As each day becomes another day,
Each year another year,
I'd trade a year in heaven
For a day with you, my dear.
"Another Time and Place,"
Dave Van Ronk

Someone tried to kill us.

I was told that right outside New Quebec was a series of natural caves hollowed out over the course of eons by the Quebec River, and that the hills overlooking the city had a sunflower-like plant that bloomed all day all year round, and grew so thick you'd think you were wading in sunlight when you walked through the meadows.

I was told that New Quebec was founded by explorers from the *Winnipeg Dave,* which still stood in what was now the center of town, and that the Town Hall built from its remains was considered an architectural masterpiece. I'm told that the Science and Agriculture Building was a combination of living space, office space, greenhouse, and outdoor park, with each part blending into the others, and was one of the things that give New Quebec its personality.

As I said, I'm told these things, but I haven't seen them, because they weren't the sort of things Souci showed me. Instead, she brought me to a little bar called Nanette's, on Champlain, where you could get a cheap drink and find a rare and delightful mixture of every stratum of New Quebec society, from panhandlers to lawyers to merchant seamen. She took me to a shop whose name I can't remember where they sold anything and everything having to do with the sense of smell, and I bought amber in a small wooden box, and I bought Souci some cologne she liked, just because I felt like it and could afford it.

Whatever the shooting was, it wasn't a fluke.

She took me to a club called En Avant, where someone famous had gotten his start. Her eyes glittered just a bit as she spoke of him, but I had the distinct feeling that she didn't have the hots for him, she had the hots for fame and success. The place was nearly empty, so we climbed onto the stage (a five-foot riser) and walked around, listening to our feet echo. That was fun.

There are things I've been ignoring that I can't ignore any longer.

Later she took me to a restaurant with an Italian-sounding name where they specialized in pastries, and we split a meat pie, then each had dessert—mine was a chocolate mousse torte that I'll remember as long as I live.

As we left, I said, "Nice town."

She nodded. "I thought you were not from here. When did you arrive?"

I came back to reality. I cleared my throat and said, "A few days ago."

"Visiting?"

"We just came in to play some music at Feng's."

"That's all?"

"Pretty much."

"Oh." Then casually, "Going to be here long?"

"I'm not sure. Maybe not more than a month or two."

"What's wrong?"

"Nothing."

"All right. Where are you from?"

"Originally? Off-planet."

"Really? I've never been off-planet. Where?"

"Am I from?"

"Yes."

"It doesn't matter. It's gone now."

"Gone?"

Ooops. "Well, you can never really go back."

"What do you mean?"

"When you leave something and then come back to it later, you find out it's changed into something else."

"Deep," she said ironically.

I winced. "Well, all right, I slipped. I originally meant something a little more practical than that."

"Oh?"

I studied her for a moment, then said, "Why do you care?"

She shrugged. "You've made me curious. Where are you from that doesn't exist anymore?"

I licked my lips. "Would you believe the Earth?"

"No."

"Good."

"Would you expect me to believe it?"

"No."

She looked at me, but only said, "Where do you want to go?"

"Back to the apartment?"

"I don't really want to see what's his name, Tom, right now. How about my place?"

"Sure," I said. "Which way is it?"

"Same direction as yours, about a half mile closer to the river."

After a while, I said, "Thanks."

"For what?"

"Showing me the town. Helping take my mind off things like bombs and bodies." She nodded. I said, "It all feels so unreal— the killing, bomb scare, all that. I keep expecting to wake up."

She nodded. "A friend of mine had her husband die, and she said it was like that. She was walking around knowing it had happened but not really feeling it, and knowing it would all hit her, and wondering when and how hard."

I said, "That's it, yeah. It's been like that since the first time we jumped, and that was more than two years ago."

"Jumped?"

I caught myself. "Never mind."

"No, tell me about it."

"You won't believe me."

"So?"

I had lost count of the slips I'd made to her. The events of the last day had shaken me, but I knew myself well enough to know

I couldn't make that many by accident. So all right. I started from Earth in the late 1980s and worked forward from there.

Twenty-four hours later Tommy and I were sitting next to the window in the back booth at Feng's. Jamie and Rose were gossiping with Libby in the taproom while we waited for our food to arrive. I realized that I'd be seeing Souci again in less than four hours and my heart leapt. I cleared my throat and said, "So, how are things going with Carrie?"

"I think I'm in love," said Tom.

I said, "Is that what it is? And here I thought you two hated each other."

"What about you?"

I felt a sudden tension that I couldn't account for. "I enjoy her company," I said carefully. "She seems to enjoy mine. That's pretty much it."

Tom nodded. He said, "I told Carrie about us."

"What do you mean?"

"I told her about how we're from Earth, and keep getting moved around by being nuked."

"You're kidding. You really told her?"

"Well, yes and no."

"What do you mean?"

"I told it like a story, like I didn't expect her to believe it, and then I just kept filling in details about Old Earth and stuff like that."

"Do you think she believed you?"

"I don't know."

"Do you care?"

"Yeah."

"Would you rather she did or didn't?"

"I don't know. Except—" He caught my eyes and suddenly looked very earnest, almost angry. "If this place goes, I want her with us."

"Yeah," I said. "I understand. I keep wondering if, when we hear the alert, we should try to fill up Feng's with as many people as we can. But—" I shrugged.

"It's hard," he said. "Who do you grab? How do you convince them? We don't even know where we're going."

"It really sucks," I said. My matzo ball soup arrived. I started to have some, stopped, and said, "I told Souci, too."

"What?" He looked torn between disbelief and laughter.

I said, "I told it straight, but I said I didn't expect her to believe me. I don't know, I just wanted to have told her."

"You enjoy her company," he said, nodding sagely.

"Shut up, asshole."

We didn't practice again that week. Thursday, a local band whose name translated, according to Eve, to "Pan's Dream," came in to audition. Libby asked Tom and me to judge them, and Rose and Jamie and Carrie and Souci were around as well. They were a three-piece outfit with a tall guy with brown curly hair playing flute, a short, dark, long-haired fellow swapping between six- and twelve-string guitars, and a big guy with muttonchop sideburns playing six-string guitar, acoustic bass guitar, and balalaika. We listened for half a song, then Tom turned to me and said, "Jethro Tull." A few minutes later I turned to him and said, "Hot Tuna."

Their approach was traditional, and I suspect most of their music was "traditional" for this colony; sixty years is plenty of time to build up a body of music. It had its own style, too, not very similar to the French Canadian music I was familiar with. It seemed to emphasize minor-key verses changing to major-key chorus, like old Slavic folk songs; and had far more complex chord patterns than traditional American, and a lot of switching time signatures from four-four to eight-four and occasionally something in nine or eleven. All of this made their material far more musically challenging than the stuff we did, and they managed to pull it off. I was also grateful that they didn't do much of what passed for folk music there, mostly interminable, monotonous ballads, like "The Wreck of the Gordon Lightfoot" which went back and forth between two notes for about fifteen minutes.

I sometimes got the impression that Pan's Dream couldn't decide what they were about musically, but that made Feng's just the right place for them. They also surprised me a great deal by breaking into a traditional Irish tune, "Follow Me Down to Carlow," which they executed with a great deal of musical dash and style, if not much vocal commitment—perhaps because none of them spoke English well. But it charmed the hell out of me.

Souci didn't think much of them, Rose wanted to play fiddle for them, Carrie wanted to sing with them, Jamie was in awe of them, and Tom and I decided that they were better musicians than we were, even if they never looked as if they enjoyed playing. I told Libby to go ahead and hire them, which she did, giving us the weekend off.

Souci got Friday night off and took me dancing, then Saturday we walked along the Quebec, which was amazing mostly for its lack of insect life. I asked Souci why that was and she just looked at me funny.

She said, "You seem distracted."

I said, "There's some stuff happening that's got me worried."

"Can you do anything about it?"

"I don't know. Probably not."

"Then don't worry about it."

It sounded so easy when she put it that way. I wondered what would happen if I gave it a try. She leaned her head against my shoulder as we walked and my arm fit so well around her waist. Yeah, maybe I could try not worrying for a while.

It was a strange time, that next week—or was it two? Three? A month? Even while it was happening, I had an idea of how strange it was—like being in a dream and knowing you're dreaming; hoping desperately that you'll never wake up, knowing that you'll have to someday. There were things I needed to be doing, and I didn't do them, and while there were still a few lingering effects from the jump, I can't use that as an excuse for all of it.

She.

She was the center of everything, for that brief time. None of us in the band felt like practicing, Rich and Eve were off in a library somewhere, and I didn't want to hang around Feng's because I knew if I did I'd drink too much. So I spent time with Souci. I can't tell you everything we did during that strange timeless time, but it was all—I don't know, *fun* seems like such an inadequate word.

Dancing? Hell, I think we saw every band in New Quebec. One that consisted of two synthesizer players, trading off different roles not just between songs, but during each song; a three-piece band that sounded like a power trio except their material was taken from old, old, Tin Pan Alley standards; a particularly weird combination of American square-dance tunes and rock with a fifties sound that Souci told me was pretty much the leading edge thereabouts; Souci teaching me dances that had set patterns, which I'd never learned in my life, and then I got to show her the slide and the cathop, and be proud when she turned out to like them.

Shopping? Watching other customers in the big department store and making snide remarks to each other about how they were dressed; juggling oranges at a produce stand; stopping in a

Christian bookstore where Souci pretended she was trying to convert me; sneaking away to buy each other the sort of inane greeting cards that I'd hoped had died out with Old Earth.

Drugs? Guilty as charged. Up for two days straight doing speed, where reality became psychedelic in stages so gradual we weren't aware of it until we realized that we were babbling to each other about the stupidest things; making love standing up in the shower as the two hundred mics of LSD started to come on, then, later, staring in amazed delight at the patterns the rain made on the window; doing shots of tequila and realizing that there were a lot of Old Earth jokes that she hadn't heard, and watching her dissolve into giggles over the pig with the wooden leg.

She.

She hated Tom, pretty much ignored Eve, got along well with Rich, and seemed to connect with both Jamie and Rose. Sometimes when I was tied up for an afternoon, she'd spend the day with the two of them, and I was pleased that they seemed to get along so well. I met few of her friends, and at first I thought she was ashamed of me, then I realized that she just didn't care what they thought, and it was almost more ego inflation than I could stand.

She.

It was only slowly that I discovered how much she was coming to dominate my thoughts and actions. If she was happy, I was happy. If I wanted to do something she didn't like, such as play "Goin' Down that Old Dusty Road," she could take the pleasure out of it, and her scorn pierced like needles.

She.

She had more moods than anyone I'd ever met, and at times I found myself just standing back and watching them: the imp in the bookstore; the seductress who first propositioned me from beneath her eyelashes; the bitch who nearly tore my throat out the second time we argued about Hags disease (which story I'll skip, thanks); the Star to Be, with her eyes gleaming and her voice calm as she spoke about the future; the personal secretary and valet who helped me figure out my budget, cut my hair, and advised me on clothes that would look good to her without offending my twentieth-century Earth sensibilities; and, very, very occasionally, the warm, vulnerable human being who wanted to be cherished and loved.

She had as many different personalities in bed, too, but those aren't any of your business, and I don't think knowing will help your understanding of the strange events I've chosen to relate, so they'll stay here in my heart where I can keep them safe. But once or twice, she'd hold me so tight I could hardly breathe and say, "I'm crazy about you, you know," as if she couldn't believe it herself.

I guess maybe I couldn't believe it, either.

I was sitting in my favorite booth one Tuesday, when Libby signaled me over to her. She was wearing black jeans and a loose pink top that set off her pale skin and brown hair. I said, "What's up?"

"Not much. The most important man in the world was here earlier."

"Oh?"

"Yeah. Only I didn't realize he was the most important man in the world, so I was serving someone who got here first and I didn't jump fast enough."

"Did he complain?"

"Yeah. I told him I was sorry I hadn't known he was the most important man in the world."

I nodded. "So, what does the most important man in the world drink?"

"Brandy and lemon sour."

"Ah. Well, there you have it."

"Yeah. How about you? You look like you've got something on your mind."

"Me? No."

"You sure?"

I turned away and surveyed the room. A middle-aged woman leaned back in her chair, coffee neglected, eyes closed, newspaper in her hand. A little girl of about nine or ten sat alone near the door in the restaurant, probably waiting for her parents. A fat guy in a grey suit and grey hat with bushy white eyebrows sat alone near the door, like an extra in a De Laurentiis spy film. I wondered if he had woman troubles. When all you have is a hammer, everything starts looking like nails. Where did I hear that?

There was a group of four business types, three men and one woman. I could now safely conclude that business wear in New Quebec, sixty-one years after its founding, involved light-colored sports coats with thin lapels, dark shirts in solid colors (button-down was okay but not mandatory), slacks in light colors with a bit of a looser fit than I was used to, ties that were narrow and fairly tame, and suede shoes. Hair, decreed the Lords of Fashion for this time and place, must be short in back and at the sides; it may be long in front, but must be carefully groomed.

I turned back to Libby. "Yeah, I guess there's some stuff on my mind."

"Like what?"

"I think I've been doing too many drugs."

"If you think so, you probably have. So cut it out. What else?"

"Souci."

"What about her?"

"The other day she started in on me. About how stupid it was to play Irish music, and she just really let me have it. She apologized the next day, said she was just in a bad mood. It bothered me how, I don't know, *devastated* I was. Does that make sense?"

She put a toothpick in her mouth and stared at me. "Look, pinhead, someone was killed in here. Someone tried to blow up the place. We don't know when a fucking nuclear bomb is going to fall on our heads. You're worried about some chickie not liking what song you play?"

"Yeah," I said. "I am. That's what's worrying me."

"So take your mind off her for a while and figure out what to do about the rest of it. Pinhead."

"You got any ideas?"

"No. We didn't tell the cops, though. Fred is trying to find out who delivered the boxes, and Rich and Eve are at the library studying up on the progress of the human race and nuclear war."

"What's the rest of my band doing?"

Libby made a crude gesture suggesting autoeroticism.

"Got it," I said. "Yeah, I guess maybe it's time I do something."

"Good," said Libby. "What?"

"I don't know. I'll talk to Rich and Eve, see if they need any help."

But they didn't; they'd already found the answers they were looking for.

Jamie pushed two tables together and Fred placed chairs around them as Rich and I cleaned up after the last pair of customers of the night. Libby brought over a pitcher of something called "plum-brego phosphate" and glasses for the bunch of us. We were in the taproom, I guess because it felt more intimate.

Rich sat down with his back to the stage and Eve at his right. I was on his left, with Libby next to me, then Fred, Jamie at the other end of the table, Rose next to him, and Tom across from me. Jamie, Rose, Fred, Rich, and Tom were all smoking the local variety of tobacco-like weed. Smoke trailed away from the stage toward the intake duct above the bar like a grey down comforter. I wondered if it could be woven into a business suit.

As we got settled I found myself studying Eve. Whatever they'd found out, she had no doubt done most of the hard work, just because she spoke all the languages and had that sort of mind. What sort of mind? She hardly ever said a word, and when she did, you could barely hear her. She had a delightful laugh and beautiful blue eyes and a habit of going into sulks. Once, when a bunch of us had been sitting around shooting the breeze, I'd suddenly been almost overwhelmed by sorrow for everything and everyone we'd left behind. I hadn't said anything, and I'm sure my face didn't change, but Eve suddenly reached over and squeezed my hand. I've never understood how she did things like that. A mystery among mysteries.

Rich said, "I suppose you're wondering—no, never mind. Eve and I decided to do what we could to predict when and if we were going to be hit by another bomb." He paused for effect. Jamie and I looked at each other and Jamie rolled his eyes. Rich continued, "We didn't exactly find out. We got sidetracked onto a study of the causes of the original war, back home."

I looked around to see if anyone was going to react badly to the mention of home, but everyone seemed to handle it all right. Rich turned to Eve, who said, "Full-scale nuclear war has occurred five times in human history." I could barely hear her over the whir of the ventilation system.

Jamie said, "Five times? Total?"

Eve nodded. "The Earth, the Moon, Venus, Mars, and Galway around Proxima, just before mass colonization started."

Tom said, "And we've been there for three of them."

I said, "Pure coincidence." Everyone looked at me. I added, "That was a joke."

Rich said, "The first war, the one on Earth, lasted about eight years."

"That's a hell of a long time for a nuclear war," I said.

He shrugged. "It's measuring from when Cairo was hit until, well, there was nothing left."

"Yeah," I said. We looked at each other. I was remembering

where I was when I heard about Cairo. I was in a hardware store, getting some brackets to mount a speaker, when I noticed everyone rushing over to the cash register and watching the little TV, and I asked someone, and I remember how weak my knees got. There was a guy next to me in a maroon raincoat, yeah, it was May, and he sat down on the floor and shook his head. There was a lady who—well, never mind. Rich gave us a moment with our memories, then began speaking again.

"We started trying to find the causes of the war, and that's when things started to get weird." Once more he paused. "We couldn't find any."

"Well," I said, "I wouldn't expect it to be that easy to conclude, after all this time."

"No," he said. "You don't understand. There was nothing. No speculation, no conflicting reports, no analyses tying it into a psychological racial death-wish, no blaming it on some country or another. No blaming it on space aliens or Elvis's ghost. *Nothing*."

"That," I suggested, "is impossible."

"I know," said Rich.

Fred said, "Methinks someone has been censoring lots and lots of things."

Libby said, "Did you try newspapers of the time?"

Eve said, "The library didn't have any."

"That seems weird," I said. "With how easy information storage is—"

"I know," said Rich. "They have papers from before the war, but none from during. Either none of them escaped, or they've been deleted or hidden."

"Wow," said Rose.

"We're not done," said Rich.

"Great," said Jamie.

Rich turned to him and started to say something, then thought better of it. Instead he said, "We started digging into the history of the resettlement, looking for patterns on what happened that led to the wars on the Moon, and Venus, and Mars. That's when Eve found the really weird thing."

"I can hardly wait," I said under my breath. Libby heard me and flashed a grin.

Eve said, "There was a Russian book that traced a particular group of colonists. They were all very powerful, and they came from different parts of the world, and they settled on Luna, well, just about the time we were getting nuked in London."

"Really," I said. "I hadn't known there was any colonization going on that early. We got blasted ahead six years, and I got the impression that there hadn't been much actual settling there until three or four years before that."

Fred shook his head. "There wasn't," he said.

"When was the book written?" asked Jamie.

"Fairly recently."

"So he could have gotten his dates wrong."

"I suppose."

"Let Eve go on," said Rich.

We nodded. She said, "This group of people—"

"How big a group?" interrupted Jamie.

"About thirty families. Big families. Extended families. Perhaps as many as a thousand people."

"All right."

"They immigrated to Venus as a group during the two weeks before Ibrium City was destroyed. Then they moved to Dockside, Mars, about four months before the war on Venus. They left Mars during the three days before we were hit in Jerrysport."

"A good group of guessers," I said. "Or else they knew something the rest of the human race didn't know."

"Or," said Rich, "they were the cause of the—"

Jamie interrupted Rich's thought by snorting quite loudly. "Are you going to tell me that a thousand people caused nuclear war on five worlds?"

Rich said, "And then removed all traces of how they did it. Yeah. That's what I'm saying."

Jamie made a sound with his lips, something like "Pffff."

Rose said, "Why would they want to?"

Rich shrugged.

Fred said, "I don't see it."

Eve said, "They were all very rich and very powerful."

I said, "Is there any evidence at all?"

"The timing," said Rich. "The fact that they could do it. The lack of any other indications as to the cause."

I shook my head. "I don't buy it."

Rich said, "Guess where they went after they left Mars?"

I shrugged. "How should I—wait. No."

Rich said, "They spent some time on Galway around Proxima, then they built a series of exploratory starships, including the *Winnipeg Dave*. At the time this book was written, they were en route following her, about six colony ships and three years behind."

"Damn," I said. "And these guys have been everywhere there's been nuclear war, and there's been nuclear war everywhere they've been?"

"Yes," said Rich.

"And now they're here?"

"Yes," said Rich.

"Wow," I said.

"I need whiskey," said Rose.

"There's more," said Rich.

"Great," said Jamie. "What now?"

"They have a name."

"A name?" I said. "Like an organization?"

"Yep," said Rich. "The book gives the name in Russian, but—"

"Sacharmedved," said Eve, or something like that.

We all took turns trying to pronounce it. I shook my head. "Does it mean anything?"

"Yeah," said Rich.

"Sugar Bear," said Eve, in her tiny little voice.

Intermezzo

You'd better get born someplace else,
Move along, get along, move along, get along,
Go, move, shift.

"Move Along,"
Ewan McCall

The Cicero Cluster became a going concern around 550 years after the founding of Ibrium City. It consisted of some fourteen star systems loosely centered around Cicero itself. It was founded by several thousand men and women who escaped from the destruction of the Triangle Worlds by matters of days in some cases, hours in others. They never learned from whom they fled, yet they were harried, hounded, and hunted, until those who escaped landed on a friendly if relatively lifeless world they called Cicero after the captain of the *Docsmith*, the flag vessel of the makeshift fleet. The sun they named Marko, and, over the course of several hundred years, they came to inhabit a belt of stars around it.

For the first few score of years they were hiding from whoever had caused the destruction of the Triangle Worlds. Later they became stronger, but they still made no effort to reach anyone outside of their own system, for fear their efforts at communication would be detected. When they finally got around to trying, nearly a hundred years after the landing on Cicero, they couldn't reach anyone. Some thought this was because communication technology had changed sufficiently that no one was receiving what they were broadcasting. Others suspected that they were using faulty information on the location of the Earth, or incorrect algorithms on the other major systems, or incorrect algorithms to update their positions.

No one seriously entertained the notion that the Earth and every other outpost of humanity had been destroyed, leaving only themselves and the enemy.

When the Cicero Cluster was discovered, or, more probably, stumbled upon by the enemy, attempts to reach anyone who might help were intensified, even as hasty defenses were organized. The theory that advances in communication technology prevented contact became more popular, so efforts to find newer, better, and more unusual means of sending information across light-years doubled and doubled again.

They never did make contact. But in the course of trying, they learned how to break down matter and reassemble it at arbitrary points in space. It was while they were debating how to use this as a weapon, and how to get the necessary amount of energy, that it occurred to someone that an arbitrary point in space was also an arbitrary point in time.

An entire world of discovery would open up, if every habitation in the cluster wasn't reduced to rubble before they had the chance.

CHAPTER
6

Seasons keep turning;
All things must die,
I just dropped over
To ask you why.
"Been There Before,"
Adam Stemple

"Sugar Bear," I repeated dumbly.

Rich nodded.

"I need whiskey," said Rose.

Tom stared at Rich.

Libby and Fred looked at each other, back at Rich, at each other, at the rest of us, and back at Rich. Silence covered the room like a London fog, broken by occasional patches of cleared throats and shuffled feet.

"Well, that was dull," I said. "Anyone have any interesting news?"

Fred cleared his throat. "Well, yes, as a matter of fact."

"Great."

"I've been making some discreet calls, trying to find out who might have tampered with those cases of whiskey."

"Ah. And?"

"It seems the truck was sitting unattended here for several hours. Unlocked as well."

"Oh."

"On the other hand, our next-door neighbor, Mr. Carob of the appliance store, saw the driver and his assistant leaving the truck to get coffee or something, and then saw two other persons near it."

Fred was the sort of person who would use "persons" in casual conversation.

"How is Mr. Carob at descriptions?" I asked.

"Quite good, actually."

"Well, bless his heart."

"Did you have to explain why we were looking for them?"

"I think he assumed some liquor was taken, and I saw no need to correct him on this."

"Bless your heart."

"Thank you." He took some notebook paper from his pocket. "The descriptions," he said.

Rich already had his hand out. He chewed his beard and grunted as he studied them. "Two men, both white, one about five-eight or nine with short red hair, walked with his shoulders hunched up, the other shorter, neat dark hair, mustache, his feet point out a bit when he walks."

"He really does have a good eye," I said.

"He does," said Rich. "I don't recognize either one from the description, though. I'll ask around."

"Discreetly," I suggested.

"What about the police?" said Rose.

I shook my head. "Whatever is going on, the local police are involved at some level, or there would be more of an investigation going on over the guy who was killed here."

"Not necessarily," said Fred. "We don't know what kind of manpower they have, or even how serious a crime murder is on a colony like this."

"It can't be legal," said Libby.

I studied the faces around me, then looked down at the table between my arms. I suspected they were realizing, for the first time, just how serious this was. I wondered how we'd all stand up to it. Fred wouldn't be shaken. I knew from talking to him that he'd been through worse. And Libby was like a rock. Rich? Eve? Jamie? Tom? I didn't know. Myself? Heh. We'd see.

". . . big explosion," Libby was saying, "and all our clothes fell off, and the lights went out. What could we do?"

I said, "What?"

"Oh, nothing. You weren't listening."

I sighed. "I'm sorry. I was distracted. What were you saying?"

"I was saying that you knew someone who knew something about Sugar Bear."

"What do you mean?"

"Souci. Remember the first time you mentioned Sugar Bear around her? She practically got up and ran from the room."

"Oh. Yeah. I thought I'd imagined that. You noticed it, too, huh?"

"Shit," said Libby. "I'd have to have been dead to miss it."

"You going to ask her about it, Billy?" asked Jamie.

I almost asked him if he had any idea what he was asking for, but there was really no point in it. "Yeah. I'll be seeing her tomorrow."

I caught Tom's eye. He stared at me for a moment, then looked away.

The next day was Wednesday, and a cold breeze came walking through the streets, carrying a smell and a tingling on the skin that's winter saying, "Hi. I'll be there in a minute, okay?" I have no great love for winter, but that first warning day of it is pleasant; it gives me a referent for the word "brisk," and makes me want to put on a leather jacket and go walking through the streets with my girl's hands wrapped around my arm as she leans toward me for warmth and my hands are in my pocket and our hair goes whipping around . . .

Yeah.

The temperature was just above freezing, and I'm told that in New Quebec this was pretty much as cold as it ever got, which was nothing compared to Jerrysport, with its incomplete terraforming, but pretty horrid compared to the tightly controlled conditions in Ibrium City.

I said nothing as we walked in toward the main drag, Souci's hands wrapped around my arm. Her hair was blown back off her face. There was that slight pout to her lips that may have been accomplished with lipstick. There were two bicycles in front of the bakery, probably the same bicycles, but I didn't see the kids. A middle-aged woman dragged groceries behind her in a small cart. A fat man sat on a wire chair outside an outdoor café; it was too cold for everyone else. Our conversation as we walked consisted of, "Where should we eat?" "How about Cecil's?" "Fine." We didn't have to talk.

There was plenty of light in Cecil's so I could keep watching her. I never got tired of looking at her. The bones on her face were not so much perfect as perfect for her; the feline curve around the edges of her eyes, the hollow of her cheek, like a work of sculpture. I thought about what I had to ask her and grimaced.

Cecil's? It was a small place with a lot of mirrors and chrome and a little bit of an antiseptic feeling. The food was good, though. We had something that tasted like oyster soup and almost was, then she had a small salad and I had something with beef and mushrooms in a sherry sauce. No complaints.

She said, "You're pretty quiet."

"I'm eating."

She said, "Ahh," which meant, "I don't believe you."

I said, "Well, yeah."

She said, "What is it?"

I said, "The bunch of us had a talk last night."

"Oh?"

"We need to know what you know about Sugar Bear."

Everything in her body seemed to tighten for a moment and I was suddenly sure she was about to leave, but then that moment passed and she just looked at me. Her eyes never left mine. She said, "Is that right?" I wish I could describe the tone of voice she used for that: the cool, distant, uninterested tone that cut like a razor and raised welts like a whip. Maybe, if I could describe it, you'd understand just how hard it was for me to continue the conversation. If you think this is a plea for sympathy, you got it, bub.

"We need to know," I repeated.

"Who is we?"

"You know what I mean."

"No, I don't."

"Jamie, Rich, Eve, Tom, Rose—"

"These people sent you to ask me—"

"Not exactly. We need to know about Sugar Bear, and I know you know something about it."

"Maybe."

"It's important."

"To whom?"

"To all of us. Maybe to everyone in New Quebec. Maybe to everyone in the world."

"Shit," and the scorn in her voice cut me again, raised more welts.

"Maybe I'm wrong about that," I said, struggling to keep my voice even. "If so, you can tell me why. I need to know."

"What about me?"

"What about you?"

"Doesn't it matter what happens to me?"

"What will happen to you?" She turned her head from me and didn't say anything. I said, "I don't understand. Would something happen to you if you told us about it?"

She didn't answer. I couldn't tell if her shoulders were shaking or not. The idea that I might be making her cry made me physically ill. I said, "Are you all right, babe? Is there something I can—"

"Leave me alone, all right?"

She got up and walked out of the place. I sat there for two hours hoping she'd come back. When she didn't I went back to the apartment, but she wasn't there, either. I sat up in the living room with my back against Tom's pillow for an hour or so, then I went into my room and slept.

Jamie woke me up the next morning with coffee with cream and sugar and cocoa. "Thanks," I said, sitting up.

He sat down against the wall opposite me. "How did it go?"

It came back to me then. I studied the wall for a moment, just to see if there were any cracks in it. I cleared my throat and turned back to Jamie. "Not well," I said. "She got upset and took off."

"You didn't get an answer, then."

"No. Not yet, anyway. Maybe after she's thought about it."

"Okay," he said, and left me to finish my coffee in peace.

Later the four of us plus Carrie trooped over to Feng's for breakfast. I had an omelette with green pepper and onions and sausage and garlic and cayenne, and a side of French toast. I had a local tea that was maybe a bit milder than the Irish Breakfast I was used to.

"Well," I said as I was finishing up. "We struck out with Souci. Now what?"

"What was the problem?" asked Tom.

"She didn't want to tell me anything," I said.

Tom said to Carrie, "Could you ask her?" Her eyes grew very wide and she shook her head.

"Guess not," I said.

"I could talk to her," said Jamie.

I looked at him. Yeah, he could be pretty persuasive. I remembered once when he convinced me to start an Irish band with him and Rose and Tom. I said, "If you think you can talk her into telling us something, go for it. I just don't want to get her any madder at me than she already is."

"This is so weird," said Carrie. "It's like you're plotting against her."

"Not against her," I said, maybe too quickly, because the same thought had occurred to me.

"What," said Tom, "*for* her?"

"We need to know what she knows," I said.

"I was joking," said Tom.

"What I'd like to do," said Jamie, "is go stir up trouble somewhere until someone does something."

"Robert B. Parker," said Tom.

I said, "When you find a good writer, you stick with him."

"It'd work," said Jamie.

"Where do we do that?" said Tom.

"Ummm. I don't know."

We sat there a bit longer, then Jamie shrugged and stood up. "I'll go talk to Souci."

"Good luck," I said. The rest of us sat and drank coffee and tea, saying very little, for the better part of an hour. Then Fred came in, saw us, and headed straight over. He had a camera case slung over his shoulder, and a manila folder in his hand.

"Any news?" I asked him.

"As a matter of fact, yes," he said. "I happened to see someone who matched one of the descriptions going into a building not far from here, so I took a picture of him, and Mr. Carob agreed that it is him."

"That's great," I said. "What building?"

"It's just a few doors down," he said. "It's called Le Bureau Théâtral du Nouveau Québec."

"That's the agency Souci works out of," said Carrie.

"Of course it is," I said.

"I talked to her," said Jamie a few hours later, back at the apartment. "I tried, anyway." I waited, watching him, wondering how he'd react to the latest news on our end. Tom and Carrie were out watching TV or something at Carrie's and Rose was in the back room running through scales on her fiddle. Jamie said, "She doesn't think it's any of our business what she knows, and doesn't feel like talking about it."

"Oh," I said. "Was she mad at you?"

He shook his head. "Not as far as I could tell. She hardly looked at me, though. She just kept packing."

My stomach did a one and a half gainer into my small intestine. I said, "Packing?"

"She said she was flying out to Dernièrebale for a week or so, to get away from things."

"Oh," I said. My voice sounded very small in my own ears. "When is she leaving?"

"Today or tomorrow."

"Maybe I should walk over there." Jamie didn't answer. I said, "She's pretty mad at me, isn't she?"

"I don't know. Your name didn't come up." He didn't look at me while he said it.

I said, "Oh."

A moment later I felt Jamie watching me, and realized that my eyes were closed. I opened them. Jamie said, "Want to play a song or two?"

"Not right now," I said. "I think I'll take a walk. I've got news for you, but it'll wait."

"Are you sure you don't want company?"

"Yeah, I'm sure. Thanks. I'll be back in a few."

It took a long fifteen minutes to get to Souci's apartment. She lived in a neighborhood of tree-lined streets, interrupted by little half-block parks and wading pools and such. She lived in the bottom unit of a new-looking duplex with a roommate whom she never saw. "That's the only way I can stand to have a roommate," she had explained. I could hear her voice when I thought about it. I remembered the inside as clean and orderly, with a couch, an entertainment console, a fibrawood table and chair set, and not much more. "The furniture is all Annie's," she had explained. "I don't have much of my own. I don't stay in one place long enough to keep much furniture." I heard her voice again.

No one answered when I rang. I thought about camping on the doorstep and decided that would be pretty stupid, so I went back. Jamie had left. I sat in the living room, hauled out the banjo, and played through "Sailor's Hornpipe" and "Arkansas Traveler," then settled down to work on "Tennessee Rag" for a while, to see if I could finally get it clean. This required a great deal of concentration, leaving me no room to think about anything else.

That evening I went to a club where Les Sons Magiques were playing. I hoped Souci might be there. She wasn't. Between sets I spoke to her friend, Christian, the lead guitarist. He confirmed that she'd gone out of town. "I'm not sure why," he said. "She seemed really weird when I talked to her. Do you know what's going on?"

I shook my head. "I wish I did."

He nodded, distracted. He put his feet up on a chair and sipped a beer. "Are you guys playing tomorrow? I should hear you sometime, and we don't play again until Saturday."

"No, we've got the weekend off. Want to get together and do some tunes?"

He gave me a sort of appraisal. "That'd be fun," he said, surprising me. "Feng's?"

"How about my place? It's just off Dupont, toward the river." I gave him the address. We agreed to make it about noon and I'd whip us up some food.

It didn't occur to me until I was walking home that Christian was a friend of Souci's, and Souci was tied into Le Bureau, which meant I ought to be at least a little more suspicious of him. I sighed. I wasn't cut out for this kind of thing.

Back home I brought Jamie up-to-date about Souci's possible connection with Sugar Bear. Since Rose and Tom were there, and I couldn't think of anything else to do, I suggested we practice.

We tried to reconstruct a couple of verses to "The Work of the Wavers," failed, and ended up learning "Chesterfields," with three-part harmonies (four, if you count the fiddle). We slapped a typical (for us) opening on it: about one-quarter speed, drawn out, overdone, and very silly. That was fun, and we got it worked out pretty well kicking into the fast part until Rose announced that she didn't want to play fiddle on it.

"Why not?" I asked, trying not to sound irritated.

"It doesn't need it."

"I think it sounds great," said Jamie. Tom was smoking a cigarette and staring at the ceiling.

I said, "What would you rather do?"

"How about bodhran?"

I said, "I think the fiddle is better." I almost said, "Why don't you learn to play the fucking bodhran before you go wanting to play it on every song?" but I didn't.

Jamie said, "I agree with Billy," but he looked uncomfortable.

Tom got up to take a walk. I don't know why that annoyed me, but it did. I decided I was developing another attitude problem. I said, "Let's can this until tomorrow, all right?"

"Good idea," said Rose.

Jamie shrugged and nodded, but looked unhappy. It was pretty late by then, and I was very tired, so I had no trouble falling asleep in spite of everything.

Christian showed up at half past noon the next day. I made some egg salad with onions and celery and peppers and stuff and he seemed to like it. Everyone else was out somewhere or another.

Seeing Christian in a well-lit room made me realize that he was younger than I'd first thought. His hair looked like he really honest-to-God never combed it, as opposed to those who spend hours every day making it look like they never comb it. His walk went with the hair: a relaxed shuffle accompanied by a bobbing, head-turning movement as if he were checking out the area to see what fun could be had, the whole overlaid with a more or less permanent smile. He swore frequently and well in French and English.

I got out my banjo, and he turned out, to my amazement, to know "Cumberland Blues." Well, if he knew that, he must know "Stealin'," right? And "Mama Tried"? We had a grand old time teaching each other songs and discovering which ones we both knew. I almost got him broken of the habit of running through blues progressions when he didn't have anything else to do. Not that I inherently object to blues progressions, you understand, but I'm fairly limited how much blues I want to play on the banjo.

Later we sat and talked, and I asked him questions about Souci, and he either evaded them or didn't know the answers. We got hungry, so I cooked something while he went out for beer. Tom and Carrie showed up, so I added some water and onions to the soup. After we ate, Tom and Christian and I played some more. When we'd exhausted all the music in the world, Christian crashed in the living room, right where the couch would have been if the place had been furnished.

The next morning I woke up to a knock at my bedroom door. I yelled, "Come in," and it turned out, to my surprise, to be Rich, looking worried.

"I'm worried," said Rich.

"I can see that," I said.

"What?"

"Never mind." I got up and threw some clothes on, trying to wake up. I stretched and said, "What is it?"

"This whole business, I don't know. It's—"

"Got you worried?"

"Yeah."

I rolled my eyes and gestured aimlessly around me. "I can't, for the life of me, imagine why. We have reason to believe there's a conspiracy which probably succeeded in wiping out all life on Earth, from which disaster we were only saved by being in a restaurant that goes shooting around the galaxy, and in which someone was murdered and which someone has just tried to blow up, which even if it didn't kill us outright would leave us stranded here when the bombs come down, as they probably will within another month. That's all. Why should you be worried?"

When I turned back to him, he was shaking his head sadly. "For one thing," he said, "because someone had been following me."

"Oh, great. That just figures, doesn't it?"

"And for another, because you've just told everything about us to whoever it is who's been sitting there in the next room during your whole speech."

"Did I hear myself referred to?" asked Christian from the door.

"It's going to be another great day," I said. "I can see that already."

CHAPTER
7

Look at the coffin
　　　　With golden handles
Isn't it grand, boys,
　　　　To be bloody well dead?
　　　　　　"Isn't It Grand, Boys?"
　　　　　　Traditional

I said, "Would you believe we were just kidding?"

"Ummm."

"Right," I said.

"Let's find some breakfast," said Christian.

"I'll go along with that," said Rich. "And we can keep an eye out for whoever was following me."

Right. I'd forgotten about that. "Are you sure someone was?"

"Yes."

"Then he wasn't very good."

"Should I be insulted?"

"No."

"All right. Where's Eve?"

"The library."

"Of course."

I finished my morning business and we went out in search of

adventure and breakfast, not necessarily in that order. We walked, or rather strolled, along LeDuc, with its wide bicycle paths and dwarf maple trees, toward Feng's. Christian was in the middle between Rich and me. Christian said, "So, is all that really true?"

"Is what true?" I said.

"Heh."

"Well," I said after a moment, "I guess you can believe as much of it as you want to."

"That's some shit," said Christian.

I sighed. "Look, I'm sorry you overheard what you did, but it wasn't any part of my plan. I was tired. Forget it, believe it, or think we're nuts, but don't expect me to answer questions about it."

He said, "Just tell me this: Does it have anything to do with why Souci left town?"

I winced. "Probably. Or maybe only indirectly. I don't know."

Half a block before we reached Feng's, we stopped. Rich pointed to a low brick building. I stopped, and the others stopped, and we studied it for a moment. The lettering on the small, hand-painted sign said, "Le Bureau Théâtral du Nouveau Québec" in stylized script. It was an interesting building, all of an odd blue brick, and only waist-high above the ground. The roof formed a gentle arc, and the stairway down to the doorway had the same arc, smaller and in reverse. I guess it was an earth-sheltered building that was not embedded into a hill, and it gave the impression of a sort of quiet efficiency.

"So that's the place," I said.

"What place?" asked Rich.

"Souci's modeling agency," said Christian before I could.

"Ah."

The door opened and two women I didn't recognize came out, unlocked a pair of bicycles, and rode off up the street. I watched them carefully in case I might need to identify some portion of them in a police lineup later.

"The one on the left," said Rich.

"What about her?"

"She's very tall."

"That's true," I said.

"Tall," repeated Christian. "Is that what you call it?"

"Yeah, I—wait a minute."

The door opened again, and a short, pinch-faced fellow came out, looked at us, turned, went back inside. I said, "Is that—"

"Yes," said Rich. "That was the guy who was following me."

"Oh," I said. "Actually, I'd been about to ask if he was one of the guys in the pictures Fred has. I've seen him before, I think with *her*."

"I haven't seen the pictures," said Rich.

"Neither have I. I guess we both ought to look at them, huh?"

"What pictures?" said Christian.

"Never mind," I said.

"Asshole," suggested Christian sweetly.

When we got to Feng's, which was just opening and already had a few people waiting for lunch, we left Christian at a table, grabbed Fred, and took him into the pantry.

"Hurry up, gentlemen," he said. "There are customers."

"Right," I said. "Pictures."

He took a plain number ten envelope from his back pocket, handed it to me, and was gone. We rejoined Christian and opened it. There were two snapshots in it, both taken, I think, from a distance with a good telephoto lens.

"This guy," I said, "I've met. His name is Justin and he's a friend of Carrie's."

"He's the one who was following me," said Rich.

"Great. And I'm sure you recognize this guy, right?"

"Yeah. We just saw him coming out of Le Bureau whatever it was."

"His name is Claude," said Christian. "I don't know his last name."

I said, "Why didn't you tell us before?"

"You didn't ask."

"Don't make me kill you."

He shrugged and smiled. I continued to look at him, considering. "What is it?" he said.

I cleared my throat. "I guess it isn't surprising that you know all of those people, I mean, if you hang around with S—, with her, you'd know the same people. It's just that—you know."

"What?"

That this guy who knew so much about us might be on the side of whoever had tried to blow up the place. "Nothing," I said. "Let's eat."

After breakfast, which in my case involved scrambled eggs and hash browns, both including green pepper and onions, the eggs also involving participation by mushrooms, sausage, and paprika,

Christian said, "So, you guys are, like, aliens from another planet, right?"

I said, "I've never really thought of it that way before. It might be more accurate to say another *time,* though. Or maybe dimension. I like that: William Kevely, traveler through dimensions."

"Can I come along?" asked Christian.

"Why?" I asked.

"Well, if we're about to be nuked . . ."

"That's right, you heard that, too, eh?"

"Yeah."

"We could be lying, you know."

"I don't think so."

I shrugged. "Always room at Cowboy Feng's."

A few cups of coffee later, Christian took off to get a few extra sets of strings—or so he claimed.

"Should we follow him?" said Rich.

"If he's with them, he'll expect us to. Do you know how to avoid being spotted? I don't."

"I guess not."

Rich and I put our feet up on the seats and drank coffee. I stared out the window. A head of red hair floated past above the far booth and my heart leapt, but it wasn't her. I thought about having a drink and decided it would be a bad idea just then.

"Something wrong, Billy?"

"Nothing important."

"What's important and what isn't? If it's important to you—"

"Yeah. I know. Never mind. I think I'll go back home and play some banjo."

"Suit yourself. Let me know if I can do anything."

"I will."

Since it was only half an hour out of the way, I walked by Souci's place and rang the bell, but no one answered.

That night I went back to Feng's to catch Pan's Dream, and I thought they were good; the flute player was especially hot. Between sets, I talked to the skinny guy, whose name was Luc. He suggested that I get together with his band sometime to jam, and I complimented him on his band, and he explained how badly they were doing that night, and later I found myself in a back corner booth drinking soda and listening until the music was over. The guy running the sound board for them was a large, bearded man with long hair, a bald spot, and a potbelly. He was pretty good, too; surprisingly good for how much cheap whiskey he consumed.

When they were done, I remained in back drinking orange juice and charged water while they packed up and left. Libby saw me, correctly deduced that I didn't want company, and left me alone. When the place finally closed, she turned the lights out without saying a word. The room became very quiet. The stage creaked occasionally as it recovered from the abuse suffered earlier. The ventilation system softly hummed the D below middle C (we've checked). From time to time, my glass thunked on the table. I decided I should probably have been drinking scotch to get the full dramatic effect from the moment, but it was better that I didn't.

After about forty-five minutes of feeling good and sorry for myself, I got up, walked outside, and found myself face-to-face with the short guy named Claude whom I had seen earlier that day at Le Bureau. He was dressed in dark clothes and had something in his hand. After a moment, it resolved itself into a large canister. We stared at each other for a moment, then he dropped it and ran. I smelled kerosene.

I don't remember deciding to chase him, but I must have because I did. It was a foolish idea. He knew the city, I didn't, he was probably in better shape than I was, and I had no idea what I was going to do if I caught him, but chase him I did, down the middle of the street, then around a building where he hid hoping I'd pass him, but I didn't, so around another corner, smack into blinding lights, a car? no, security light, and he's running *that* way, toward the door to a bar, I think, past it, a wind catches in my throat and I can't breathe for just a moment, tears in my eyes, someone opened a door, but no, not that way, around to the left, and was that him going through that window? good thing this place is empty, feet echoing slap slap up a flight of stairs I can hear him glass breaking out the window down to land rollingrolling-rolling broken glass on my shoulder makes me happy from an alley looks like fucking New York City he must be out of breath by now, good, I wish I could get more air into my lungs and my legs are so heavy, so heavy, where did he go now, can't see the runner for the tears, and he's turned down this—

He stopped. Why?

Ah! He thinks he's lost me.

"Shit," I said aloud, and leaned against a building for a while, breathing in gasps. I could practically feel him on the other side of a garbage dumpster, maybe twenty feet away from me. I pushed away from the wall after a while and started walking, trying very hard to walk quietly so he wouldn't think it odd when he could no longer hear my footsteps after about thirty paces, when I stopped, listened, and heard his.

I set out after him once more, carefully this time. I mostly stayed hidden, and once I caught him looking back over his shoulder, but I was pretty well concealed in the shadow of a church of some sort. Appropriate, if you like. I never saw him look back after that, so I assumed he never saw me.

Eventually he left the city proper, and I fell even further back as we walked along a dirt road. I could just barely see him as he came to a very tall house all done up in Victorian clothes, from which light came streaming out to collect in puddles on the road. The house was very big, and formed a nice silhouette against the sunset. I decided it would have made someone a very fine haunted house, from what I could see of the towers. Perhaps it had gables; I don't know what a gable is. It had funny things that looked decorative built up around the towers, and if they weren't gables they should have been, because it was that sort of house.

There was an iron fence, the fence set into a low wall. It made me wonder, suddenly and perhaps irrelevantly, what this indicated about the economics of the person or the colony. But I had no idea if skilled craftsmen were plentiful, or iron was rare, so it really told me nothing. I hid behind the wall and watched as Claude knocked on the door and was admitted. I got no glimpse of the person on the inside. I made a note of the house number and the name of the road, and I left.

It took me a long time to find my way home, and I might still be looking if I hadn't found the river and correctly guessed that we were downstream from my apartment. The walk home helped settle nerves that badly needed settling. I stopped by Feng's and removed the canister that did, in fact, contain kerosene. I held it for a while, thinking. A killing, a bomb, and this. The killing was successful, the bombing prevented by Rich's alertness and by luck, the burning by luck alone.

I opened the place up and stored the kerosene inside Feng's for lack of anywhere else to bring it, and because one never knows when one might need two or three gallons of kerosene to burn down a Victorian mansion or something.

When I woke up, it was early afternoon of a beautiful Sunday tra-la tra-la. Out the window of my bedroom, past lacy curtains left by Mr. and Mrs. Previous Occupant, a monster elm, Earth variety, held the ground together and the sky up and neatly bisected the unkempt green terraced and dirty-pine-fenced backside of a New Quebec residential district. The tree had to be damn near the full sixty years old that it could be. Can you imagine that? Land on a planet and start planting elms. Every once in a while I think the human race is worth saving, after all.

As I lay there that afternoon making deep, melancholy, and philosophical reflections, it came to me that this last bit—the one about saving the human race—wasn't totally out of the question. That is, whoever had blown up Earth could have had that in mind. A frightening thought, if an unlikely one. It would certainly explain the way the wars followed people around.

"But who," I subvocalized, "would want to destroy the human race, anyway?" I considered this carefully, in part because it took my mind off wondering about Souci. The more I thought about it, the odder it seemed. I did not consider myself any sort of expert on the human animal, and I'd never made a study of psychology, or maybe I'd have been able to make some sort of intelligent guess. I tried to build a picture in my mind of the sort of maniac who would be seriously trying to destroy humanity, and what his motives could be. Religious? Maybe. But what religion? I could suggest the idea to Eve, who enjoyed looking things up in libraries, maybe she'd learn something, and then I could—

—what?

I sighed and studied a knot in the elm. In wood it's called a knot; in metal it's called a flaw, because somewhere we decided that man is fallible and nature is not. This first proposition seems intuitively obvious; the second is dubious. As I studied this knot and made cynical observations about humanity and myself, I faced the fact that I had no idea what to do about any of the dilemmas I found myself amid.

But I had to know.

Maybe—probably—because the alternative was to wonder about *her,* but the reason didn't matter. There it was, and I was going to act on it, because I needed to act.

But first, I would deal with those aspects of reality that rudely forced themselves upon my consciousness; that is, I got out of bed and used the bathroom.

An hour later, showered, shaved, with notes left behind me to who may be concerned, I set out walking toward a large mansion. The notes detailed what I had discovered, gave the location of the mansion, and what I planned to do. I mailed it to Libby care of

Cowboy Feng, figuring I could get to them before it was opened
and tell them all of this in person if I survived.

It is certainly the case that I am a coward, but there was an air
of unreality about this threat that made it easy to deny it; to just go
do what I wanted to without really thinking about it. Whatever
happened, I expected it to be interesting.

The place was more impressive in the daylight. It was big and
white with red trim around the windows that should have made it
look more garish than it did. All the paint was new. All the edges
and corners were sharp. The door was big and wood and had an
ornate brass knocker that belonged there. I used it, and waited
more than a minute. The door opened with a thoughtful creaking
and a slowness that would have been more appropriate in a Mel
Brooks parody of a horror movie than in the real thing. When it
opened and I was able to get a look at the man who opened it, I
knew at once that this was not the butler I'd more than half
expected, though I cannot point to precisely how I knew.

He stood half a head taller than I. His face was heavily jowled,
heavily browed, and quite ruddy. His hair was curly and completely grey. He wore black and white, including a very long,
black dinner jacket with, apparently, velvet lapels. Jamie would
have looked great wearing it on stage. Other than his white shoes,
I thought him fairly well dressed. I hate people who wear white
shoes. Sorry if I'm stepping on any toes, so to speak, but it's a
prejudice. Don't let me get started on Trans Ams. He studied me
with an expression of mild curiosity; if I were selling encyclope-
dias, he would ask me to leave politely but without room for
argument.

I tried to forget the white shoes. He said, "*Oui, monsieur?*" His
voice was very rich and full, the sort of voice one enjoys listening
to.

"*Parlez-vous* English?" I managed, with some work.

"Indeed," he said. "How may I help you?" Clipped, yet
distinctly more American than, say, British. East Coast, perhaps.
Perhaps not.

"I am looking for the master or mistress of the house. My name
is Kevely."

As I said my name, his brow went up and my heart dropped
approximately the same distance. "William Francis Kevely, is it
not?" he said. "Or Billy, as your friends call you?"

My voice was dry, but fortunately did not crack. "That is correct."

"Please come in, Mr. Kevely. This is my home. My name is Harold Peter Rudd. You will understand if I do not offer to shake hands."

"A pleasure, Monsieur Rudd."

"The pleasure is mine, Mr. Kevely."

I crossed the threshold into an L-shaped entryway, with coat closets on either side and a mirror straight ahead. He helped me with my leather jacket, where it found a home between something white and furry and something long and tweedy. I think it was supposed to feel honored.

Out of the L and into the land of high ceilings and a fireplace in a big sitting room where we were surrounded by books that didn't look read, a fireplace that did look used, and light-colored wood paneling. I didn't see any speakers, but they could have been concealed. Two chairs sat in the middle looking lost, facing each other at an oblique angle. They were probably Louis the something or other. When he gestured me into one, I was surprised that it was comfortable.

"Brandy, Mr. Kevely?" he said. Of course. I wondered how much he was playing a role. Silly question, phrased that way. The room echoed as he spoke. The whole thing was pretty spooky, and rather surreal at the same time.

"No, thanks. I'm fine." I wasn't really; I was wearing jeans and a black tee-shirt that said, "The Flying Karamazov Brothers. There's more to to the theatre than than repetition." Such things don't usually bother me, but on that occasion I really wanted to be wearing my nice white-on-white shirt with French cuffs and the jeans with the holes in the knees. Oh, well.

He sat facing me at that oblique angle I mentioned earlier. My left eye could watch him while my right eye could look at the cold fireplace. He relaxed, his feet stretched out in front of him, crossed at the ankles, and his hands in the pockets of his jacket. His eyebrows were as gray as his hair. He noticed me looking at the fireplace and said, "Should I start a fire, Mr. Kevely?"

"I don't think that will be necessary, Monsieur Rudd."

"Very well." He cleared his throat. "I must say, I didn't expect to run into you."

"I came chasing bears," I said.

"Ah. Of course." He smiled. In another context, I would not have taken it for an evil smile. "Any particular bear?"

"We could start with the one who tried to burn down Cowboy Feng's last night. Claude, isn't it?"

"So it *was* you, and he *didn't* lose you."

"It was and he didn't."

"He was afraid of that."

"And we can go from there to whoever tried to blow it up earlier. Claude again, I think. And, perhaps, Justin?"

"You know a great deal."

I waited for him to say, "More than is good for you," or something like that. When he didn't, I said, "I don't know as much as you do, or as much as I'd like to." I decided to make what I thought was a reasonable guess at this point. "For example," I said, "I don't know why you had someone shot at the restaurant, or who he was to begin with. Or, in fact, exactly who shot him."

Rudd nodded, his mouth twitching. A very expressive mouth, it was, too. "You must understand, Mr. Kevely, that we are far from perfect."

We? Sugar Bear?

"Well, yes."

"We are dedicated people, but we are not killers, save by necessity."

"This was necessary?"

"You misunderstand. I am explaining that we bungled. More particularly, I bungled. I should have had a photograph, but, well—" He spread his hands. "I didn't. I relied on a verbal description, and there was an unfortunate man who matched the description. I *do* feel bad, although no doubt he was diseased as well, so there is no real loss."

"Oh." I cleared my throat. This raised more questions than I could handle at one time. I started with, "If it was a stranger who was shot, why did he die saying, 'Sugar Bear'?"

This time, Rudd's whole face twitched. "I told you we are not professionals. The gunman told him. I don't know exactly how, I suspect he said, 'Sugar Bear has found you, you scoundrel, prepare to die,' or words to that effect."

"Oh. In English?"

"It is still our native tongue, even though we have come a long way in space, and through many generations."

"I see. Well, in that case, who was he *supposed* to have killed?"

"Oh, come now, Mr. Kevely."

I blinked, and as I did the photographer in my mind reconstructed the dead man, and the stenographer who works in the same department rattled off a verbal description from the photo, which came out something like, "About five-seven or five-eight, big nose, long, black hair, black drooping mustache." I knew at once who else that fit, and I realized, at a quite visceral level, just how stupid it had been for me to walk into this place, unarmed and alone.

Intermezzo

When I was young I had no sense
I bought a fiddle for eighteen pence.
The only tune that I could play
Was "Over the Hills and Very Far Away."

"When I Was Young,"
Traditional

She took another hit off her cigarette and blew out the smoke in a long, thoughtful stream, watched it swirl across the booth toward the empty table next to her, and remembered the night before. She tried to form it into words for herself, failed. How can happiness be put into words? Problems she didn't even know she had were whisked away, vanished, gone. It was better than anything she'd tried before: acid, coke, anything.

Love?

A joke, that. Love was the problem, not the solution. Being hit by a car was better than love.

She took another sip of coffee. Tony had promised to have more tonight if she wanted it, and Tony could usually be relied on. Well, if you're going to break skin, there's no point in not enjoying it.

Snatches of songs came to her, dancing in the ear of her mind, making melodic suggestions to counterpoint the smoke swirls.

She suddenly wished she had her fiddle and that she knew how to play it. Maybe she'd start practicing again. She took another sip of coffee, another hit off her cigarette, exhaled, and watched the smoke. Spooky. Scary. She liked that.

She stubbed out her cigarette and refilled her coffee cup from the tacky green pitcher the all-night restaurant served coffee in. She played with cream containers she didn't use and thought about it. *Doesn't it bother me that I'm shooting heroin?*

And, *Yes, it does.*

She lit another smoke and stared at nothing.

It's me, Rose. Not some junkie. It's me.

She saw it then. This was to be her life. She'd watch Tony burn his brain out and turn into a vegetable, and Julie would get quieter and quieter, until she shut down altogether, and Margaret would lose touch with reality until everything became so Significant that nothing mattered, and she, Rose, would join them, and that's how it would be.

They're all losers. They're going nowhere. I've got my music. That makes it different.

She could stop. Stay away from needles, and fill in the void with music. She shook her head. No. She could, maybe, stay away from the needles, but she'd still be around Julie, and Margaret, and Tony, and that meant being around the candy, and that meant using it.

The sickly pale sun was coming through the restaurant windows. Morning already? She paid her bill and walked through snapping winter winds, deciding that she was beginning to feel the effects of a whole night spent drinking coffee.

She walked up the two flights to her apartment and let herself in. Margaret was sitting on the floor on sofa cushions. She smiled dreamily, her head on Tony's shoulder. "How did you like it, Rose?" Margaret asked.

"It's great," she said honestly. "It's better than coke, it's— excuse me a minute."

She used the bathroom. It was small and the sink and mirror were cracked. She splashed water on her face, then went out and picked up her fiddle case. Rose walked to the door and opened it again. Julie, who had rejoined them in the living room, said, "Where ya going, hon?"

Rose took a deep breath and looked at the three of them. She said, "I love you guys more than anyone or anything in the world, but I can't see you anymore. Good-bye."

She shut the door quickly so they wouldn't see her tears, and walked down the two flights of stairs to the street, clutching her fiddle case like salvation. It was very cold.

CHAPTER
8

And when I'm dead, aye, and in my grave
A flashy funeral pray let me have.
With six bold highwaymen to carry me
Give them good broadswords . . .
And sweet liberty.

**"The Newry Highwayman,"
Traditional**

Startled, surprised, and shocked do not mean quite the same
things. Startled is when you walk around a corner and almost
bump into someone. Surprised is when you look down the block
and see someone you thought was out of town. Shocked is when
you walk around the corner and bump into a dead man. It is
impossible to control what your face does when you're shocked,
it is difficult when startled, but, actually, fairly easy when
surprised, if you try.

I realized that I'd just placed myself into the hands of a man
who had tried to kill me. I was surprised, not startled or shocked.
My mind raced, tried to come up with some means of escape,
failed. I was going to have to just play it by ear, and hope my
mouth could think clearer than my brain. So, where were we? Ah,
yes: He assumed I knew he was trying to kill me. "Of course," I
said.

"You do not," continued M. Rudd, "have a listening or recording device upon your person, or it would have been detected when you entered my home. Similarly, you do not have a weapon. Thus I conclude that you are here neither to trick me into saying something that you will record to use against me in some way"—here he smiled as if the notion was amusing—"nor to attempt violence against my person. I am curious. Why are you here?"

"I'm afraid you will have to remain curious, for the moment."

He frowned, the disapproving look of the stern parent. "Come now, Mr. Kevely. I've answered all of your questions. You could at least tell me why you have come."

"To get the answers to those questions you've just answered."

"Rubbish," he said. "I haven't told you anything you didn't already know, or couldn't have discovered, or even guessed."

"All right, if you really haven't told me anything, why should I tell you anything in exchange?"

He laughed, and it seemed quite genuine. "Very good, Mr. Kevely." He shifted in the chair, crossing his ankles the other way. "Well, then, is there something I can tell you that you didn't already know?"

"Sure. Who exactly do you work for, and what are your goals?"

His eyebrows climbed once more. "I work for the Physician, as I'm certain you are aware, and we are attempting to cure the patient. You should know that; you are part of the disease."

"I am?"

"You are. It is why it is necessary to surgically remove you."

"Ah. As I am certain *you* realize, I don't look at it quite that way."

"That is irrelevant."

"No doubt."

"Can you be more specific about this disease, or what the cure for it might be?"

He stared at me speculatively. "No, I don't think so," he said. "But that does bring something to mind. Perhaps you could tell me something." He pulled his right hand from his jacket pocket. "Why in the world should I not simply kill you now and have done with it?"

I'd never had a gun pointed at me before. The novelty of the experience impressed me more than the particulars of the weapons, so, if you are one of those who are curious about such things, you'll have to be content with my impression that it was a small, blue automatic. My unease notwithstanding, I'd been more or less expecting this ever since I realized who the dead man looked like. I'm proud to say I didn't bat an eyelash or miss a beat. I held his gaze and said, "What would *you* have done before walking in here?"

He stared at me, his eyes narrow, and I'd bet he would have traded several weeks out of his future allotment of paradise to know what I was thinking. Then his eyes widened, and his face broke into a smile. "Ah," he said. "I see. Very good. A stalemate."

"I think so."

"You are a brave man, Mr. Kevely."

"You are a clever man, Monsieur Rudd."

He bowed his head and stood, still pointing the gun at my stomach. "Under the circumstances, I'm afraid I must ask you to leave."

"As you wish," I said. "It has been a pleasure meeting you."

"And you as well." He conducted me to the door and opened it. I looked out at a piece of rural New Quebec. Except for the smell of livestock, it was not materially different from my piece of residential New Quebec. It smelled of freedom and safety out there, as well as of horses and goats, and I badly wanted to bolt. M. Rudd still had the gun in his hand, though it no longer pointed at me, so I held myself still and tried to act calm. "No doubt," he said, "we shall meet again before everything is settled."

"I expect we shall. My compliments to the Physician."

"And mine to Mr. Feng."

"Indeed."

I walked out onto the street at last. My legs, bless their souls (sorry), held me steady until I was a good mile away from Rudd's. I didn't stop there, but I did allow myself the twin luxuries of letting my knees shake and looking over my shoulder once or twice a minute from there until I reached the door of Cowboy Feng's.

As I walked, amazed and delighted that I continued to breathe and that my heart continued to beat—which it did, and made sure I knew about it, too—I wondered what in the world he thought I had on him that had prevented him from killing me. If I could figure it out, it might do so again.

Feng's was almost empty, it being between the lunch and supper rushes. Before supper? It was still before supper? Amazing how time stands still when your life is in danger. I sat where I could watch the door and I ordered some coffee in order to calm down. It didn't work, but I don't think Valium would have, either, right then.

Rich showed up a bit later. He took one look at me and said, "What happened?"

"It's a long story," I said. "Is Eve still at the library?"

"Yeah."

"Well, here's some current stuff for her to look into, if she wants: Harold Peter Rudd. He lives at sixteen Saint Marguerite Road. Here's another one: the Physician."

"Sounds like you've had an interesting day."

"To paraphrase Dalkey: You damn betcha, ratface."

"Who? Never mind. Tell me about it."

"Not now; I want to relax for a while."

"Okay. I'll go talk to Eve."

"All right. And, Rich, keep looking over your shoulder. Be very careful. These people really would kill us."

He stared at me. "You're going to have to tell me about this."

"I will, Rich, just not right now, okay? And be careful."

Jamie and Rose showed up an hour or so later, sat down next to me. "Where have you been?" said Rose. "We misseded you." I didn't know anyone else who could get away with saying *We misseded you.*

"Oh, I was sort of busy," I said. "Wandering around, telling everyone I met about who we are, getting shot at, that sort of thing."

"Are you serious?" said Jamie.

"Well, I'm exaggerating a bit. Where have you been?"

"Exploring the city," said Rose. "They have this big park that's full of rocks. Big rocks. You can climb all over them, and slide down the—"

"Wait a minute," said Jamie. "I want to know what happened to you."

I shrugged. For some reason, I felt a reluctance to tell them about it, perhaps because I'd been so stupid in walking into it. "Never mind. How's Tom?"

"Depressed," said Jamie, as if the word tasted bad.

"Huh? About what?"

"What do you think?"

"I have no idea."

"Carrie."

"What about her? I thought the two of them were twin songbirds upon the tree of mutual rapture, winging their way, together, through the forest of true love, to find the—"

"Blllaaahhh," said Jamie.

"I thought that was pretty good, for a spur-of-the-moment thing."

"You should be a performer," said Rose.

"No, I just play banjo."

"*Man,*" said Jamie.

"What's the deal with Tom and Carrie?"

"Oh, they spend half their time being cute at each other and the other half tearing each other to shreds."

"Ah. I hadn't noticed that other half. But, then, I guess I've been pretty much involved in my own world lately."

"Shit happens," said Jamie.

"You've been hanging around with Libby, haven't you?"

"Yeah. And speaking of Libby . . ."

"Yes?"

"There's something that's been on my mind for a while."

"Talk to me."

"Do you have any skills to speak of, other than music?"

"That's a weird question."

"Just answer it."

"All right." I considered the question carefully, answered more or less honestly. "As far as I can tell, I don't even have music. If I could sing—"

"I think you sing real good, for a boy," said Rose, blinking.

"Thanks."

"I'm serious," said Jamie. "Do you really do much of anything except play banjo and sing?"

I decided that he didn't really intend to be insulting. I said, "Well, not really well. I sort of write songs, sometimes, but not well enough that I'd list it as a skill if I was going to apply for a job."

"Right. Same with me, and Tom, and Rose. Music is all we know, as far as marketable skills go."

"So, what about it? It's kept us eating so far."

"Did you know that Libby was hired as a paramedic and as a bartender?"

"Yeah. I was there when she mentioned it. What about it?"

"Did you know that Fred is a marksman, and was in a Marine Corps Special Forces unit?"

"Really? He seems too thin for that."

"It's true. He mentioned it one night when he was drunk and coked up. It was part of the job description he applied for. He and Libby didn't get together until after they were both here."

"Okay, I believe you. What about it?"

"Did you know that Rich isn't just hanging around, he's employed by Feng's as the maintenance man?"

"I think he mentioned that, yeah."

"And his girlfriend happens to speak about six million languages, as well as cooking as well as Fred?"

"Okay. I don't see what you're getting at."

"Check this out: The people here at Feng's consist of the four of us, who ended up here by accident, really, and four others, who might have been handpicked to go trucking through the galaxy doing whatever it is they've been doing."

I chewed this over, looking at it from several different angles. Then I said, "You *have* been thinking, haven't you?"

"Yeah."

"So you believe the four of us have stumbled into something the four of them know about, and they aren't letting us in on it because we can't be trusted, but they let us hang around because they like us?"

"Or maybe they just haven't told us yet, but they're going to. Or maybe they aren't, but they think we'll be useful. I don't know. But think about it, isn't it a little weird? And wouldn't that explain it?"

I nodded slowly. "Yes, it would." Then I smiled. "You like the idea of charging through time and space battling evildoers, don't you?"

"Well, um, yeah. Don't you?"

"Not particularly," I said, with complete honesty. "How about you, Rose?"

"I want whiskey," she explained.

"Don't you think it's possible?" said Jamie, sounding excited.

"Maybe. If so, what do we do about it?"

"I don't know."

"Maybe we should ask Rich to his face."

"Or Libby. She wouldn't lie to me."

"Are you sure?" I asked.

"Yes. Well, no. But what the hell?"

"Do you want to ask her, or should I?"

"I will. You talk to Rich."

"Good enough. We'll compare notes later."

"Want to eat?"

"Yeah."

"Food," said Rose.

I wasn't especially hungry, so I settled for deep-fried mushrooms and a glass of mango juice. Then we sat at the table for a while, saying little. Jamie didn't seem inclined to pick today to talk to Libby, and Rich didn't show up. At one point I went back to talk to Libby, but I didn't mention any of Jamie's ideas to her because that was his job.

"Having a good day?" she said.

"In a way. I'm alive."

"That's always good."

"It was a close thing, today."

She stopped moving, looked at me. "Go on," she said.

"Last night, someone tried to burn the place down."

"Keep talking."

And I did, leaving out nothing. She crossed her arms and listened with an intensity I could almost feel. When I finished, we spoke a little more, until at last she said, "What a mess. Well, look, don't worry. Fred and I will take care of things."

"What do you mean, take care of things?"

"Don't worry about it, all right?"

"How can I help worrying about it?"

"Yeah, okay. Go ahead and worry. I have to figure this out."

"Okay. Let me know when you have something."

I rejoined Rose and Jamie. I said, "I think you're right."

"What just happened?"

"Never mind."

We drank coffee until the evening rush started, then we walked home slowly. As we went past Le Bureau, I felt my back muscles tense. I had actually wanted to leave a couple of hours before, but I didn't want to walk home alone. Based on the day's experiences, I felt this was honest cowardice, rather than paranoia. I resisted the impulse to keep looking over my shoulder, because I didn't want to have to explain it to Rose and Jamie. It was a very long walk, but we got there and Tom was lying on a mattress in the living room, his arm over his face. He didn't look up when we walked in.

I said, "Hey, buddy."

He moved his arm. "Hello."

"What's new?"

"I'm tired," he said.

I nodded. "Where did the mattress come from?"

"Carrie."

"Oh. Well, that's good."

"Yeah."

That was all I could get out of him, but it was enough to make a point of some sort. Jamie and Rose and I exchanged glances, then we went into Jamie's room. Jamie and Rose both slept there, but it was emphatically Jamie's room. It was interesting how it had become more and more his own as the days went by. First, there was nothing but carefully folded clothing and a guitar in the corner. Then a cavalry saber, one that had been an antique when we left Earth, appeared on a wall. A few days later he acquired a model of the spaceship in the New Quebec television serial *Star Trek: 3100*. I wasn't sure where he'd been watching it.

Candles began to appear, most of them in ornate iron holders, and then a small but elegant mahogany bookcase showed up. Rich gave him a toy car (1953 Dodge) to set on top of the bookcase, and Fred found him a leather-bound collector's copy of *Conan of Cimmeria*. Libby gave him an eight-by-ten topless photo of her, which took a place of honor at the head of the bed. I wondered how he explained it to his visitors. He probably didn't.

Anyway, Jamie seated himself beneath Libby's breasts, Rose next to a model of an extinct piece of marginal technology, and myself below the Sword of Damocles, and we spoke softly about many things, far into the night. We spoke of travels on Old Earth, people we knew and missed, music, love; and it was as good as a meal at Feng's.

The next morning, we were awakened at an obscene hour, like eight o'clock, by some sort of loud buzzing noise originating from somewhere within the apartment. The operative word here is *loud*. It had two or three simultaneous pitches, and they were all designed to grate on the human nervous system. Jamie and I met in the hallway, he in his red terry cloth, I in my red silk. Rose came out behind him dressed in a sheet. "It isn't the doorbell," she said. Tom was sitting up in the living room frowning a frown of puzzlement and staring at the kitchen, whence the noise seemed to originate. He got up (black briefs were his fashion statement) and walked into the kitchen, his arms dangling.

The sound was coming from a small black plasma terminal set into the wall next to an attached handset. Right. He looked back at me. I picked up the handset, the sound stopped, and a machine-generated voice said something in French while displaying it on the screen. I strongly suspect it said that we now had phone service.

"We now have phone service," I announced. "I forgot I ordered it. The phone came with the apartment, and local service doesn't cost much, so what the hell?" Had we only been here a few weeks? It seemed like much longer.

"Will it make that sound again?" said Rose.

"There's probably a way to change the tone or turn it off."

"You should find it," said Rose. "That's the important thing."

"I understand that now."

The four of us went after the instruction booklet, and the "?" button on the phone. Well, the three of us. Rose made coffee and helpful comments. I suspect that the instructions would have been pretty obvious if we spoke French. Fortunately most common mistakes routed one to someone who knew what to do, so we eventually got hold of a "Service Center Representative" who spoke English and filled us in on name codes, place codes, title codes, voice activation, preselect, recall, and the rest of the details concerning the operation of the easy-to-use private-band-series ground-to-ground Personal Communication Console Workstation and Dishwasher.

Well, I made up the part about the dishwasher.

"Great," I said an hour later, feeling the same satisfaction either Joshua or Delilah must have felt when the Earth moved. "Now what?"

"Sleep," suggested Jamie.

"Breakfast?" said Rose, pronouncing it "bref-tist."

"Why don't you call someone?" said Tom.

"Who?"

"How about Feng's? Fred or Libby will be there."

"Do you know the number?"

"What number? Hit 'Commercial,' spell out C-O-W—"

"Oh, yeah, that's right."

"Should we put it in memory?"

"You guys do that later; it's too complicated for me." I made the call, and Libby's face appeared on the screen.

"Cowboy Feng's, this is Libby, can I help you?"

I turned on the local camera. "Hi, there, sex goddess."

"Billy! You all right?"

"Yeah, fine. We just got a phone installed."

"Oh. Well, you guys coming in for breakfast?"

"Give us an hour or so."

"That's fine, we won't be open for a couple of hours, at least, so we can have the place to ourselves."

"Sounds good. See you in a bit."

"Later."

There followed one of the few arguments we ever had over use of the shower. We normally avoided these arguments by getting up at different times. This one I won because it was my apartment. But then I felt guilty so I hurried. After several minutes of hot running water we were all prepared to be civil to each other, and agreed that breakfast at Feng's would be a good thing. Tom even seemed a little happier. I think the phone cheered him up in some strange, unfathomable way.

On the way over, I thought about trying to figure out an alternative route, that didn't take us past Le Bureau. It wouldn't be all that hard, just an extra block down LeDuc to Pompidou, then up Valois. But it would be annoying. Maybe it was silly. And then it came to me that Souci had helped me find the apartment, so perhaps it wasn't a coincidence that we had to walk past the place every day. I kept these thoughts to myself, but they were disturbing.

In spite of all the wasted time, it still lacked half an hour of Feng's eleven o'clock opening when we arrived at the door. Fred greeted us with, "Good morning, gentlemen," as he let us in. "We have presents for you."

We stopped and looked at each other.

"Presents?" ventured Jamie.

"Courtesy of Mr. Feng himself," said Fred.

We trooped in hesitantly and saw Rich, Eve, and Libby staring solemnly back at us. On a table behind them was the largest collection of firearms I'd ever seen in one place at one time.

Jamie spoke for all of us. "Holy shit," he said.

Intermezzo

So come, all you weavers, you Calton weavers;
Come all you weavers, where e'er you be.
Beware of Whiskey, Nancy Whiskey;
She'll ruin you like she ruined me.

"Nancy Whiskey,"
Traditional

The mirror was dirty.

Tom stared into it as if to see something deep and significant in the hollow-cheeked face that stared back at him—maybe a *Picture of Dorian Gray* effect, where he could identify rot that lay somewhere behind his eyes—or *something* to give him some clue as to why he was in this fucked-up trash-heap of a life. If he could only be sure he deserved it, it might be easier to take. Probably not, though.

And, in any case, the mirror was dirty, so that was about it for significance.

He had a sudden urge to smash his fist into it, and, for once, didn't. He wondered where Sara was this morning, and almost smashed his fist into the mirror yet once again. He thought about having a drink, and made himself look into the mirror again, just to think about something else. By now, he knew better than to have the first one. But then, by now, Sara should know better than to be gone all night like that. Didn't she care about him?

And the answer to that was: Yes, too fucking much.

It was almost as if she were doing everything she could to make him drink, as if she were trying to—

But she wasn't. Everything she did, she had a reason for doing that made sense while she was doing it. And that was pretty much as far as it needed to go. She was who she was, and he was who he was, and if they were going to spend a few months or years sticking knives into each other, then that's just how it would be.

He didn't decide to go into the kitchen, but somehow there he was, standing in front of the refrigerator wishing there were some beer. He dug around in the pockets of a few old jackets until he found enough money for a six-pack. He stared at it for a long time, then checked the clock above the sink. It was late, he'd have to settle for the sort of beer convenience stores sold. He shrugged.

Before he left the apartment, he put a few things in his old duffel bag, not even half filling it. When he walked out, he noticed that his hand was trembling as he locked the door. That was funny, in a detached sort of way.

Then it was down three flights of stairs to the bus stop, and a timeless time until the bus came. Someone on the bus spoke to him, but it wasn't until several minutes later that he realized it, and then he wondered how he'd responded.

When it let him off, he walked straight into the treatment center. He didn't look at the name above it, and he didn't pause dramatically to have second thoughts or wonder if he could take it, or if it was a good idea; he just walked through the door and checked himself in.

CHAPTER
9

We put that car in motion
    And filled it to the brim
With guns and bayonets shinin'
    Which made old Johnson grim.
           "Johnson's Motor Car"
           Traditional

What really stands out in my memory from that moment was not, in fact, the collection of firearms that was getting grease on three of Fred's nice clean tables; but rather the instant split, as with an axe, between those who were waiting inside and those of us who were just arriving, between those who, as Jamie had suggested, worked for Feng and those who were just along for the ride. Between those who might in some way be responsible for all of this and those who were inarguably innocent. We were no longer simply a group of eight friends, we were now Feng's people and the band, and we stared at each other as we looked at the piles of weapons occupying the tables.

Jamie, Tom, Rose, and I looked at each other. Then Jamie said, "*Yeah,*" and charged forward to get his hands on the gear. Rose slunk back. Tom and I walked slowly up to the table, and Tom picked up what looked like a service .45, ejected the clip—excuse me, the "magazine"—and did things like he knew what he was doing. I just stared. You want a description? There were lots of guns, most of them brown or black or blue.

Rose came up behind me and put her arms around me. She said very softly, "Billy?"

"Yeah, sis?"

"Do I have to have one of those?"

"No, because you have your fiddle."

"That's good. Those things scare me."

"Me, too."

"Are you going to take one?"

"No. I don't need one, either, because I have a banjo."

As we stood around the table, Fred cleared his throat and began speaking in a distinctly professorial tone. "We have," he said, "managed to procure a good variety of firearms. Each of you should be able to find a weapon or weapons suitable to your own needs. You may note that most or all of these were in use when we left the Earth. This is because there has not been, so far as I can tell, a great deal of advance in firearms technology, and because I picked out weapons with which I was familiar. Some of these were purchased here, although many were brought from home in anticipation of just such a requirement."

He paused, during which I exchanged looks with Rose. *Just such a requirement.* I shuddered.

"For myself," Fred continued, "I have selected an H&K MP5 machine pistol for area control, and a Winchester .30-06 with a 6X scope for distance work. For a handgun, I have my own U.S. Government-issue Beretta nine-millimeter semiautomatic pistol.

"Tom, you seem familiar with the Colt Government Model .45. Is that correct?"

Tom closed his mouth, opened it, and said, "I used one in the Navy."

"Very good. I suggest you stick with it."

"No, you stick with a knife. You shoot with a gun."

Fred continued, "For you, Jamie, with your size, I would recommend a large handgun." He picked one up. "This is the Smith & Wesson .357 revolver with the eight-inch barrel. It is highly accurate, has good stopping power, and is extremely reliable. I'll check you out on the quick-loader later."

Jamie took it like he knew how to handle it, then said, "Do we have an Ithaca pump-action shotgun, like Hawk has?"

"Hawk?"

"In the Spenser books."

"Oh." Fred took him seriously. "We have a Remington pump. But I would recommend the Ithaca side-by-side double-barreled twelve-gauge, since it can be sawed off, which a pump-action cannot."

"Uh, okay."

"For you, Eve, I would—"

"I don't want one," she said almost inaudibly.

"Very well. Rose?"

"No, thank you."

"Rich?"

"I know how to use a revolver."

"You're also pretty big. Do you want the same thing Jamie has? We have a Colt model—"

"I'd rather have something smaller. Like that, say."

Fred nodded and handed it to him. "This is a Ruger .38-caliber revolver with a four-inch barrel. There is also a quick-loader that will work with it."

"Check," said Rich.

"Billy?"

"No, thanks."

"Libby?"

"That one."

"Are you sure?"

"Yep."

"All right."

He gave it to her. She held it up and said, "This is a .44-caliber automag, the most powerful handgun in the—"

"Clint Eastwood," said Tom. "*Dirty Harry*."

"Even I knew that," said Jamie.

There followed a few minutes of picking out boxes of ammunition, extra magazines, holsters, shoulder harnesses, and that sort of thing. I said, "Boy, we're really having fun now."

Rich caught my eye. "Is something wrong?"

"Yeah, but it isn't your fault."

Eve said, "Do they have to enjoy it so much?" But she said it so softly only I heard her.

Libby said, "We should all get together and talk, but we have to open the place up right now. How about after close tonight?"

No one disagreed. We helped get all of the firearms out of the way and clean up the tables. As I was wiping one of them off,

Fred approached me. "I don't like the idea of you being unarmed," he said. "Libby told me they tried to kill you."

"Yes, they did. I wish I knew why, and what it meant, and like that."

He shrugged. "I'm sure you do. But, in the meantime, you should—"

"Look, Fred, if I take one of those things, and I get in trouble, I might be tempted to use it, and I'd just hurt myself."

"I talked Rose into taking a derringer. It seems to me that you can—"

"How did you do that?"

"It was pearl-handled and had an engraved dragon's head."

"Ah. She likes monsters."

"In any case, why don't you—"

"No. I wouldn't know what to do with it."

He licked his lips. "Just a minute." He disappeared into the back for a moment. I continued cleaning the table. When I came back there was something in his hand. "How about this, then?" I stared at it. "It's a British commando knife. Don't try to throw it or you'll snap the blade. You can cut with it, but it's best used straight into your target."

"Target," I repeated softly.

He nodded, his eyes locked with mine. Our eyes were very communicative, that day. I took the knife.

After the tables had been cleaned up and Feng's opened, I pulled Rich and Eve aside and gave them the details of what had happened yesterday.

"I heard most of it from Libby," Rich said, taking off his jacket in order to put on the shoulder rig for his pistol. I helped him with this. Eve did not.

I said, "It scares me how natural you look in that thing. Do you know how to shoot?"

"You point it and squeeze the trigger."

"I—"

He held up his hand. "I know. Yes, I've had gun safety courses and I've done target shooting."

I nodded. "I'm just freaked, I guess. For one thing, the notion of putting a loaded weapon into Jamie's hands frightens me."

"Me, too. But he told me his father used to take him hunting, so he knows how to use them, at least."

"Yeah. And he really isn't as irresponsible as he pretends to be. At least, not all the time."

Eve shuddered and squashed herself against Rich. Her hand came in contact with his holster and she jerked back like she was burned. She stared at him for a moment, then turned and fled toward the pantry. I looked at Rich and he stared back, as if daring me to make a comment.

I said, "Do you know if she found out anything about Monsieur Rudd?"

I saw him mentally shift gears. "Yes. The Rudd family is mentioned in the Russian book. They've been in New Quebec for forty years, as far as we can tell. She's still trying to track down what they—and Harold especially—have been up to. These people don't leave many tracks."

"I think 'spoor' is the appropriate term. Or maybe 'fewmets.' "

"Right."

"Keep at it. I want to know why he tried to kill me. Hell, maybe we can convince him not to."

"Right," said Rich ironically, and headed out into the street.

I sat down at a table that had recently held about a hundred pounds of weaponry and drank more coffee than was good for me. I thought about having a cigarette. I spent a great deal of time thinking about having a cigarette, although not as much time as I had six months before. Stupid way to spend your time, not smoking. "Hi there, whatcha been up to?" "Oh, I've been not smoking. You?" "Not drinking. Whatcha gonna do tomorrow?" "Oh, I thought I'd not drink coffee, without cream and sugar, you know. Maybe in the evening I'll not gamble for a while." Crap. I was wearing my jacket indoors now. I was wearing a shoulder rig, from which a very sharp, black dagger hung upside down, so I could get at it quickly. I felt the weight of the thing and hated it a lot.

I sighed, and mused, and drank coffee, and presently Tom showed up next to the table. "How are things, Billy?"

"Okay," I said. There was a slight bulge in his jacket about belt level, where he had the .45 stashed, and his pockets were heavy with extra magazines. He sat down across from me.

"What's up with you?"

"I'm going to have a talk with Carrie."

"That's good, I guess."

"Yeah. And she has a message for you."

"Oh?"

"She said to tell you that Souci's back in town."

"Great," I said. "That's all I need."

Just about then we were joined by Christian, who put his feet up on the booth and lit a cigarette. "So, how are you gentlemen today?"

"Getting by," I said. Tom nodded.

Christian said, "Has there been something happening lately?"

"Why do you ask?"

"From the looks on your faces, I'd say you were upset about something."

"We're both pinheads," explained Tom.

"I see."

There was silence, then Christian cleared his throat. "So, what's a pinhead?"

"Ask Libby," I suggested.

"Who?"

"The bartender."

"Oh. Bartender. Beer. Now, there's an idea. See you gents later." He strode into the taproom and sat at the bar. Tom and I continued our commiserating, the details of which I will spare you. But an hour or so later, as I got up to leave, I noticed that Christian was still sitting at the bar, presumably learning what a pinhead was, according to the wisdom of Libby Sangretti. I made a mental note to ask one or the other of them what she'd said, but, with one thing and another, I never got around to it.

I found Jamie looking out the window of our apartment. Leaning against the wall next to him was an Ithaca 12-gauge side-by-side double-barreled shotgun. I said, "Is it loaded?"

"Huh?" He snapped his head around. "Oh. You startled me."

"And you didn't go for your gun?"

"Should I have?"

"Maybe. I don't know."

"Yeah, it's loaded. But the safety's on." He indicated the big black .357 lying on the counter as if it were just another kitchen utensil. "That's loaded, too, but there's no round under the hammer."

"That's a great comfort to me. What were you thinking about?"

"Guns."

"What about them?"

He shrugged. "I was shot once, you know."

"No, I hadn't known that. What happened?"

"Nothing. Never mind."

"You seemed to enjoy picking out your toys."

"I did. You would have, too."

"Maybe."

"But I was standing here thinking that I might actually have to use one of these. I mean, point it at someone and pull the trigger."

"Think you can?"

"Yes."

"I couldn't."

"You sure?"

"Not completely, I guess."

He stood there a moment longer, then turned to me. "Libby once told me she was afraid of guns, because it would be too easy for her to shoot someone. Now I know what she means."

"I understand."

He nodded and turned back to the window. I came over and stood next to him. "Like, for instance," he said, "wouldn't you kind of like to just open up the window and blow that little motherfucker away?"

I followed his gaze. Short, curly-haired Claude was leaning against a tree, watching our apartment from just across the street, arms folded, as calm as you please. I didn't answer Jamie, in part because I found myself agreeing with him.

"Souci?"

"Yes."

"This is Billy."

"I can see that."

"Oh, right. You don't have your camera on."

"Mmmm."

"Umm, welcome back."

"Thanks."

One . . . two . . . three . . . four . . .

"So, should we, um, get together or something?"

"What do you want to do?"

"I don't know. Have lunch? Some drinks?"

"I'm on a diet."

"Take a walk?"

"Where?"

"I don't know. Want to talk?"

"What about?"

"Ummm. Never mind. Look, I'll, uh, call you again, all right?"

"Sure."

"Bye."
"Bye."

Fred told me that there are many imitations of the British commando knife of World War II, because in spite of the brittleness of the blade it is one of the best antipersonnel knives ever invented. He also said that it is easy to identify the real thing by the imprint on the guard. I couldn't read the tiny writing of the imprint, so I don't know what the real one said or why a fake one couldn't say something equally illegible which would fool me.

He called it "a very sexy weapon," which may give you some idea of what he's like. The phrase made me shudder, in part because I could almost see what he meant. The knife, all twelve inches or so of it, was painted with nonreflective black paint. The hilt was cigar-shaped and fit my hand better than I'd have thought just looking at it, and better than I sort of wished it did. There was a little nob at the end, which I guess was a screw or a nut that held it together.

The guard was small, because, according to Fred, this was not primarily a knife-fighter's weapon, but one intended for sticking in the backs of one's enemy. Certainly the blade had that look; it was very slim, and had a flattened-out diamond shape. It really did have a good edge, and as I ran the point along my inside forearm directly above the artery and watched the impression the blade made, I realized how incredibly easy it would be to just exert a little more pressure there. It would take hardly any effort.

Hardly any effort at all.

Eventually I put the knife in its sheath, took the harness off, and set it on the floor, and I went over to my futon and lay on my back, staring at the big, beige, soundproofing tiles on my ceiling.

"How's it going, Tom?"
"All right. Carrie and I talked and got some things straightened out."
"That's good."
"How about with you?"
"I'm doing all right. I talked to Souci today."
"Oh, really? How is she?"
"Fine. She says she's on a diet."

Libby wiped out a·last ashtray and turned the key on what was now an antique cash register. Her hair looked jet-black in this light, her face pale, her eyes very bright. "Okay, I'm done," she announced.

"Very good," said Fred, pushing a pair of tables together. The last customers had left fifteen minutes before, and we'd all helped out getting the place ready. No one said anything about what we were gathered for, because they were afraid to, because they were enjoying the suspense, because they were busy, or, in my case, because I wasn't terribly interested.

Rich ran a bug detector around the room. Jamie said, "What about microphones from outside the building?"

"Any microphone pointed at this building will only hear the D below middle C," said Rich.

"Ah," said Jamie, and sat down at one end of the double table, Rose on his right, me on his left. Tom sat next to me with Fred across from him, next to Rose. Eve sat next to Tom, Libby next to Fred, and Rich took the other end, his back to the bar, facing the stage and Jamie. We all drank coffee, some of us with cream and sugar.

Rich and Jamie stared across the table at each other, and I had a sudden premonition that they'd end up shooting each other before the meeting was over. I almost suggested that everyone put his gun behind the bar, but I couldn't think of a way to say it that would have been taken seriously.

"There are things some of you probably want to know," said Rich. "Maybe you should begin by asking them."

"I'm up for that," said Jamie. "I'll start. What the hell is going on?"

Rich looked at his fellow conspirators, if you will, then back at Jamie. "Would you care," he said, "to break that down a little?"

"All right. First of all, why is it this place keeps getting nuked, and, second, why is it that every time it does we end up jumping to another city or planet or solar system or galaxy or dimension—"

"And don't forget time," put in Rose.

"Yeah," said Jamie. "Like she said. What about it?"

"Some of that," said Fred, "we don't know ourselves. I was hired originally as a waiter and bouncer, and I didn't know any of the rest of it until Rich told me. I've never met Feng."

"Who has?" asked Tom.

Rich held up his hand, as did Libby.

"Where is he now?" asked Tom.

Rich looked uncomfortable. "You know we're dealing with time travel here, right?"

"Yeah," said Jamie, as if he'd been traveling through time all his life.

"Well, then, *now* is a funny concept. I think I can say that he's not anywhere—"

"Look," snapped Libby. "If you could go shooting through time and space anywhere you pleased, would you hang around in a restaurant that might get hit by a nuclear bomb any second?"

"I would," said Jamie.

"You probably would," said Rich.

"I thought this place was safe," said Rose.

The four of us looked at each other. "Well," said Rich slowly. "It *is* radiation-proof. And it does have means of jumping away from trouble very quickly as long as it has sufficient power, and it does have means of taking that power from a nuclear explosion."

"So," said Libby, "as long as the bomb doesn't hit so far away that we don't get enough of the energy, or so close that we're toasted before we can jump—"

"And as long as everything works—"

"We're okay," concluded Libby.

"Oh, that's just great," said Jamie.

"There's a pretty big window for how close it has to be and how close it can come," said Rich.

"It's worked so far," added Fred.

Rose said, "Can I have a—"

"No," said Jamie.

"What else do you want to know?" asked Rich.

"What it's all about."

"Saving the future," said Libby. "Is that noble enough for you?"

Jamie stood up—no, rose to his feet—turned so we had a profile of his face, stuck his chest out, and deepended his voice. "Yes," he declaimed, "Captain James Lindhal of the Time Travel Rangers shall go forth once more to—"

"Will you sit down?" said Rich.

"I was enjoying it," said Tom.

"Me, too," said Libby.

"I want a whiskey," said Rose.

Jamie sat down.

Fred suddenly turned to me. "You haven't said anything."

"I'm just listening. I'll ask any questions I think of."

"Very well."

"Do you think," asked Jamie of Libby in particular and the table in general, "you might be persuaded to be just a trifle more specific about what you mean by saving the future?"

"It isn't that easy," said Rich.

"What's not that easy?" said Libby. "He wants to know what the whole thing's about. Tell him." She turned to Jamie. "A few hundred years from now a large group of nut cases are trying to wipe out all of Feng's people. We have to fix things."

"What do you mean, Feng's people? How many?"

"As I understand it, the population of several worlds."

"Wow. So, you mean, find these guys and kill—"

"No. This is time-travel stuff. Nothing works that easy. We can't do anything that would change history, or, rather, the future history that allowed us to be here."

"Huh? Oh, I see what you mean. But then how—"

"Feng," said Libby, "says that, up to a point, history will correct itself, and beyond that point it is impossible to do anything that will change it."

"Okay, then—"

"The exceptions are things he calls nexus points, which are intersections of—" She stopped, looked puzzled, stared at me, then at Fred, and finally turned to Rich and said, "You explain it."

Rich said, "They can trace effects, so they can find places where if you do this thing, it won't change history until after the time you left, from the future. Does that make sense?"

"It almost does," said Tom. "That's scary."

Rose nodded.

Tom turned to me. "Do you believe all this?"

"Yes," I said. "I'm not sure why, though."

He nodded. "That's about how I feel."

Jamie said, "So, what do we do?"

"Each time we've jumped," said Rich, "it's been to a nexus point. Unfortunately at most of them we didn't stay long enough to accomplish our mission. On the plus side, with all the jumping, we've been lucky enough not to lose anyone on the team."

Jamie said, "How does it know where to go when a bomb hits?"

"Got me," said Libby. "Rich? Eve? Fred?"

They all shook their heads.

Jamie said, "But what's the job?"

"We don't know exactly. Doing whatever we have to to save Feng's people."

"You're sure they're the good guys?"

Rich said, "Would you grow up?"

"It was a joke," said Jamie.

"Do you want in?" said Libby.

"If you didn't think we did, why did you give us the guns?"

"Because they tried to kill Billy, which means you guys are in danger whether you want to be or not, so we owe you the chance to defend yourselves."

"Who tried to kill Billy?" said Rose, staring at me. Jamie and Tom were also doing the wide-eyed thing.

"That guy who was killed in here," I said. "I found out that someone thought it was me. They also tried again last night."

"Why didn't you tell us?" said Rose.

"Because I was stupid."

"So what else is new?" said Jamie.

"Shit."

"But that's another thing," Jamie continued. "Why *did* they try to kill Billy?"

He looked from Rich to Libby to me, but it was Fred who answered. "I have a theory."

I said, "I'd like to hear it."

"I'm not certain of this, but it seems to me that if Feng's people can go into the past, so can the other guys, and it may be that Billy is the one who will stop them. They have to kill Billy in particular."

I studied the tabletop. It had a nice mosaic pattern of black against green.

"Well," I said after a time. "That really sucks."

Intermezzo

I'll tell me ma when I go home
The boys won't leave the girls alone.
"I'll Tell Me Ma,"
Traditional

The motherfucker has a gun.

It just kept going over and over in his head like that, like a
chant. He couldn't explain it the way he'd be able to years
later—in terms of unwritten rules, customs, and so on—he just
felt the outrage.

He was in an alley next to a park with six of his friends. They'd
started in the park, and then the, he didn't know, five or six or
seven or eight of them had taken off down the alley. They were
fighting because they were fighting, and he would win his fight
because he always won, but, *The motherfucker has a gun.* It
almost overshadowed the other statement that pierced his thoughts
like a dagger: *He's pointing it at me.*

One of the things he most enjoyed was those delicious moments
when he could step back and just watch himself in action; when
thinking and planning were beside the point, and the motions of

121

his fists, the sounds of flesh striking flesh, the blur of action around him, all became—as he wouldn't be able to express it to himself until years later—surreal. It went beyond being impressive to someone else or to himself; it was strange and mystical and like nothing else, and the people he was pounding into the ground were beside the point.

There was a tug, high on his right leg, and somewhere—way, way back—there was pain.

The motherfucker has a gun. The motherfucker just shot me. The motherfucker just fucking tried to fucking kill me.

And, *I'm going to kill him.*

There was a baseball bat in his hand so he threw it, and he wasn't surprised until later that, after turning four and a half lazy circles, it actually connected, *bam,* right in the head. He hoped he hadn't killed him yet, so he could do it again, and so it was, because the motherfucker was starting to stand up already. But then he was there, and then he had the gun, and it was pointing at the motherfucker's head, and he was slowly, so slowly, squeezing the trigger, and eyes were wide with fear, and he knew he was about to die, and—

"Don't, Jamie. Don't kill him."

Tip's voice. Shit. What did he want? Well, fuck it, then, and Jamie threw the gun down the alley and started pounding. He'd beat him to death, then. That would be more fun, anyway.

He was gone. So far gone that he was no longer even watching himself; it was just happening, and he was never fully aware of what went on between then and when Tip's voice finally penetrated for the second time.

"Jamie. Stop it. Jamie, Jesus, you're killing him. Jamie—"

And, somehow, he did stop. "Okay, Tip." He felt like he wasn't even breathing heavy. He wondered when his leg would start hurting, and realized the pants were ruined.

"We gotta split, Jamie. Now."

"Right," said Jamie, sounding and feeling just a bit stupid. He looked at the guy he'd been pounding on. Shit. A kid, maybe sixteen, Jamie's age. And smaller. Why the fuck had he brought the—

Jamie stared. "Tip, is he . . . is he breathing?"

"Huh? Shit, yes, man. Now let's go." Tip had his arm and was starting to drag him. Jamie stared, ignoring the mass of blood over the kid's face, trying to see some sign of life. He didn't, but he was in no state to really tell, either.

"Jamie."

"Yeah, all right." He allowed himself to be dragged away. He noticed in passing that they were the last two combatants in the area. Then he connected the sirens to the fight they'd had and took off in earnest.

"I'm afraid I killed him," said Jamie, but so softly Tip didn't hear him. He didn't repeat it aloud, or, really, to himself, either. Except that for years, in his mind, he'd see the kid lying there. Sometimes, he would see the kid breathing. Other times he would see that the kid was not. The fight never made it into the papers, and Jamie never ran into any of them again, so he never found out. By the time two months had passed, Jamie had pretty much stopped hanging out with Tip and his friends. Looking around for something to do instead, he picked up his father's old Gibson and started wailing away at it.

But sometimes, for years, the kid still made his way into Jamie's dreams, and on those nights Jamie didn't sleep well.

CHAPTER
10

If my true love she should go
I will surely find another.

"Will Ya Go, Lassie, Go"
Robert Burns

"I could be wrong," said Fred.

I nodded.

Jamie said, "We'll have to be careful to protect you."

I said, "Let's not get carried away with this. We should *all* be careful, and not wander around alone, or late at night. They were going for me the first time; they might go for someone else next time. Or for Feng's itself," I added, "which they've done twice already."

"This is true," said Fred.

"Which brings us," said Libby, "to the question I asked before: Do you want in?"

I said, "It would be pretty silly of me not to, wouldn't it?"

Libby smiled. "How about it, Jamie?"

He laughed. "What, saving the galaxy? I'm up for it."

Tom just nodded. Rose said, "Well, if the rest of my band is going to, I guess I will, too. I'll be the fiddle player."

"We'd figured you for the whiskey taster," said Libby.

"I can do that, too."

"You know," said Tom, "that does bring up a question: Just what do you want us for? I mean, are you going to give us jobs or something?"

The four of them exchanged looks. "We don't really know," said Rich. "Just knowing that we can count on you is the main thing. Other than that, we'll have to see what happens."

"One thing," said Jamie.

"Yeah?"

"About those guns: Do you know what it's legal to carry in this colony?"

"That's a tricky question," said Rich. "For one thing, there are no laws about carrying firearms at all. But you have to understand, most people don't carry guns, so if Fred wanders around with his Uzi—"

"H&K," said Fred.

"—whatever, he's going to get looked at. But the other end of it is, well"—he turned to Eve—"why don't you tell them?"

She cleared her throat. "Billy, do you remember the sergeant who questioned you after the shooting?"

"Umm, not really. I was pretty much in a daze."

"Well, his name is Iverness, and—"

"That doesn't sound very French," accused Tom.

"Not everyone who lives here is French," said Rich.

"He was joking," said Jamie.

Eve continued patiently, "There are several Ivernesses in the local police department."

"Okay. And?"

"Iverness is the maiden name of Harold Rudd's mother."

"Oh, great," said Jamie, beating me to it. "Does that mean the whole police department is on their side?"

"Pretty much," said Rich.

"Then we've had it," said Jamie. "They can just walk in here—"

"Let them try," said Fred.

"But they can't," said Rich. "It isn't that easy. They control the police department, and most of the city, but it isn't anything like absolute. It means they didn't really investigate the shooting of whoever was shot here, and it means if we're found dead one day

it won't be investigated too heavily either, but, no, they can't go
blatantly ignoring their own laws. I hope."

Jamie said, "So if they shoot one of us they can get away with
it, but if we shoot one of them—"

"They'll probably come after us with the whole department.
Yep."

"Oh, that's great."

"No one said life is fair," said Rich.

After that there wasn't much to say. We sat for a while, staring
into empty coffee cups while trying to think of encouraging things
to tell each other and failing.

"I think we should get some sleep now," said Fred at last.

"Good idea," said Rich.

Fred continued, "Those of you who are living at the apartment
should walk home together, and try to find routes which do not
take you past that agency. Ideally, find several and mix them up.
Also, you may want to consider moving back here."

"A thought," said Jamie, and looked at me. I shrugged. The
original reason why I wanted a place of my own had very likely
vanished.

"I'll think about it," I said.

"Let's go home," said Jamie.

The four of us walked together, looking over our shoulders all
the while. I couldn't escape the feeling that I was in enemy
territory, and I was starting to be glad that I had the knife with me,
after all.

Tuesday we all stayed in, and, miracle of miracles, got some
practicing done. Not a great deal, and we didn't play very well,
but I felt better for having done it. Ditto for Wednesday. I also
read a few summaries of recent history that Eve had found in the
library's English-language section. One was mostly political, and
too dry for me to force my way through, and the others too
technical for me to get much out of.

Later, Rose went into the bedroom to work on some fiddle
tunes. Jamie and Tom and I drank coffee. "So, how are things
with Carrie?"

"Better," said Tom. "I don't know. Sometimes it's great, and
sometimes we just tear each other apart. I know she's been
sleeping with other guys. I can tell. But she denies it. And—"

"I don't understand that," I said. "Jealousy, I mean. So, she's
sleeping with other guys. Why does that matter?"

"It wouldn't bother you?"

"It never has. I don't know, maybe I've just never been in the kind of situation where it would."

Jamie said, "I used to get jealous, but it was sort of beat out of me by—well, it doesn't matter. She's history now."

"Literally," said Tom.

Jamie shuddered and we fell silent and began to get depressed.

"All I know," said Tom, "is that it drives me crazy that she's sleeping with other guys."

"It isn't that I think you're wrong, it's just that I don't understand. It's different with me. It just hurts that she's not with me."

"You're a pinhead," said Tom.

"That's what Libby tells me."

"It'll take a while to get over it," said Jamie.

"I know," I said. "How many times have you been burned?"

"Like that? Three times. It's easier after the first."

"Well, that makes me feel much better. I suppose, though, that it's pretty surprising it hasn't happened before, all things considered. Your basic broken heart. Shit. It's so stupid."

"It is," said Jamie. "There's so much else in life. I mean, take a walk and look around."

"I'll get over it," I said.

"Women," said Tom.

"Here, here," said Jamie.

"Well, what about Rose?" I asked.

"What about her?"

"She's in love with you."

"Yeah," he said miserably. "I know." After a long moment of silence, Jamie said, "You see why I'd rather just worry about people shooting at me? Hell, at least I can shoot back."

"You know, I almost do understand," said Tom.

"Me, too," I said. "That scares me."

Jamie went out that evening. He took his pistol with him but left the shotgun. I had no idea how worried about him I was until he came back, the next afternoon. Rose, of course, was frantic, and dealt with it by picking on him for the whole rest of the day, mostly about how ugly his beard was. He, of course, responded by calling her various vile and disgusting things, all of which escalated until Tom and I had to leave.

"Be careful," said Jamie.

"Drop dead," I suggested cheerfully.

"That's a great idea, Jim," said Rose as the door closed behind us. "Why don't you do what he—" and their voices mercifully faded into the distance. Once out on the naked street, I wanted to bolt back inside. I forced myself to relax, and said, "Well, where to? Feng's?"

"How about Carrie's?"

"Sounds good," I said, and we set off in a direction I hadn't gone before.

It was more than two miles, but the weather was good for walking. The danger began to take on a feeling of distance and unreality, which made it actually sort of fun; I could almost understand some of how Jamie enjoyed picking out weapons. Tom was, I think, more alert than I, and kept looking around, but nothing untoward happened.

Carrie had rented a tiny little house set in the middle of a big lot. The lot had a lawn that looked ignored and several apple trees that looked even more ignored—a few limbs had broken from the weight of unpicked apples. The house itself, however, seemed to be well tended. The wood stain was new, at any rate, and there were no signs of disrepair that I noticed as we approached. It was incongruous, as if someone had bought a big lot but could only afford a small house. Tom knocked directly on the door; there was no screen. It was opened almost at once.

Carrie stood there in a bathrobe, a look of shock on her face. We could see past her into the house, where Justin sat, wearing only a towel. They both had wet hair. Justin was holding a razor blade over a mirror, on which was a white powder that must have been coke. There was a Baggie next to the mirror with a small quantity of powder in it. I wanted to say, "This is a raid," just to see what sort of reaction it would elicit, but I didn't have the chance even if I'd chosen to.

Tom moved quickly, stepping into the house and shoving Carrie aside with the same motion. I came in behind him and he already had the .45 out and was shoving the magazine home with a practiced hand.

"Tom, don't," I said as he took aim at Justin's head. Justin just stared at him.

Carrie began screaming. Tom hesitated, and his hand trembled. "Why the fuck not?" he asked.

I tried to think of a reason and couldn't. "Don't do it, Tom," I said. "Please." Carrie kept screaming. And Justin—well, he had balls, I'll give him that. He just stared down at Tom with a superior smirk on his lip, his beady eyes squinting, as if a bullet or two in the head didn't phase him in the least. *I* wanted to blow him away.

And Carrie kept screaming, and Tom's hand still trembled as he held the gun pointed right into Justin's face. "Tom, don't," I said once more.

"Shit," he said. I could hardly hear him over Carrie's screaming. He turned and looked at her, then took a step forward, and kicked, upsetting table, mirror, and coke. Then he turned and walked out of the house. I backed out after him. Justin still hadn't moved.

Tom was considerably ahead of me when I closed the door of the house. Carrie's screams abruptly ceased, but I thought I could hear her starting to cry. I caught up with Tom, looking back over my shoulder in case Justin was armed and decided to try to get us. He wasn't or didn't. Tom was taking long strides and still holding the gun. I hoped we didn't meet up with anyone before he thought to put it away, and, in fact, we didn't.

When we reached the apartment, Tom sat down in the corner and closed his eyes. Jamie said, "What happened?"

"Never mind," I said. "Just never mind."

Later that day Jamie and Rose started in on each other and Tom and I stood up at the same time, and the two of them promptly shut up.

"Hi."

"Oh, it's you."

"Don't you ever turn your camera on?"

"Not often."

"Oh. Well, want to get together sometime?"

"And do what?"

"I think we've had this conversation before."

"Look, you called me."

"That's true. I must have had a reason."

"I understand your friend Tom made an ass of himself with Carrie."

"Is that how you heard it?"

"Well, didn't he go barging in there, and almost beat Carrie to death, and then break down and start bawling?"

"Hmmmm. That's not exactly as I remember it."

"Well, then, what *did* happen?"

"It doesn't matter. Tom shouldn't have gone over without calling first, in any case."

"Why tell *me*? He's *your* friend."

"Yeah."

"Look, I have to go. I'll see you later."

"When?"

"I don't know. Sometime. Bye."

"Bye."

The next day was Friday, but Fred called and explained he'd found a solo Irish act to play for us that weekend.

At first I was outraged. "Why did you do that?"

"Billy, can you think of what you guys will be like, standing on that stage for three hours?"

"What do you mean? We—oh. Targets."

"Can you say, sitting ducks?"

"I get it. Shit. I'll tell the others."

I did, and they didn't like it but they understood. Unfortunately it not only left us with nothing to do, but it took all the wind out of our sails for practicing. Tom and I took a walk so we could talk about what had happened, but then we found we didn't have anything to say, except Tom kept repeating, "I should have killed him. I should have killed him," like a litany.

Jamie took off again that night.

The next morning, when he wasn't back, Rose said, "I wonder where Jim is?"

"Who knows?"

"Well, I mean, I wouldn't want him to be killed. By anyone except me, that is."

I looked at Tom, who rolled his eyes. "I understand," I said. "I'm sure he's all right."

"But where? I wish he'd let us know."

I shrugged. Was I supposed to tell her he was safe with some woman, or that he was no doubt out alone all night? "I'm sure he's fine," I said. "How are you?"

"Grand," she said. "Couldn't be better. This place is so much nicer when that man is away."

"I mean, aside from him."

"Fine. I've been working on a new song that man wanted me to learn."

"Great," I said. She sat down next to me and I put my arm around her, and I think it may have helped her. In any case, thinking I was helping her helped me.

Later, being my usual stupid self, I called Souci, hoping she might have changed her mind, about what, I'm not sure. As usual, she had her camera off. When she answered, I said, "Hi. How's it going?"

She said, "All right. I'm sort of busy." At the same time, in the distance, I heard a voice saying, "Who is it?"

A man's voice.

Jamie's, to be exact.

I disconnected.

Intermezzo

Wildly o'er Desmond the war wolf is howling;
Fearless the eagle sweeps over the plain.

"O'Donnell Abu,"
Traditional

It happened on another long, dull night, out near the west gate,
where nothing ever happened. He was doing a favor for Gary, a
corporal in Toot-toot's platoon. Toot-toot was a dumpy, balding
little sergeant from New Jersey who wheezed constantly. His real
name was Ker-something-insky, and Fred's sergeant, who was
called Mumbles, was always telling him Polack jokes, just to see
if he'd react. He generally didn't.

Gary, for whom Fred was doing this favor, was a thin cowboy
from Arizona or New Mexico who was always in trouble, but
never in deep trouble. Fred was standing guard on this windy but
not unpleasant June night because Gary had asked, and he, Fred,
was never able to say no. He scowled into the desert and lit a
cigarette.

When he saw the headlights, it took him a few seconds to grab
his M-16, just because he couldn't believe anything at all was

happening. Then there was that delicious, cold wash, which he'd hardly ever felt since he'd gone into Special Forces training. He knew that there was, still, hardly any chance that he'd be called upon to actually do anything, but there was that slim chance, and he was bored.

The headlights came closer. Fred stood next to the guardhouse, just behind it, his hand near the alarm. The headlight stopped at the gate. Where most would have tensed, Fred relaxed. The jeep stopped, but no one moved.

"Who's there?" called Fred, his voice strong and even.

"It's me." Gary's voice. Weak. "How you doing, buddy?" Drunk.

"Very well. How did you come to be out?"

"We have our secrets. Oh, shit. Look, can you let me back in, and not mention it to anyone?"

Fred stared. "Gary, this is a maximum-security installation. Leaving the base is a major breach of—"

"I know. Can you just do it?"

"I don't believe I can. How did you get out in the first place?"

"Rover let me out."

"Ah." That almost wasn't surprising. Rover was in Gary's squad. He had a dog's face, and the brains to match. "Why did you do this thing?"

"I had to. There's this girl—"

"I think you have done a bad thing."

"If you'd met her—"

"This is a problem, Gary."

"Look, we've only got a couple of weeks at this post. I can stand that. I won't go out again. Just let me past, all right? There's no one around—"

"Get in. Quickly."

"Thanks, Fred. I owe you. Really."

As the jeep sped past, Fred reflected that he was going to have to learn to say no eventually.

There was a certain justice, he decided later, to the fact that Gary pulled down ninety days, as well as the bad-conduct discharge that he and Rover got.

CHAPTER
11

I said, "By the fires
I see this is Hell
And by the looks on your faces
You're damned here as well."

"More Thumbscrews,"
William Kevely

Let's talk about love.

I sat in my room with my back to the door, my legs straight out in front of me, my feet limp, and I stared at the ceiling and thought deep and profound thoughts from which wisdom emerged, as by magic. Well, okay, maybe not. But answer this for me: Why should the end of a fling with someone I hadn't even met two months before leave me more dejected and, well, *alone*, than the destruction of the birth world of the human race, the place imprinted into my psyche and very genes as being and containing everything that was home?

Imprinted into my psyche and very genes. Aye, there's where it's used as a polishing cloth. Exactly *what* has been imprinted into my genes and very psyche? I dunno. Standing here, at the door to yet another epoch of humanity, with a view that spans from one end of the hall to another, I say to you that I have no idea in the world, or worlds, what this thing is, except that I got it and I can't shake it. But some things are learned, and, in fact, are learned so thoroughly that they'll never be pried out of the mind in which they have taken root.

Love, to pick an example at random. Romantic love.

To be a human being born into the mid-twentieth century is to inhale ideals of romantic love with your first breath, to drink it with your mother's milk, to eat it with your Gerber squashed peas, and to have it drummed thoroughly into your skin and vital organs by every children's tale, television serial, Hollywood movie, work of popular music (and unpopular music), and back-alley conversation.

But here's another one, just to confuse you: To reach maturity in the late twentieth century is to learn that romantic love is a myth, created by the needs of the spirit and the skill of the songsmiths and the confusion of a spiritual being left, for a time, with nothing spiritual to believe in. Perhaps I overstate the case, as most people of that time were not aware of all of this—certainly not consciously. But nevertheless, romantic love was in the process of being discredited, even though the generation of man doing the discrediting was its slaves.

It's quite a concept, all in all. It tells us that that love must be hot instead of warm, or the sharp peak of a mountain instead of the gentle slope of a hill. Yet we all know that too much heat can burn, and that mountain peaks, while pleasant to stand on for a while, do not make as good dwelling places as hillsides. At least, for most of us.

We are a very creative race, you know. And an imaginative one, even when we don't know it. It seems that those individuals who most bemoan their own lack of imagination are the ones who think they have met the perfect mate and spend hours spinning daydreams of how it will be and what it means. These people, along with their spiritual brothers who are waiting for the perfect mate who must be out there somewhere, are using their imaginations to find new and ingenious ways to hurt themselves.

I'm referring, of course, to myself.

We could tell ourselves that what we wanted was the warm familiarity of the lover we knew, who knew us, with whom we had grown together and could continue to do so, that security was part of love, rather than its anathema. We could tell ourselves this, but even as we did, a persistent voice whispered from our souls, *This isn't right. There's something more.* And there is the other side, perhaps worse: When we achieve, out of nowhere, the explosive infatuation reflected in a hunger that cannot be sated, the voice says, *Yes, this is right, it must be like this forever.*

Infatuation, as a phenomenon, can never be fully exorcised. Infatuation, with a person, an idea, a flower, a mountain, a starship, will exist as long as man. People who find their reason to exist in other people will exist as long as man. But be grateful, you who stand with me at the end of man's infancy and the beginning of his adolescence, that no longer are such things held up as a virtue for which we all ought to strive.

All this I have learned, and much of it I learned there and then, as I sat and thought deep and profound thoughts, from which wisdom emerged, as by magic. I am thus immune from causing myself needless pain over what cannot be and should not be, and I am able to go on with my life and with those things that are inarguably far more important than who is sleeping with whom at any given moment.

I sat with my back against the door, my legs straight out in front of me, my feet limp, and I cried until I was exhausted, and eventually I slept.

I'm so fucking wise.

When I awoke it was around midnight. My back hurt, and I felt like I'd slept sitting up in my clothes. The apartment was quiet. Rose slept in Jamie's room, dreaming of Jamie, Tom in the living room, dreaming of Carrie. What a team. What a band. I wondered if Christian would be interested in forming a duet.

I picked up the harness with the knife and looked at it for a while, then put it back down. No, I wasn't really feeling suicidal, I just didn't want to be carrying it. I walked down the hall and out the door, breathing cool New Quebec night and wondering if it, too, would be reduced to radioactive rubble. God, I was in a cheerful mood.

No one tried to shoot me down as I stepped out onto the street, no one seemed to be following me as I made my careless way along, and I was not attacked as I walked into Feng's.

I went back into the kitchen and helped Eve finish closing it. Neither of us spoke; I just started wiping down counters and sweeping while she threw charged water on the grill to polish it. We carried the garbage bags (they had biodegradable plastic bags here) out to the dumpster, and as we were walking back in she put her arms around me and hugged me. I'd never noticed before how nice her hair smelled. "It'll get better," she said almost inaudibly, then with one last squeeze she led me in.

By then it was around twelve-thirty. I sat at the bar and drank water with lemon in it until closing, which, this being Sunday, was only half an hour away. By one forty-five the last customers were out of the bar and had moved into the restaurant where they could sit and drink coffee and eat while they sobered up enough to walk home.

Libby said, "Are you being a pinhead, Billy?"

I nodded.

"Want to tell me about it?"

I did so.

She shook her head. "That's harsh."

"Yeah."

"But you know he doesn't mean anything by it, don't you? Jamie's just a whore. He doesn't understand what he's doing."

"I know."

"I suppose that doesn't help, does it?"

I shook my head.

"Is there anything I can do?"

"Yeah, Libby, there is. Explain it to me. You know I don't understand this stuff, tell me why this is happening to me, why I feel like I just want to roll over and die."

"Because you're a pinhead."

"I know that. Why else? Why is she so vicious whenever I talk to her?"

"Because she loved you."

"Bullshit."

"No, it's true. That's why she has to act like that, so she can break away from you."

"I don't get it."

"That's because you aren't like her. She can't go from loving a man to liking him, she has to hate him first."

"That's crazy. Why?"

"Because she's scared, and she'd rather hate someone than risk getting hurt. She probably doesn't know it, but there it is. Lots of people are like that." She gave me another glass of water with lemon. "You wanted the wisdom of Libby the shrink, I hope you like it."

"The whole thing is stupid."

"Yeah. So's being a pinhead. But you are one, anyway."

"That," I said, "is for damn sure."

She tousled my hair. I stood up and leaned across the bar to give her a hug. She squeezed me, then kissed me, then we were kissing for real. I slid over the bar top and held her so tight it must have hurt, but she didn't complain. When we came up for air she gasped, "Upstairs."

"Yeah," I said. "Yeah."

We stumbled up there to the bed she shared with Fred, and clumsily got rid of our clothes. Her eyes were so brown and wide, her legs were strong and gripped me while she made hissing sounds and low rumbling noises, or maybe that was me. I touched her breasts and her hips and her legs, and brushed her hair from her face, and she responded, and I remember frustration that I couldn't keep my mouth locked with hers while looking into her eyes. The eyes won eventually, brown pools of lust, of love, of fever; I went crazy for a while, but it was a good crazy, and she matched me until that moment we held each other so tight we might have just compressed into the same space, which would have been fine, if you ask me.

We breathed heavily, and sweated, and sometime later Libby had the same thought as me: "At times like this," she said, "I really miss smoking."

We lay quietly for a few minutes. Sometimes I think that sex is only a necessary prelude to good cuddling. But it grew late, and it would be embarrassing, even if nothing else, for Fred to find us like this, so I stood up and began to dress. She said, "Where the hell are you going, pinhead?"

"Home. I need some more sleep, I think."

"You're walking home alone?"

"You coming with me?"

"Fred will."

"That's not quite the same."

"I know."

"I'd rather you did."

She looked at me soberly and began to get dressed herself. "Maybe one of these days I will," she said. We went back downstairs, and she called for Fred, who was in the dining room talking to Rich. The two of them showed up, bulges under their jackets.

"Yo," said Libby. "The pinhead here needs to get home."

"Very well," said Fred.

"I'll come, too," said Rich.

"More help is always appreciated," said Fred.

The three of us left Cowboy Feng's together.

We spoke little as we walked. Fred suggested taking a wide detour around Le Bureau, and we did. Fred was alert, I was lost in thought, and Rich was watching me. Fred continued to look around. We went past a place where a church across the street faced an apartment complex on our side, which I always enjoyed because the apartment complex was built in a really fine Baroque style, with a big arch over the wood door, and windows with boxes and decorative stonework around them, while the church looked something like what on Earth would have been an "office park." That's a phrase I love: "office park." Is it where offices go to play? Or where you park your office when you're not using it? Le Bureau, at least, had a bit of style. I wondered if Souci was there now. No, it was late. She'd be at home, maybe with Jamie.

Rich said, "Something on your mind, Billy?"

"Huh?"

"You were gritting your teeth."

"Oh. Women troubles, still or again. Nothing new."

"Souci?"

"Who else?"

"Billy, I don't know how to tell you this—"

"But she isn't my type. I know. Thanks."

"It's true."

"Of course it's true. We are, quite literally, from different worlds. We have almost nothing in common. She doesn't even like Irish music. Even if circumstances were different, we'd have absolutely no future. I know all that. It doesn't change the fact that it hurts like a motherfucker."

"Yeah. When I was married, I—"

That time, I could tell, it was a gunshot. Something hit me and I realized that it was Fred, pulling me to the ground. Rich fell next to me at the same time. Fred lay across me, keeping me pinned. All I could see was Rich, who caught my eye and gave me an okay sign as he pulled his gun out.

It was very quiet. Fred said, "You all right, Billy?"

"Yeah. I think I might have heard something go past my ear right before the sound, but I might have imagined it." I wondered if my heartbeat was really as loud as it seemed.

"Rich, you all right?"

"Yep. Did you see?"

"No."

"The hedge?"

"Pretty much has to be."

"Check."

"Good. You two make a run for that apartment building, go through it, duck around the corner, and take off and head for your place in as roundabout a way as you can."

Rich said, "Will the apartment be open?"

"I haven't run into any security locks yet."

"Okay."

"I'll give you cover and keep an eye out for muzzle flash. If whoever it is fires again, he's history."

"Right."

"Whoever it is, is still behind that hedge, so you make sure you keep yourself between it and Billy."

I said, "Wait a min—"

"Shut up," they both said together.

"It's you they're after," said Fred. "If they can't get a clean shot at you, they might not even fire."

"Might," I said.

"Shut up," said Rich.

"Shit," I suggested.

"Go," said Fred, and Rich took my arm and hauled me up. We sprinted for the apartment building, just a few doors away.

I could do nothing except concentrate on speed. My eyes were focused on that door. It came to me that they might have placed a second killer somewhere, but I couldn't do anything about that now, so I just ran.

Rich was just a bit behind me and to my left. We were almost there when he stumbled and fell against the door, his palms landing flat against it, and I heard the shot, followed an instant later by several that were crisper, louder, and came in quick succession, and I figured were Fred's.

Rich sank to his knees against the door. He had been shot from behind, but there was a bloodstain on the door where he'd struck it with his chest. I knew that was a bad sign. Then I saw the hole in the window next to the door, and realized the bullet had passed completely through Rich's body and broken the window. This was a very bad sign.

Rich managed to turn himself around. His eyes were open very wide. He rested against the door of the apartment, legs straight out in front of him, feet hanging limp. The bloodstain on the front of his shirt must have been three inches in diameter and was still spreading. I took off my shirt and held it against the wound. He coughed, flecks of blood appeared on his lip and beard.

"It stings," he said.

"Don't talk," I told him. "We'll get help."

He said, "I'd like to thank all the little people who made this moment possible." He gave a small, bloody laugh, then leaned his head back and closed his eyes, breathing deeply and unevenly.

Fred came up a moment later. He said, "I got her."

"Her?"

"I've seen her before. I don't know where."

My heart and stomach did an amazing series of quick acrobatics. "Souci?"

"No, I'd remember her."

"Ah. We need to get help for Rich."

He shook his head. "Too late, Billy."

"No, he—" I looked at him. He was no longer breathing. "Damn," I said, my voice quivering.

I think he may have had more hats than anyone I knew. Three top hats (two black, one grey), a bowler, three leather caps and one woolen cap, and others. The one I remember best was a brown leather cap, with a snap. I don't remember anything else that was going on that day, or even where we were, but I remember Eve kept pulling the cap down over Rich's eyes, while he tickled her. I remember his big crocodile grin.

He had a strange fascination for the sounds people made during lovemaking, which was his biggest failing as a housemate. He would not only fill you in on what your other housemates had been up to, but what he thought of the sound effects you and your lover had made last night.

One Christmas we were in London, and the bomb scare was very real, so we didn't dare leave. Rich brought the motorcycle into the dining room and decorated it with bulbs and lights and strings of popcorn. At midnight on Christmas we killed all the other lights in the place and he turned on the emergency flashers.

He had a nasty, unpredictable temper, but he always seemed gentle.

He spent a great deal of time thinking up ways to get rich. He very badly wanted to be wealthy. Now he never would be.

"Let's go, Billy."

"We can't leave him."

"You want to explain all this to the cops?"

I shook my head. Fred helped me to my feet. He took Rich's .38 and put his own Beretta in Rich's hand. "It might fool them," he said. "At least for a while."

I nodded and took a last look at Rich, sitting with his back to the wall like he was resting, Beretta in his hand. My ears began to pound as I turned away.

We made it back to the apartment without being stopped, although about halfway there we started hearing sirens, so we took a longer, more circuitous route. Tom and Jamie and Rose were all there.

As we walked in the door, Jamie said, "What is it?"

I opened my mouth, then closed it. I realized that I wasn't wearing a shirt, but that I was still holding the bloody bundle in my hand. Fred took it, said, "I'll be back in a moment." He walked out.

"What the hell happened?" said Jamie.

The phone buzzed. I stared at it, wondering if it could be Souci, and I felt a flash of cold, black rage that I would want it to be, that I could think of her at a time like this. I marched over to the phone and picked it up—at least in part in order to avoid speaking with Jamie. If it had been Souci, I don't know what I would have said to her. But it wasn't.

"Billy!"

"Yeah, Libby?"

"Where's Fred?"

"Fred is fine. He stepped out for a few minutes."

"Okay. The police were just here. About Rich. They said he's—"

"Yeah. I was there. How's Eve?"

Libby shook her head. "They've sedated her and taken her to the hospital."

"Damn."

"Are you and Fred going to be all right?"

"Yeah."

"The cops are on their way over to you now."

"Thanks for the warning. Any idea who shot him?"

"The girl who was in here with Carrie. Danielle."

"I remember. The photographer."

"Was she? That's funny, so was Rich." There were traces of tears at the corners of Libby's eyes.

"Thanks for the warning," I said again. "I'll see you later."

Fred came in as I disconnected. I said, "That was Libby. The police have been there."

Jamie said, "Would someone please tell me—"

"Rich is dead," said Fred.

Jamie stared. "Oh, man."

Rose sat down. Tom's mouth dropped open. At that moment someone knocked at the door. I opened it and found myself face-to-face with the light grey uniform of the New Quebec Municipal Police Force, or the Munis, as they were called.

"Good afternoon, Mr. Kevely. Do you remember me?"

"Um, vaguely. Sergeant Iverness?"

"Yes. May we come in?"

"Certainly. Please."

"Thank you. This is Officer Devenois. I believe I've met all of you before."

"Sit down."

"Thank you." His eyes fell on the shotgun by the window and his eyebrows rose.

"It's mine," said Jamie. "There are no laws against it, are there?"

"No. Not yet, at any rate. Is that also yours?"

Jamie followed his glance to the .357 Magnum on the counter. "Yes."

"You like guns, eh?"

"Big guns," agreed Jamie.

"I see." He turned back to me. "Do you know why we're here?"

"I just got off the phone with Libby down at Feng's, and I've just passed the word on to my friends."

His mouth tightened. "Indeed? She wasn't supposed to call you."

"Oh. Are you sure she understood that?"

"Hmmm. Perhaps not. Well, I'd like to question each of you separately. Is there a place we can do this, or need we go to the station?"

"No," I said. "My room will work, I think."

"Excellent. We'll start with you."

I led him back to the room. His eyebrows rose when he saw my knife and harness. He looked a question at me, but since he didn't actually ask it, I didn't see a need to answer. He began asking questions and I answered them as best I could. I lied a lot. I think he knew it, but he didn't bring me down to the station, so that was good enough for me. I was very exhausted when he finished with me and started on Jamie.

After a long time they left, and we stared at each other. "Wow," said Jamie. "They get anything from you?"

I shrugged.

"Rich," said Rose, her eyes wide. "And poor Eve."

"I know," I said.

Tom said, "What happened?"

"We were attacked," said Fred.

"They were trying for me," I said.

"They'll try again, you know," said Tom.

"I know."

"I'll stay with you," said Jamie.

I said, "Are you sure your attention can be spared from—never mind."

"What?"

"It doesn't matter. Look, I've got to sleep, all right?"

I felt curious eyes on me, but no one said anything.

I went off to my room, but I didn't sleep until almost morning.

Intermezzo

She's a big, fine, strong, lump of an
Agricultural Irish girl
> **"The Agricultural Irish Girl,"**
> **Traditional**

It started simply enough, as always.

Her father said, "Libby, find the quarter-inch wrench for me," and she went off to do it. The workbench had been a strange and wonderful place when she was younger, and even now, at fourteen, there was a certain fascination. She looked around for the wrench but didn't see it. While looking, her attention was captured by a red box, with three wires coming out of it and a dial in front. One of the wires had a dull needle-like thing at the end.

She wondered at its purpose. Her first idea was that it had to do with testing car batteries, but she had seen her father do that, and he didn't use this thing. It obviously had something to do with electricity. She wondered what would happen if she stuck the needle into a socket, but decided that it would probably be a bad idea.

The other two wires, one red and one black, had clips at the end. She attached one clip to the handle of the clamp, the other to the workbench, and began gently touching the needle to the saw, the wall behind the workbench, one of the nail jars, the—

She was grabbed from behind and swung around. Her father slapped her on top of her head, hard, and the box fell onto the floor. *Good. I hope it's broken,* she thought.

"I told you to get the wrench, not play with every tool I own." He slapped the back of her head hard enough to make her teeth rattle, looked around for the wrench, and finally spotted it on the paint shelf. He took her by the arm and roughly dragged her over to the shelf, took the wrench, and threw her across the garage, where she banged her right elbow painfully against the old cedar buffet.

What finally did it, she decided later, was that the wrench hadn't even been where he said it would be. As he turned away, she grabbed the nearest thing to hand, an old push broom, and charged him. He turned around at her footsteps, and she swung, the big end catching him in the side. "Ufff," he said, and took a step backward.

"You're never going to hit me again," she screamed. "I'll kill you if you hit me again."

He yanked the broom from her hand, snarling, and threw it off to the side. As he stared at her, she realized that she had never seen him this angry before. The thought came, *He's going to kill me. He's really going to kill me. I'm going to be dead, and maybe go to Hell.*

As he took his first step forward, the flight reflex took over and she was gone, into the house, slamming the door behind her. When it opened, she was down the hall. His footsteps clattered behind her like the Four Horsemen, and when she looked back she saw Death, and it was gaining on her.

She opened her bedroom door and dived up onto the top bunk, squashing herself into the corner. By accident, it was the right thing to do, because the bed was so wide and her room so small that no one her father's size was able to get past it, and the bed was long enough that his arms couldn't reach her, although he kept trying, like a creature out of a monster movie.

She never watched monster movies after that, but he did go away and, like all the other times, the incident was forgotten by suppertime.

Forgotten by him; never by her.

CHAPTER
12

Hunted from our father's home
    Pursued by steel and shot,
A bloody warfare we must wage,
    Or the gibbet be our lot.
  "The Rapparee,"
  Seamus McGrath, Tom Brett,
  Michael O'Brian, and James English

Breakfast the next morning was a portion of prepackaged pudding that the label claimed was chocolate, served with a helping of mutual quick frost from each fellow roommate to every other. But the coffee was hot and there was milk to lighten it and sugar to make it sweet. A tense stillness, a deafening quiet, made the little apartment stifling. No one spoke, no one even looked at anyone else, we just watched the walls close in.

At one point Jamie stood up, got out his Gibson six-string, and started singing "Sir James the Rose," but no one responded, and soon he became quieter. Presently he stopped.

What is there to say?

I slipped into my room to play my banjo, but I couldn't manage to feel any enthusiasm for that, either, so I stopped after three or four plunks. I went through the list of things I wanted to do, mentally crossing them out as I came to the ones that broke some natural law, could get me arrested, or I was certain to regret in a few hours. When I found one that survived all of the cuts, I went back into the living room and said, "I'm for Feng's. Anyone else?"

"I'll go along," said Jamie, I think figuring to protect me.

"All right," I said, because I couldn't think of any way to say no.

"I might as well," said Tom, since the rest of us were. Rose was already there, waiting on tables so Fred could cook, since Eve . . .

Jamie put the shotgun into a canvas bag and stuck his pistol under his jacket. I took along my knife so Fred wouldn't give me any shit about not having it. Tom had his .45.

"Should we bring our instruments?" said Tom.

"I don't much feel like practicing," said Jamie, which was unusual for him, but understandable. I didn't feel like practicing, either, but I was feeling contrary. I said, "I'm bringing mine. I might not want to come back here for a while, since every time we do we have to worry about getting shot at."

"That makes sense," said Jamie, so we all packed up our instruments. Nothing untoward happened on the way to Feng's, except that it was a real pain to carry a banjo all that distance. We arrived just before the dinner rush. I'd mostly skipped breakfast, and it had been several hours ago, anyway, so I ordered lamb paprikache, with spaetzle, lemon-grass soup, and an appetizer of celery root. Everyone sat down at a booth, but I was feeling antisocial, so I asked Fred to bring me my dinner in the bar. As I walked away, I felt three pairs of eyes on me.

I waited for the food and watched Libby work. I wondered if we were now something different than we'd been before last night, but Libby kept being her cheerful self, which I guessed meant not. This was almost certainly just as well.

As I sat there, Rose, in her stupid white waitress uniform, came up behind me and put her arms around me. "How's my brother?" she said.

"Why is it, with all this great food, Feng couldn't have found waitress uniforms that didn't look like something out of J. C. Penney's Old People's Sale?"

She kissed my cheek. I said, "I'm all right, I guess. How about you?"

"I'm worried about my little band." She pronounced both *t* 's in little.

"Are you? Why?"

"I don't know, I just am."

"Have some whiskey."

"I will."

She sat down and did this.

"Are we ever going to play again?"

"I don't know," I said. "If we get out of this alive, we might. If we all die, then probably not."

"I do not wish to die," said Rose, as if she had considered the matter carefully and just reached that decision.

"All right, then you won't."   .

"That is a good thing. But Jamie has to live, too."

"All right, I'll take care of it."

"And we need Tom to play mandolin."

"That's true."

"And Fred and Libby to bring us food and whiskey."

"Right."

"And Eve and—oh." She stopped, looking stricken.

Fred arrived with my celery root. It was very tangy and had a trace of lemon in the dressing, so I suspected it would go well with the soup. Libby brought me a glass of burgundy, and it was okay.

"It seems like you're angry at Jamie," Rose said.

"Well, there was some stuff, but I don't think I'm angry. I don't know."

"That's good, because I'm the only one who gets to be mad at Jim."

"I understand that now."

"I think we need to get you a girl."

"Yeah? Okay. Find one for me."

"She has to be a good one, because you're my brother."

"Pick one out for me. I'll trust your judgment."

"I will. You know that girl Souci, she wasn't very good for you."

"People keep telling me that. I wonder if her friends are telling her the same thing."

"You know, it isn't any of my business, Billy—"

"Oh, go ahead and say it."

"Well, I just wonder if you didn't arrange for things to fall apart between you and Souci. I mean, it almost seems like—"

"Yeah, I know. I've thought of that, oddly enough. Maybe it's true. It's certainly a lot easier to be hurt than to, oh, hell with it. I'm not a shrink. Maybe it's true. Either way, it doesn't help."

"I know."

She dried the corners of my eyes, downed her whiskey, hugged me, and went back to the restaurant.

Presently Tom sat down next to me. "Did you know that James Cagney never actually said, 'I'm gonna do to you what you did to my brotha, you dirty rat'?"

"As a matter of fact," I said, "I *did* know that. And Bogart never said, 'Play it again, Sam.'"

Libby said, "Get something for you, Tom?"

"Orange juice."

"Coming up."

I said, "You going to call Carrie?"

"Why? She's a whore."

"That's harsh."

"It's true."

"So you're not going to call her?"

"I don't know."

My salad bowl vanished and my soup appeared. Yes, it complemented the salad very nicely. It went well with the wine, too, in an odd sort of way. Slurp slurp. I'm a very loud soup eater.

"It's Justin," said Tom. "I hate him. Did you see how he was looking at me? Like I was dirt."

"I was pretty surprised you didn't blow him away.

"I almost did. Right there. You know, he treats her like shit."

"How do you know that?"

"She told me."

"When?"

"Last night. I called her."

"Ah. I think Libby would say you're a pinhead."

"Libby would be right. Billy, you ever cry about Souci?"

"Yeah. You ever cry about Carrie?"

"Yeah. If she ever found out, she'd probably be proud of herself."

"I don't think she would be. Souci would, though, if she knew I had. She probably guesses."

"Yeah."

"But I can't help thinking she really cared about me."

"God, are we ever pinheads."

"Yep."

"Are you pissed at Jamie?"

"How do you know about that?"

"Souci told Carrie and Carrie told me."

"Oh."

"Well, are you?"

I thought about that and tried to answer honestly. "I don't know. I'm hurt. I've never been jealous before so I'm not used to it. Jamie's my brother, I couldn't hate him. But I don't know. Suppose she made a pass at him. He could either say yes and feel guilty about it, or say no and feel resentful. I guess I'd rather he felt guilty than resentful. It'd help to know he felt guilty, though—at least a little."

"He probably does, in his own way," said Tom.

"Probably."

"But what if *he* made the pass at *her*?"

"Then," I said firmly, "I don't ever want to know about it."

After a moment, Tom said, "Man, I still can't believe that Rich is dead. It's like it isn't real."

"I know what you mean. I keep turning around, expecting him to be there. And every time I walk by his bike, it hits me again. It sure is weird how the brain works."

"You mean how we're bummed out about our love lifes when what we're really upset about is Rich?"

"Yeah."

"I hadn't noticed."

"Heh."

We said nothing more for a while, then Tom wandered off into the restaurant. I finished my soup and had more wine. Jamie joined me. He had a beer, I switched to coffee. I decided I was drinking too much coffee lately.

He said, "How you doing, bror?"

"All right. I'll live, anyway."

"You seem kind of down."

"Yeah, I guess."

"Is it about Souci?"

"Yeah."

"Well, look, Billy. I know her pretty well—"

"Yeah, even biblically."

He looked at me. Then he cleared his throat. "Would you believe me if I said she isn't good enough for you?"

"No. She good enough for you?"

"Huh?"

"Never mind."

"How about—"

"Let's not talk about her."

"All right."

The food showed up and Jamie was politely silent out of respect for my pleasure. Business in the bar picked up and then slacked off while I ate. Libby brought Jamie another beer, then leaned on the bar and said, "So, how's it going, gentlemen?"

"All right," said Jamie.

I said, "How's Eve?"

She shook her head. "Not catatonic, but not responding to anything. On the other hand, she's still sedated, so that may be part of it."

"I hope she comes out of it," I said.

"Me, too."

"I wish I didn't feel responsible for it."

Jamie said, "Did you pull the trigger?"

"Well, no."

Libby said, "Did you order Rich to go along? Did you even *ask* Rich to go along?"

"No."

"Then why feel responsible?"

"Because they were protecting me. Whoever it was, was probably shooting at me, and if he'd let me get shot, he—"

"Rich figured he was doing something important. It was his choice."

"I know."

"If they want to kill you that badly, we'd better not let them."

I said, "I just wish I knew why they were doing it—what their goals were. That's what I've been racking my brains with and I can't figure it out."

Libby nodded. "Yeah. If we knew what was in it for them, it would help."

I shook my head. "I don't think anything is in it for them, exactly. I think they believe in what they're doing, at least on some level."

Jamie said, "Destroying entire populations? They believe in that?"

Libby said, "I heard a rumor today that war broke out on Mince. Nuclear war, every city on the planet. If Sugar Bear is behind it, that's another, what, eight, nine thousand people they've wiped out? You think they believe that's the right thing to do?"

"What's Mince?" said Jamie.

"A colony world around a star somewhere between here and the Fishbait Cluster."

I said, "From talking to Rudd, I do think they believe in what they're doing."

"That doesn't make sense," said Jamie. "Are they religious nuts?"

"I don't know. He referred to the Physician, and a cure, which could be a religious reference of some sort. But I ought to have seen symbols of his religion if there was one, or heard something in what he said. I don't know."

"Well," said Jamie, "let's make a list of all the possible reasons why a group of people would want to destroy humanity, and—"

I said, "That's a joke, right?"

"Right."

I sighed.

Libby said, "Why does anyone want to kill anyone? It's probably the same reason, only bigger."

"Money figures in there pretty highly," I said.

"So does jealousy," said Jamie. I winced.

"Hate," said Libby.

"Power," I said.

"Revenge," said Jamie.

"If we're making a list," said Libby, "put money in twice."

"Yeah," I said, "and if we're going to mention hate, we should mention fear, like you said."

"That's true," she said.

"Fear of what?" said Jamie.

"Hell if I know. Besides, they probably aren't all like—shit."

"What?"

I stared off into space for a moment.

Libby said, "What is it, Billy?"

"Maybe they *are* all like Souci."

Jamie said, "What do you mean?"

I gestured to Libby. "She was telling me about hate and fear."

"What about it?"

"That Souci got angry because she was afraid."

"I could believe that," said Jamie. "What about it?"

I ignored him and asked Libby, "When's the first time you ever saw her mad?"

"I don't think I've ever actually *seen* her mad."

"Yes, you have. The first time you two met."

"That was right here. You two were sitting at that table and—oh, right, she got mad and walked out."

"Do you remember why?"

"Ummm, it was a political argument, wasn't it? No, I remember, it was Hags disease."

"Right. It was something that scared her so much, she got angry, because that's what she does."

"Well, and?"

"Maybe these people are scared about something."

"Like what?" said Libby. "What's going to scare someone so badly he's willing to help destroy entire populations?"

"It's a quarantine," said Jamie. "They're trying to prevent infection."

"From what?" said Libby.

"Now that I think of it," I said, "why not Hags disease? They had it on Earth, they still have it. It's a one hundred percent fatal communicative disease. Isn't that enough to scare someone?"

"Well, yeah."

"Scares the shit out of me," said Jamie.

"So, how do you protect yourself from a disease like that?"

Libby considered this. "To start with," she said, "I'd pour shitloads of money into research, to find a cure."

Jamie said, "And be as careful as you can of people you don't know—"

"How about this?" I said. "You select a group of your friends and peers, and isolate yourselves from everyone else."

Libby looked thoughtful, then shook her head. "I don't think it would work. You'd need a whole planet."

"So? They're rich."

"It wouldn't work over the long run," said Libby. "How do you ensure there isn't any contact between you and the rest—oh."

"Yeah. First you isolate yourselves, then you get the rest of humanity to blow themselves up."

"A little extreme, I'd say."

"What," I said, "history doesn't have any examples of nut-case fanatics?"

"A point," said Jamie.

"I don't know," said Libby.

"Take it a step at a time, then. Hags disease appeared just about the same time it became possible to consider colonizing the Moon. So they secretly arrange to have a colony, then they start a war on the Earth. But they aren't quite fast enough, and some people escape and set up on the Moon. So they try Venus, and wipe out everyone on the Moon, but two colony ships make it there, and the Earth is still able to send some ships out, too. So they try for Mars, while wiping out Venus, and the same thing happens, and there they are, looking for their own colony, planning to destroy everyone else."

"Wow," said Libby. "It's weird, but it sort of fits."

"It sure does," said Jamie. "But, then, what does Feng want?"

"As I understand it," said Libby, "what they're looking for is some sort of handle on the enemy."

"Handle?"

"A weakness. Some means of striking back at them. In Feng's time, they're trying to wipe out Feng's people, and Feng's people know nothing about them. We're supposed to find something that will help."

I nodded. "They," I repeated. "Sugar Bear. The enemy. Wow."

Jamie said, "Then we haven't really accomplished anything."

"On the contrary," I said. "This is it."

"What do you mean?"

"We've figured out that they almost certainly have a single home world, rather than being spread throughout the galaxy. If that world can be found, Feng's people can counterattack, or threaten to counterattack, or something like that." I turned to Libby. "Can't they?"

"That sounds right to me, Billy," said Libby carefully.

"Well, great," said Jamie. "How are we going to find their home world?"

"Whose home world?"

I spun around. Libby said, "Oh, hi, Christian. We didn't see you there. Get you a beer?"

"That'd be nice. What's going on? Whose home world are you looking for?"

"Whose do you think?"

"The bad guys?"

"Good guess."

"I thought you thought I was a bad guy."

"It's a possibility," I said.

"Does that mean you have to kill me?"

I wasn't sure if he was joking or not. I said, "I don't know. What's the location of the rebel base?"

He shook his head. "If you're the good guys, I have to ask that."

"Don't bother," said Jamie. "The bad guys already blew it up."

"That's harsh," said Christian.

"That's Libby's word," I said.

"I've been hanging around with her a lot. Did you mean the Earth, that the bad guys blew up?"

"Yeah," said Jamie. "How did you know that's what I meant?"

"It's where you guys are from," said Christian.

"Oh."

"You think they destroyed the whole place?"

"It looks that way," I said.

"Wow. That's scary. Why do you have to find out where they live? So you can blow up their planet?" He didn't seem especially serious about this blowing-up-planets thing. We looked at each other, then at Christian. "All right," he said, "*how* are you going to find it?" Again, we didn't answer. "*Man,*" he said. "You guys really think I'm with them, don't you?"

Libby said, "How are we supposed to know, one way or the other?"

"I guess you're right," he said. "But who are *they,* anyway? I'm curious."

"Well," I said, "if what I've just figured out is true, they're a bunch of nut cases who think the only way to protect themselves from Hags disease is to kill off anyone who might be infected, which means anyone but themselves. I'm not sure how they manage to be sure none of them have contact with a carrier."

"Scary," said Christian. "That means killing a lot of people."

"The whole human race," said Libby.

"And what are you guys doing?"

"Trying to save them."

"Save everyone?"

"Why do you ask?" I said. "Got someone in mind you don't want saved?"

"No, I just wondered who appointed you guardians of humanity."

"Shit happens," said Libby.

"Yeah," said Christian. "I guess it does at that." He finished his drink and walked out of the bar.

Jamie got another beer. "What the hell got into him?"

"Hmmm," said Libby. I agreed with her.

"All right," said Jamie. "As I was saying, how are we going to find their home world?"

"I don't know," I said. "But now that we know what we're after, we're closer."

"I just hope they don't kill us all before we find out," said Jamie.

"Amen to that," I said.

In the next room, there was a tinkle of broken glass. I mentally tsked. Then I heard the distant report of a firearm. Someone screamed.

"What's the secret of comedy?" I said to no one in particular, as Jamie took his pistol from his belt and walked into the next room. Libby didn't answer, she was too busy turning the key in the cash register and pulling her .44 from under the bar.

"I've wandered into a western," I said. "I don't believe it." There were more screams from the next room and I began to be convinced.

CHAPTER
13

He was a braw galant
    And he rode at the ring.
And the bonny Earl of Morray,
    He might have been a king.
        "The Earl of Morray,"
        Traditional

Chaos engenders confusion springs from disorder; the gentle whitewash of remembrance fails me, and I relive too much. What is this quintessence of dust, as the man said, and on bad days I know why. I wanted to huddle in the bar and hope anybody who didn't like me wouldn't come looking, but I'm curious as well as cowardly, and sometimes the former dominates, for a time, for a time.

I stopped beneath the arch, on the taproom side, and stuck my head out to get a glance into the dining room, whence came the tinkle of broken glass et al., and I retain the flashes of sight/sound passing through the tunnel we call memory, the better to cushion the blow, my dear, but the eardrum rings and the retina burns, even now, when the fixer of all contusions should have twisted its rope enough.

They were standing in the doorway, holding the sorts of

weapons that it takes two hands to hold. We had somehow moved from a western to a gangster film, which is only a difference of props and stage setting, I suppose, but I didn't like it.

I ducked back, breathing hard.

In that confusion of fear and adrenaline, I doubted what I had seen, so I looked once more, ducked behind my wall again, and the screaming resumed, accompanied this time by a shower of splinters marking the spot where my head had just been; I resolved at this point to stop sneaking peeks. But I recognized two of those who had come in as Justin and Claude, and I had no reason to think that their intentions toward me were any friendlier than they had been before.

There was more shooting, and I looked again, my decision forgotten in the heat of the moment. All right, then. Forget the sights and sounds and memories and emotions, I'll just tell you what happened, as I was able to reconstruct it later, and you can supply your own reactions, since you will, anyway.

The plan involved three of them walking in the front door with automatic weapons, just seconds after two others were to appear from the back with hand weapons, and the group was to simply go through the place shooting any of us they saw until they found me, and then they could leave after making certain I was dead.

How were they to get in the back door, normally kept locked? A "customer" slipped back there and unlocked it, after making certain where I was in the restaurant. The plan was good, and would have worked except that Fred happened to be taking out the garbage. A few days before he was killed, Rich had installed a small light in the back door, just to let us know the door was unlocked. The light was on, and Fred knew that it shouldn't have been. Fred was not the sort to let this kind of thing slip by.

He picked up his machine pistol and returned to the door to check things out, just as it opened, and two heavily armed persons attempted to, as they say, gain entrance. Fred fired, knocking out a window and making someone scream, but not actually hitting either of them. It is much more difficult to hit someone you're firing at than you may think, especially when you're in a hurry and he's shooting back. Fred was good enough that he might have been able to drop them both by taking his time and picking his targets, but he chose, on this occasion, to just fill the air with so much lead that they had to leave, which they quite reasonably did.

Jamie and Libby appeared right as they were slamming the door shut. Fred told them, "Guard the hall," and turned to deal with the front, correctly guessing what was about to happen, but not wanting to leave the back way unattended.

There were three of them, as I said, all with full-automatic rifles. Tom took out his pistol, but Fred was ready. They saw Fred as he saw them, and everybody fired. When the smoke cleared, one of the attackers, someone I'd never seen, was wounded and running up the street as fast as he could and Justin had dived out the door, leaving Claude alone in the room.

By this time, all of the customers were on the floor, most of them screaming. Claude ducked to the side, losing his weapon in the process. He came up with a small pistol and, from a prone position on the floor, shot three times at Fred, then he got up and ran out the door himself as Tom emptied his automatic in Claude's general direction.

Fred slumped against a wall and no one moved. Apparently one of Claude's shots had hit him, though not badly as far as I could tell. I saw a wound high on his right leg, which hadn't been as obvious as Rich's wound had, I suppose due to differences in weapon, bullet, and location. The customers gradually stopped screaming, although one of them continued to moan softly.

Jamie and Libby appeared in the room, just as I walked in. "I've locked the back door," said Jamie.

"Good work," said Fred. Sweat was pouring down his face, and I realized that he was in a great deal of pain. Tom put another magazine into his .45, walked up to a window, and looked out it. There was no trace of humor on his features.

Libby knelt next to Fred and said, "You all right, babe?"

"Fine," he said, gasping.

Libby turned and said, "Get him in the back room, and I'll look at that leg. We also need to get these people out of here."

Tom said, "Better put them in the bar. I don't think it's safe to send them outside."

I said, "Oh?"

"I saw Justin meet up with Claude, and they're sitting in the bakery across the street, probably going to shoot at us."

"Wonderful."

I came forward, wanting very much to feel useful. The room was thick with the harsh smell of gunpowder. There was a blue haze in the air, like and yet more sinister than tobacco smoke. Jamie and I carried Fred upstairs where he could rest on the bedding where Libby and I had made love twelve hours before.

Rose and Libby coerced the ten or so customers into the bar.

Fred seemed to be losing a great deal of blood. I pressed a shirt against the wound as hard as I could. Fred's face was covered with sweat and he winced as I applied pressure.

He held out his gun to me. "You want to use this?"

"No. Now shut up."

"Yes, sir."

I went back out. Libby was just finishing getting all of the customers into the bar. Tom yelled, "Watch it!" and ducked. There was a spray of glass, and someone screamed again.

I told Libby, "He's upstairs, lying down."

She nodded and set her pistol on a table, disappeared in back. Tom stood up, fired out the window, and ducked again. Jamie did the same thing. I stayed down. There was a thunk somewhere above my head and off to the right, and I was sprayed with particleboard as a bullet hit the wall. I tried to swallow but my mouth was too dry. Rose huddled on the floor next to Jamie's right leg. This continued for a while. Tom selected a magazine from the pile by his feet and reloaded. Jamie used the quick-loader for his revolver, tossing it over his shoulder as if for luck. They both fired out the window again.

There was a pause, during which I crawled over to Tom and said, "What the hell's going on?"

He shrugged. "There's at least a couple of them, in the bakery across the street. They shoot, we duck. We shoot, they duck. No one's going to hit anyone."

"Great," I said.

"I wonder why the police haven't shown up?"

"Hell if I know."

Jamie said, "Maybe we should rush them."

At that point Libby, who had just emerged from tending to Fred's wound, walked past him. She said, "Good idea." She picked up her pistol and carried it loosely at her side. Then she just walked out the door, turned toward the bakery, and started shooting.

Jamie was the first one after her, with Tom right on his heels, then me, then Rose. What Rose or I thought we were going to do, I don't know. There wasn't anyone on the street, except one grey sedan with the Muni insignia on the door.

The bakery was small and ugly, with exterior brick up to three feet, then plate-glass windows perhaps four feet long and three feet wide, separated by thin metal strips. The windows displayed loaves of bread and pastries. All of these windows were broken.

Most of the pastries were ruined. As we came out, Libby, Tom, and Jamie fired.

Justin and Claude emerged and began running down the street, I guess deciding that the bakery was a poor place to have a gunfight, after all. Jamie and Libby shot at them and missed, and we all set off. I wondered what I thought I was going to do if we caught them. It was growing dark, and I wondered if that would make a difference.

Claude, in front, reached the door of Le Bureau Théâtral du Nouveau Québec. It occurred to me that, once inside, they would know the place really well, and that they might have reinforcements waiting. I guess the same thoughts occurred to the others, because they put on a burst of speed and we were right behind them in a narrow hallway, with no possibility of cover for anyone. If they stopped, I think they could have had us all then, but instead they continued past a receptionist's desk to what looked like a copying center, with several machines and a sturdy bookcase or two. There was a window in the back, and at first I thought they'd go through it and keep running, but instead they stopped below it and turned to face us, like boars at bay. I was just outside the room, Rose was behind me, Libby and Jamie and Tom were almost in the door.

Squat, curly-haired Claude fired a shot at Jamie, and tall, long-haired Jamie went down behind a copier. I couldn't tell at the time if he had ducked or been shot, and neither could Claude, who kept shooting into the machine, hoping to pierce it and hit him. Claude's pistol was small, but in that room seemed much louder than the bigger weapons had in Feng's. My ears hurt.

Justin had a machine pistol, but Tom moved too quickly. He rolled behind a bookcase, came up, fired several times. He missed, but I saw where the bullets hit near Justin's head. Justin ducked down. The .45 was very loud, as well.

Libby fired at Justin, and, well, for noisemakers, you'll have to put the .44 automag up there with Spinal Tap and 747s. She fired at Claude, and I stayed down and figured that ear damage was the least danger I was in. She kept alternating shots at Justin, who was behind a machine, and Claude, who was behind the counter. There was a lull while she reloaded, during which Justin stood and went crashing out the window. Tom leapt through the window after him, .45 flailing about in his hand.

I guess this was too good a chance for Claude to pass up, because he stood suddenly and carefully aimed for Tom's back. A sick feeling hit my stomach, and I yelled and so did Rose, but we needn't have bothered. Jamie stood up from behind the machine and fired. Claude spun and slammed against the wall, looking very surprised, and I saw an exit wound in front of his shirt, just like Rich's, and I was glad.

Claude was working on raising his pistol when I heard the hammer fall on Jamie's revolver. It was empty. Claude's face lit up. There was another gut-wrenching frozen moment, but then there was another ear-shattering explosion as Libby put a shot into Claude's stomach. Claude dropped the pistol and crumpled to the ground, and now the look on his face wasn't surprise, it was pain, and I thought of Rich again and I liked that, too. Libby fired again, then again, then kept putting bullets into his body until her gun was empty. I turned away before this point.

I started to shake in the deafening silence. "Let's get back to Feng's," said Jamie after a moment. I realized that I was having some trouble hearing him for the ringing in my ears. His face was slack and he looked very tired. Libby didn't answer; there was an expression on her face that I couldn't read.

Rose said, "What about Tommy?"

"I don't think he'll come back here," I said. "Let's just get back to Feng's where it's—well, safer."

Jamie and Rose and I left the office. I heard Libby's footsteps behind us as we reached the door and stepped out onto the street. We turned up toward Feng's in the growing twilight, and stopped cold.

Sergeant Iverness stood in a crouch, his pistol held in both hands and pointed at Jamie. Christian stood easily in an ankle-length leather coat, cigarette dangling from the corner of his mouth, a pump-action shotgun pointing loosely at Libby. I was glad Tom, at least, wasn't around, and I hoped he'd be all right.

"Toss your guns to the side," said Iverness crisply. His voice came as through a distance due to the ringing in my ears, and this added to the sense of unreality about the entire scene.

Jamie sighed and let his gun drop. I heard the sound of Libby's dropping as well. What the hell, they were empty, anyway. Christian moved the shotgun to cover Rose, who had her hands jammed into her jacket pocket. The rest of us stood with our hands well away from our bodies.

Iverness said, "Where's the skinny guy?"

I shrugged. He studied me for a moment, then turned to Christian and nodded. "Let's get it done," he said, again as from far away. I knew it couldn't be real.

Christian swung his shotgun until it was pointing at Libby

again. Then Iverness faced me and pointed his pistol dead at my chest, and I saw his face tighten just a little, and I could actually see, or imagined I could see, his finger squeezing the trigger.

I closed my eyes, just to show how brave I am, and waited for the bullet. Next to me, Jamie had time to say, quite clearly and distinctly, "Well, shit," then I heard the sound of a shotgun, twice in quick succession, and I winced and waited for the impact.

And waited.

Presently I looked. Iverness lay on the street, and I averted my eyes from what was left of his face. Christian's shotgun still pointed at him. He pumped another round into the chamber, walked over to the body, and touched it with his foot. I think he was checking to make sure he was dead, but I averted my eyes once more.

None of us moved; none of us spoke. We stood there in the spreading darkness and looked at one another and at Christian, who returned our looks from slitted eyes.

Rose said, "Perhaps we should go inside now."

"Good idea," I said. "And you can put that thing away anytime."

"What? Oh, this." She put the derringer back in her pocket. "I never got to shoot it, anyway," she said. "Christian shot first."

"I noticed that," I said. And to Christian, "Why?"

"I've never liked cops," he explained.

That was as good as I needed just at that moment. Jamie and Libby retrieved their weapons and left Iverness lying there. We walked back to Feng's. Did I mention before that I'd wandered into a western? It felt like it more than ever as we walked through deserted streets back to Feng's. It would have been funny if it weren't so spooky.

When we got there, Jamie stepped in ahead of me, though he wasn't armed, either. I stood inside and looked around. There was still the faint smell of gunpowder, but the blue smoke had dispersed. There was a fair amount of broken glass, chipped woodwork, and smashed crockery, and I could see it would take some clean up, but it was home. We sat down at a table, and I said to Christian, "Well, when are the police going to show up?"

"I don't know," he said. "You weren't supposed to live through today, so no one made any contingency plans."

"Sugar Bear really does own the police department, don't they?"

"Pretty much the whole city," said Christian.

"Damn."

Jamie nodded thoughtfully, then suddenly turned to Libby. "By the way," he said, "why did you charge out there like that? That was crazy. You could have—"

"Fuck off," said Libby, acid in her voice.

"Well, shit," said Jamie, but didn't push it.

To change the subject, I asked her, "How is Fred doing? We should tell him what—"

"The bullet hit an artery in his leg," said Libby. "He's dead."

Intermezzo

Now with this loaded blunderbuss—
The truth I will unfold.
He made the mayor to tremble
And robbed him of his gold.

"Brennon on the Moor,"
Traditional

He lived in a single room, sharing bathroom and kitchen with the junkie to the right and the prostitute across the hall. The mattress took up one corner of the room, his hollow-body electric and acoustic took up one corner, his antique, honest-to-God, real, two-hundred-year-old Fender Stratocaster got the guitar stand. Next to them was his shotgun, two pistols, and ammo boxes. On the other side of the room were his piles of clothes (one dirty, one clean; he could usually tell them apart). Next to them books: Flaubert, Dickens, Hugo, Hawthorne, Dumas, a few contemporary novels, some current works of political studies, music theory.

Just at the moment, he was working on soloing over thirteenth formations, playing with the mixolydian scale, emphasizing the seventh in the lower octave and sixth in higher. He was lost, as he always was. The rest of the world did not exist, music was all there was: the music in his head, and the music from the guitar, as he concentrated on making every note speak, on phrasing and dynamics, and the creation of beauty.

There was a sharp rap at the door. He stopped playing. What the hell?

"Who is it?"

"Municipal Police Force."

He frowned, set the guitar down, opened the door. The big one, in front, said, "Sir, we've had a complaint about noise—"

"From who?"

"I'm afraid we can't say. Someone in the building." Here the cop sniffed.

"Jesus Christ, it's not even ten o'clock. What's the problem?"

The cop's face changed then, and he said, "Look, punk, I don't give a—"

"Hold it," said his partner, a shorter guy he almost recognized.

"What?"

The partner said, "Aren't you Christian Drewry?"

"Yeah. So?"

The two of them had a hasty, whispered conference, then the short one said, "Excuse us. Never mind."

Another one who took orders from Rudd, Christian decided, which made him a friend of Iverness'. Christian smiled to himself. He mostly helped Rudd out because he liked Ivy and because it was fun to test his nerve from time to time, to get out some of his frustrations, but every once in a while, it paid off in unexpected ways. He said, "Before you go—"

"Yeah?"

"Who was it?"

"Huh? Oh." The cop pointed straight down.

"Thanks."

"Forget it."

When they'd left, Christian went back into his room and picked up his .38, replaced one live round with a blank load, and cocked the pistol with the blank under the hammer. He walked down the stairs and kicked open the door to the guy's room. He didn't know the guy, who had just moved in, but he didn't really care. He was fat and balding and very surprised as he sat watching the TV. Christian stuck the barrel practically up the guy's nose and said, "You got a complaint, motherfucker?"

"Huh, wha—?"

"I said you got some noise complaint to make? Am I interfering with your peaceful enjoyment of the evening?"

"N-no."

"Good. You're interfering with mine."

Christian smacked him across the face with the gun while simultaneously firing it. Then he put a round into the TV and left without looking back. He went up to his room, set the pistol down, and picked up his guitar again, began laying down melodic phrases on top of chord progressions in his mind.

CHAPTER
14

Up the long ladder and down the short rope
To hell with King Billy and God bless the Pope.

"Up the Long Ladder,"
Traditional

"He's dead," said Libby, toneless, even, distant.

Leave it there, just for a minute.

Why? Perhaps as a gesture of sympathy made out to whoever needs it at the moment. We'll find out soon enough, I suppose, and cash it then. Fill in the amount with your chosen investment, in the coin of love, hate, excitement, disgust, intrigue, boredom, or however you spend your life. Leave it there; we'll come back to it.

When Rich died, scenes had returned to me—incidents which had captured who he was, to me, and this had brought his death home, and yet kept it at a distance and begun the healing process.

But I guess I never really knew Fred. There was a distance about him at all times, a formality that was not cold, but didn't invite closeness. He was good at what he did, and he was dependable, but he was almost more of an automaton than a real

person. Jamie, I guess, was closer to him than anyone except
Libby, and that was perhaps because they were so different. Jamie
was loud where Fred was quiet, Jamie was warm and emotional
where Fred was cold and rational. But now Jamie was alive, and
Fred was not, and I wished I'd known him better, that I might
mourn him as he deserved.

Those were thoughts at the time, in that first instant after
Libby's announcement. I don't know what thoughts the others
had, but there was silence for a long, long moment, broken
suddenly by Tom's arrival. He walked in the door so cautiously
that it would have been comical if it weren't so reasonable.

Then he looked around and said, "What is it?"

We told him. He went up to Libby and held her. It looked like
she was about to start crying, then she caught herself and said,
"I'm all right. What happened to you?"

Tom opened and closed his mouth, still holding Libby, then he
said, "Justin outran me, which was just as well, since I realized
that my gun is empty and I left all my spare magazines back here."
He shook his head like it was a joke, but I couldn't help
shuddering. "What happened with you guys?" he said.

I said, "Did you go by Le Bureau?"

"No."

"Well, if you do, you'll find a few bodies in the area."

"Oh?"

"Claude, for one."

"Good work. Who got him?"

"Jamie and Libby."

"Good," said Tom, like he meant it.

"Claude's the one who killed Fred," said Jamie.

"Oh," said Tom. "Who else?"

"Would you believe, the cop, Iverness?"

"Really? We're going to have the whole city on our asses. Who
shot him?"

Jamie gestured with his head toward Christian, who was sitting
in a far corner. Tom stared at him. "I thought you were on their
side."

"I was."

"What happened?"

"I don't know," he said. "I was just standing there, about to
shoot Libby, and I couldn't. I had to shoot Ivy instead. I don't—"

"Ivy?" said Rose.

Christian shrugged. "I've known him for a long time."

"You *are* with Sugar Bear," said Jamie softly.

"I was. I don't think I am anymore."

"But I don't get it. Why did you do all that stuff?"

"What stuff?"

"Why were you with them?"

He lit a cigarette and turned away. I thought he wasn't going to answer us, but he finally said, "That's a hard one. I never thought about it much, I just did it. I was brought up that way, like we were special because we were still going to be around when all the sickies killed themselves."

I said, "You mean, when you guys wiped out—"

"I didn't know about that until you guys told me."

"Oh. What did you do?"

"Pretty much what I was told. Security stuff, making sure people didn't find out about us, helping to keep the organization safe. It didn't come together until just now, when I had to kill Libby and couldn't. Even when Ivy and I charged in the back door, if Fred hadn't been there, we'd have gone through and shot you down."

"You sure kill easy," I said.

He said, "Yes, I do," looking me in the eye. After a moment I looked away.

Jamie said, "Well, I believe you."

"Me, too," I said.

"I guess you're with us now," said Tom.

"I guess so."

"I don't suppose," I said, "you could tell us where the home world is?"

"No. I hadn't even realized there was one until you mentioned it. I've never been very high in the organization."

"Hmmm. So we still have to figure out how to find it."

"The Physician would know."

"Who's the Physician? Rudd mentioned him."

"The big boss. I don't even know if he's on Laurier or somewhere else."

"Oh. How do we find him?"

"Souci would know."

"Oh, wonderful," I said. "I have real doubts that she'd tell us."

"Yeah. Me, too."

"We could ask her, though," I said. "I know where she lives—"

"She's moved," said Christian.

"To where?"

"I don't know."

"Wonderful."

"But I think her friend Carrie would."

Tom shook his head. "This just keeps getting better, doesn't it?"

"At least we know what we have to do," I said. "If the cops don't show up and drag us all in."

"I think we're going to be safe for a while," said Christian. "Only those at the top really know what happened, and it'll take them a while to figure out what to do."

"Good," I said.

"Tell me something," said Jamie to Christian. "How did Sugar Bear find out about us?"

"I don't know, exactly. I got word of you from Monsieur Rudd, and was told to keep track of you, and—"

"What were you told about us?"

"That people here were on the side of the sickies, and might have to be stopped."

"I see," I said. "That's worth knowing."

"But," said Jamie, "why were you after Billy in particular?"

Christian shrugged. "I don't know. Word came down. If you want to believe it, there's a rumor that the Physician has means of communicating with the future."

"I believe that," I said.

"Me, too," said Jamie. He looked over at Libby, who still hadn't spoken. She was trying very hard not to be upset. Jamie went over to her. I started to, but found I couldn't. Rose did.

I caught Tom's eyes, and we went upstairs, where the body lay. She had folded his hands on his stomach, and a silver ring I thought I recognized as Libby's was on the little finger of his left hand. I thought about her slipping it onto his finger and folding his hands like that, and I couldn't see for a little while.

Tom and I finished wrapping him in one of the spare blankets and took him outside. It had gotten quite dark, and there was no one in sight. I wondered about the customers who had been trapped inside for several minutes, and what happened when they'd called the police.

But one thing at a time. We took care of Fred's remains as well as we could, which wasn't very, and I'll spare you the details. When we got back to Feng's we were both in pretty ragged shape. Libby hadn't moved, except that she and Rose had their arms around each other and Jamie was next to her. Christian, to my surprise, was also talking to her.

Tom and I sat in the far corner. I said, "Well, are you going to get hold of Carrie so I can get hold of Souci so we can maybe get this over with?"

"I suppose," he said. "But, Billy, is this ever going to be over? I mean, are we going to be able to just live someday?"

"Maybe. Why ask me?"

Tom shrugged and watched the clump around Libby. It was impossible to read his expression. I checked the clock, but a bullet had stopped it at 6:22. I went into the bar and read nine o'clock. It was amazing that no more time than that had passed. I looked out one of the windows, but the rest of the block was still silent, like everyone was huddling inside his house for fear of being caught up in something dangerous. Pretty reasonable, when you thought of it.

"I can't believe the police haven't shown up," said Tom.

"I know. We need to decide what to do, though."

"Go back home?"

"Maybe. Want to call Carrie?"

"No. I will, though."

He walked back to the bar to do this. Jamie got up and went into the back, carrying his shotgun. I resisted asking him what he was doing, and a bit later I heard sawing noises and didn't need to. Tom came back and said he couldn't reach Carrie.

Rose and Libby got up and disappeared into the back. Libby's eyes were red and she looked tired. Christian joined Tom and me.

"How's she doing?" I asked.

"As well as you can expect," said Christian. "I think she'll be okay. She says she could have saved him if she'd gotten to him sooner, but from hearing her describe the wound, I don't think she could have, and I think she really knows that. Give her time; she'll be all right."

"We don't have time," I said, but only under my breath.

The sawing sounds stopped, to be replaced by filing noises that were just as loud.

"I hope she can sleep over the racket," I said.

Tom said, "Do you think any of us will have a full night's sleep tonight?"

I shrugged and looked at Christian. He said, "I don't know. If they haven't shown up yet, they might not, but there's no way to be certain."

"You keep saying we," I said.

"They speak French here," said Tom.

"If I go back home they'll kill me," said Christian.

"I understand," I said. "I was just checking."

A little while later Jamie emerged. His shotgun was now about a foot shorter and looked very nasty. Christian said, "Twelve-gauge?"

"Yes."

"Good. We can share ammo. I'm getting low."

"We're gonna kick some ass," said Jamie, more grimly than enthusiastically.

"We're going to sleep first," I said.

Jamie said, "Someone should stay awake in case something happens."

I sighed. "Yeah, you're right. I'll take the first watch."

"Wake me in an hour and a half?" said Jamie.

"Right."

"I'll be next," said Christian.

I looked at him for a long time, then said, "All right. Then Rose, then Tom. We'll let Libby sleep. If she can. If we all can."

But, for whatever reason, we could.

My first thought upon waking was, *We actually made it through the night without trouble.* Then I began to wonder what would happen today, and started to realize just how big a fix we were in. A depressing way to wake up, but there was something satisfyingly familiar about lying in the pantry of Feng's on a pile of coats and spare blankets. It reminded me of happier times, lying there with Rose and Jamie and Tom and everyone, with nothing to worry about except our next night's set list and when the next bomb would hit. Hah.

I got up and found Tom sitting in a booth with his arms folded and his legs stretched out in front of him. He was wrapped in a blanket. He turned around and said, "There's coffee."

"Good."

"I made a 'Closed' sign and hung it on the door."

I nodded. "I notice someone also put plywood over the broken windows."

"Jamie did that."

I said, "I've never seen the place closed during business hours before."

"Neither have I. Libby's going to have to have some words with Feng." Then, "She's the only one of them left, isn't she?"

"Yeah, I guess she is, with Eve being in the hospital. I'm getting myself some coffee. Want some?"

"Yeah. Thanks. Speaking of Eve, as soon as things settle down even a little, we need to go see her."

"Yeah."

I got the coffee, came back. "Maybe I'll make us some breakfast. I enjoy working in a professional kitchen."

"I like your cooking."

"Thanks. Should we wait until everyone else is up?"

"Maybe. But then you can't use mushrooms because Rose and Libby don't like them, and you can't use onions because Jamie doesn't like them, and God knows who doesn't like whatever else you'd want to cook with."

"What don't you like, Tom?"

"Being a pinhead. Being stuck in here. Worrying about whether we're going to be killed. Worrying about nuclear war. Not being able to just relax and play music. Should I keep going?"

"We might be able to do something about the last. We all have our instruments."

"That would be good, if we can find the time."

There was a knock. Tom picked up his .45 from where it was sitting on the table and walked over to the door. He looked out, carefully keeping his body to the side. He yelled, "Sorry, we're closed." He came back and sat down, setting the gun back on the table. "Yeah, I'd like to play a few songs. It's been a while. What's wrong?"

"Nothing. It's just that you—nothing." Presently Jamie and Rose got up, and shortly after, Christian joined us. We drank coffee until Libby got up. She nodded hello to us and there was an anger in her walk and the tilt of her head. I retired to the kitchen.

I turned the big grill on low. I found a large cast-iron skillet and melted some goose fat over one of the gas flames while I took the medium French chef's knife and sliced half a dozen onions and two big green peppers and crushed some garlic cloves. When the fat was sizzling I threw the garlic in along with a little salt. I cleaned some mushrooms, put the onions and peppers in the hot fat, then sliced the mushrooms to the happy sizzling sounds.

I took out two dozen eggs and beat them, then put the mushrooms in the skillet. I added milk to the eggs, whipped them a bit more, and dumped them into the skillet when the onions

looked almost right. I turned down the heat, buttered twelve
pieces of sourdough bread, and put them on the grill. Then I added
some chives, salt, and pepper to the eggs as well as a little
cayenne, and, just before they were done, I added a tablespoon of
half-hot Szeged Noble Rose paprika, which would never exist
again. I buttered the other side of the bread and turned it on the
grill, then dished the eggs onto six plates along with the sourdough
bread and brought them out three at a time. Fred could have
carried all six without a tray.

Rose and Christian complained about the mushrooms, Jamie
complained about the onions. Libby didn't say anything. Tom said
he liked it. After we'd eaten, Rose said, "I'll wash the dishes
since you made the bref-tist."

"Bref-tist," that's what she said.

I explained that I would not try to talk her out of doing the
dishes. She gave me a kiss and said, "You cook good, even if you
do use fungus."

There came another knock at the door. This time Jamie got it,
holding his sawed-off shotgun down at his side. I noticed that
Christian's shotgun was near to hand. No one else seemed
concerned.

Jamie said, "It's Carrie."

I looked at Tom. He raised his eyebrows. "Well, should we let
her in?"

"Might as well," I said. Jamie opened the door and Carrie
slipped inside. She was wearing a long coat of some white fur.
She started to walk toward Tom, but stopped when she saw
Christian. Her eyes widened.

"It's all right," said Christian. "I've switched sides."

She stared, and her mouth worked.

Christian said, "Have *you*?"

"I—" She looked puzzled. "I don't know."

"Figures," said Christian. He spat.

Tom said, "We need to know where your friend Souci is."

"I can't tell you that."

"Why?"

"I just can't. She doesn't want anyone to know. She'd kill me."
Tom turned away.

She said, "I came over to see you."

"About what?"

She looked at us. The rest of us moved away to give Tom and
Carrie room to talk privately. The two of them spoke softly

together. Tom's face was grim, and his fists clenched several times as they spoke. I got tired of watching very quickly, so I went back to the pantry and got out my banjo. I played "Cripple Creek," and for a short time the world looked brighter than it had—brighter than it was, I guess.

Tom joined me. I stopped playing. Tom sat down. I said, "Well?"

"I'm a pinhead."

"So what else is new? Has Carrie heard about the big fight?"

"Justin told her." There was no mistaking the bitterness in his voice as he pronounced that name. "I guess Sugar Bear is really mad at us now, but they don't know what to do."

"Why haven't they sent the police in after us?"

"She isn't sure. Or at least she says she isn't sure. I think there's a lot of stuff she isn't telling me."

"Hmmm. What else did she say?"

"Personal things."

"Ah."

"Nothing new. Nothing good."

"Oh. Any luck getting her to tell us where Souci is?"

"She won't say, she's too scared."

"Damn. We'll have to keep trying. Has she left?"

"No. She wants to know if she can stay here with us."

"Why?"

"She's frightened."

"Of whom? Or what?"

"I'm not sure. She wouldn't say."

"That, as Christian would say, is some shit." I walked out there. Libby and Christian were in a corner talking in whispers, I could hear Jamie and Rose in the kitchen cleaning. Carrie looked up, and her blue, blue eyes looked very wide and frightened. I sat down next to her and said, "Why is it you want to stay here?"

"Because . . . I do. Do you have to know why?"

"Yes."

It looked like she was about to cry. She said, "I don't have anywhere else to go. I can't be with Justin anymore, and Souci is hiding—"

"You know where?"

"I can't say."

I said, "Why not?"

"You don't know what she's like."

"Yes, I do."

"No. She terrifies me. It's like, when she's around—"

"I know about it. Believe me. But that isn't why you aren't telling us, is it?"

"Yes, it is. I just can't do something that would make her angry."

"Great," I said. "Then you sure as hell can't stay here."

"I—"

"Tell me why I should trust you. If you're here, how do I know you won't open the doors in the middle of the night? If you're so weak you can't risk making someone angry at you, how can I be sure that a little pressure, especially from *her*, won't make you sell us out completely? Don't you realize that they're trying to *kill* us?"

She didn't say anything, she just stared at the ground, and her shoulders shook. There are times when you just have to be a hard-ass, and this was one. Unfortunately I've never really been up to the job. I sighed. "Okay, here's what I can do." I dug around in my pocket for a while. "Here's a key to our apartment. We aren't using it, so you—what is it?"

"Nothing."

I looked at her. There had been no mistaking that reaction. "What is it, Carrie?"

"Nothing, I just—"

"Don't bullshit me. It's something about the apartment, isn't it?"

"No, there isn't any—"

"Is it bugged, is that it?"

"No, I was just—"

"Are they waiting for us there?"

"No!"

"Are they going to burn it down?" She looked away. I said, "Is that it, Carrie? Are they going to blow the place up? Do they think we went back there instead of here?"

She buried her face in her hands. After a moment she nodded.

"When?" I asked her.

"It's set to go off at noon."

"Jamie," I yelled. "What time is it?"

"About five after twelve," he yelled back.

I licked my lips and stared at Carrie, who sat there and shook. "How precise was the bomb? Was it just the apartment or the whole building?"

"I don't know. It was Justin. He's good with bombs. He might have just gotten the apartment."

"Might have? Great. Or he might not have. There were six apartments in that building, Carrie. How many were just blown up? Is there a fire going? How many people are going to die from *it*, Carrie? How many people just burned to death because you're too scared to tell anyone what's going on in time to stop it?"

She was crying now, very hard. This didn't bother me at all. I was dimly aware of the others gathered around, but didn't care about them, either. I said, "Here's another question for you: How many more are going to die? How many that you could have saved, if you weren't running around in terror of a bitch-goddess? Is she going to run you all your life?"

"I don't know."

"Decide, right goddamn now. Are you your own master, or are you living as the shadow of someone else? And if you *are* your own master, then how can you justify letting as many innocent people die as are going to die if you don't help us?"

Christian came back into the room. He had apparently been out making some phone calls. "Yeah, it blew up," he said. "It'll be a while before they know how many were killed. They've already found three bodies, though."

Carrie was sobbing loudly. My heart was not breaking for her. I said, "So, three people just died. At least three. How many more, Carrie?"

She stopped crying but didn't look up. "Lots," she said softly. "Everyone on the planet."

I stood up. "*What?*"

"There's nothing anyone can do about it," she said. "The missiles have been launched already."

Tom, Christian, and I looked at each other. The silence stretched from one end of the room to the other several times, until you could have hung your linen on it to dry. At last I swallowed and said, "From where?"

"I don't know. Somewhere in space. They'll be here sometime tomorrow. Late in the afternoon, I think."

"We need to warn people."

"Why? There isn't any way off the planet, and there are enough missiles to make the whole planet uninhabitable."

"I can't believe there's no way off the planet."

"The reason the police have ignored you is that they're investigating the sabotage of every space-going vessel in the city and on the planet, which occurred just about the same time you were attacked yesterday. Half the reason for the attack was to make sure you couldn't do anything about it. I guess they thought you had better sources of information than you have. There's only one carrier left, which is hidden somewhere for the rest of us to use. Most of us—"

"Us."

She swallowed. "Sugar Bear."

"Right."

"Most of us on the planet left two weeks ago."

I licked my lips. "Damn," I said. I discovered then that knowing a nuclear attack was coming and being unable to prevent it was much, much worse than being hit by surprise.

"We've got to do something," said Rose.

"I'm open to suggestions," I said.

"There are more than five thousand missiles headed for this planet," said Carrie, almost tonelessly. "Each of them is more than powerful enough to destroy a city, and leave hundreds of square miles around it uninhabitable. The missiles are programmed by the Physician. Not even Monsieur Rudd can call them off or change their course."

"That," said Libby, "is very harsh."

"You know a great deal about this," I said. "More than Christian, for instance. Why is that?"

"Justin works directly for Monsieur Rudd, who is in charge of Sugar Bear of New Quebec, and in command here on Laurier. Justin talks a lot when he's coked up."

"I see. How does Souci fit in?"

Carrie bit her lip. "She used to go out with Justin. He told her even more than he told me."

"Oh."

"She was never involved in Sugar Bear activities, any more than I was, but she grew up with it, so she knows a lot."

"So, she was seeing me to get information?"

Carrie looked at me, and slowly shook her head without ever breaking eye contact. "She didn't know who you were when you met—didn't figure it out until you mentioned Sugar Bear that day. She and I went along with Claude and Danielle. I guess they'd figured out something about the way the place first showed up. They didn't tell us until much later. Then they told her to stop seeing you and she told them to fuck off. I guess they almost had her killed, but Justin talked them out of it. She loved you."

This, as you can imagine, made me feel just glorious. I cleared my throat. I said, "I'm surprised they let Justin live, with how much he talks."

"He knows people. And he's actually pretty careful who he talks to."

"I guess he must be, at that. So, where is the home world?"

"I don't know. The Physician knows."

"And Justin and Souci both know where the Physician is."

"Yes."

"And you know where Souci is."

She nodded.

I said, "Well?"

A shudder went through her whole body. "She and Justin are staying with Monsieur Rudd."

"Shit," said Christian. "I should have guessed that."

"So should I," I said.

"Doesn't matter," said Jamie. "We know now."

"Justin," said Tom. "Justin is there."

Libby didn't say anything, but she picked up her pistol, and, for the first time since Fred had died, a smile crossed her lips.

Intermezzo

Her eyes, they shone like the diamonds
You'd think she was queen of the land.
"The Black Velvet Band,"
Traditional

Carrie woke up shivering, with dawn just barely hinting its arrival. The sheets were soaked with sweat; she pushed them off the bed. She opened the window, suddenly in desperate need of air. When the window wouldn't open she almost smashed it, then she almost screamed. It opened at last, and the air tasted good, but was so cold that it sent chills through her. She shivered for a moment and looked for something to pull over the flimsy gown she was wearing. After a while she found a big, thick, blue terry-cloth robe. After that she felt a little better. She lit a cigarette and stared at the purples of the night sky. She couldn't remember what her dream had been, and she wasn't sure she wanted to.

The cigarette and the robe suddenly made her feel like an old woman, and she had a vivid image of herself that way, old, alone, wrinkled, alone, alone, alone. She stubbed the cigarette out and walked back and forth, driving the thought from her mind. Then sat in the fuzzy orange chair and rocked back and forth, singing softly to herself, until she felt better.

Once again, as it had so often, she wondered if she could be a singer. Everyone said she could. Even Mme Jeanne, her voice coach, who would rather die than give someone a compliment, had as much as said she could make a living doing popular music, if she was willing to give up bel canto (sniff, went Mme Jeanne).

And Carrie wanted to, she knew that.

To be in front of people, pouring every last, hidden secret from her soul out through her voice, and watching them light up, or cry, yes, that's what she wanted. And she could do it, too, but—

But you can't please everyone. Some people wouldn't like her. They would say she was too breathy, or too free with her melody lines, or didn't move well. And they would be wrong, but they would say those things, and would say them to *her*, and she couldn't stand that. It would destroy her.

Well, it would.

Wouldn't it?

As she lit another cigarette, she realized that if she had any more, Mme Jeanne would be able to tell she'd been smoking and would bawl her out.

The thought made her wince.

She put the cigarette out and went back to bed.

CHAPTER
15

"I'll fight but not surrender,"
Said the wild colonial boy.
"The Wild Colonial Boy,"
Traditional

Jamie said, "You know what I don't understand?"

"What?"

"If Feng came from the future, he must be sending us back, er, forward, to do something that will help him, right?"

"I suppose," I said.

"Well, if Sugar Bear can really communicate with the future, like Christian says, then they can tell if they've won or not just by checking a little further. And for that matter, so can Feng and his people, right?"

Libby cleared her throat. "As I understand it," she said, "no one can actually communicate with the future. All you can do is send messengers back to find your people and tell them things. It is a very difficult process, and very expensive, even for them. Sugar Bear must have learned that Feng had found us—Fred, Rich, Eve, and I—and that we were on their trail, and sent

184

someone back to have us stopped. At the time, we didn't know what we were looking for, but they couldn't have known that."

Jamie said, "I still don't get it. If they're from the future they must know how it turns out. So it's like, whatever we do doesn't matter."

Libby shrugged helplessly. "I don't know. I'm just a hired hand. They never told me any of the technical stuff."

"They," said Jamie. "You mean Feng?"

"Yeah, I mean Feng."

"He recruited you himself."

"I would have said 'hired,' but maybe recruit is more accurate."

Jamie looked up at the picture that adorned the arch that connected restaurant to bar. I did, too. His smile no longer looked cheerful; now it was evil, manipulative. "Man, I'd like to meet him," said Jamie.

"Why?" said Libby.

"He's from the future. Who wouldn't like to meet someone from the future? I mean, aren't there things you'd like to ask him about?"

"I'd rather meet someone from the past," said Libby. "Most of the things I'd like to know from Feng are things he won't talk about."

"But what's he like?"

"He's a pinhead," said Libby. "Any more questions?"

"Shit. Yeah. I still don't get it. What about Feng's future? I mean, the future to him? Don't they know how it came out?"

Libby said, "Think of this: Time travel is really hard to pull off, and risky to the people doing it. They wouldn't send anyone back if they didn't have to. I mean, the guys from the far future, where it's already decided. So, one side can't send anyone back because they lost, and the other side either doesn't want to waste the energy, or sending someone back to say it worked out would prevent it from working out, so they can't do it."

"That makes sense," I said. "As much as any of this does."

"Okay," said Jamie. "So what we have to do is get information back to the future that will give Feng's people a chance against Sugar Bear."

"Right," said Libby. "And we've already got something, because they didn't, I mean, don't, or won't, or something, know who the enemy is and what the whole thing's about."

Tom said, "Is it enough?"

Libby said, "I don't know. Probably not. If we can tell them where Sugar Bear's home world is—"

"What if it moves?" said Christian suddenly. "I mean, what if they change it?"

"Why would they do that?"

"I don't know. It's just that you're assuming that the place that's their home world now is the same as what will be their home world in however many hundred years."

"A point," said Libby. "In fact, that's just what they've been doing."

I said, "It seems to me that anything we can find out is bound to help. If we only learn where they used to be, that may help them track down where they went. And what I'm hoping is that the Physician is from Feng's time; which means he'll know the answer we actually want."

Christian nodded. Libby said, "Anything else?"

"Yeah," said Jamie. "I think we should get on with it."

"I'd wait until nightfall," said Christian. "They might have people keeping a watch on that house, although I doubt they suspect anything."

"It'll have to be tonight, though," said Carrie. "They'll all be gone by tomorrow."

"You, too?" said Tom.

She nodded. "That's the plan. I just needed a place to stay tonight."

"How is it you were planning to get off-planet?"

"I was supposed to meet them at Monsieur Rudd's tomorrow morning. But he wouldn't let me stay there because they don't trust me anymore."

"I see. Well, you may as well stay here. We is gonna be busy."

"Doing exactly what?" said Libby. "Or is it too much to ask for to come up with a plan?"

"Well," said Jamie, "it wouldn't hurt if we had a floor plan for the house."

"That," said Christian, "is not a bad idea."

"Oh, Lord," I said. "I'll do the best I can, but I was only in one room—"

"That's all right," said Christian. "We have an expert here." He looked at Carrie.

Carrie said, "I—"

"Just do it, all right?" said Tom.

She licked her lips and nodded. Rose found her a place mat and a pen, and Libby began asking pointed questions about the layout of the place. We sat down and drank coffee while they worked.

Less than an hour later we were all looking at the more or less finished product. "Well," said Jamie after a while. "This does us a world of good."

I said, "We know where to find the back door, anyway. Carrie, are you sure you have no idea where Souci is?"

She shook her head. "One of the bedrooms on the second or third floor; that's all I can guess."

Rose said, "Couldn't he have built a smaller house? He doesn't need that many rooms."

"Conspicuous consumption," I agreed. "Shameful. Well, any ideas?"

"Two of us go in the back," said Christian, "and three in the front. There's a certain symmetry to the idea that I like."

"How do we slip past the guards?"

"We don't," said Christian. "We just get up to the wall, at night, then move fast."

"Won't the doors be locked?" I said.

"Hmmm. Right. Anyone have any explosive?"

Libby got up and left. I said, "How about the windows? We could throw something at them—"

"Unbreakable," said Carrie. "You'll have more luck going through a wall."

"Hmmm. All right. We'll—" I stopped as Libby came back and set down a wooden box. She pulled the top off, and I saw six hand grenades, lying neatly in packing material, looking like a Christmas present.

"Fred had these," she said.

"All right," I said. "Next problem?"

Tom said, "Do we have any idea at all what we're going to do once we get inside?"

I said, "If something happens to Monsieur Rudd I won't shed any tears, but the important thing is that we have to get Justin or Souci to tell us how to find the Physician, so we can get him to tell us where the home planet is—unless we're real lucky and Justin or Souci knows."

"I doubt it," said Carrie.

Tom said, "Does that mean I can't kill Justin?" Carrie made a small noise.

I said, "Not before we find out what we have to find out."

Tom looked unhappy but didn't argue.

"How do you figure to get them to talk?" said Christian. "Torture?" He looked skeptical.

"I don't really know anything about torture," I said. "I don't know if I could go through with it if I did. Would you like to volunteer?"

"What, you don't have the balls to do it yourself, but you can ask someone else to?"

"Yep," I said. "You got it. Can you do it?"

We were momentarily interrupted by Carrie getting up and making a dash out of the room, either to cry or to throw up, I never bothered to ask.

To Christian I said, "I don't know."

"I have a better idea," said Libby.

"Yeah?"

"We'll just keep them in the house until they tell us how to find the Physician. I think they'll tell us if it's that or miss their ship."

"Then what?" I said.

"Once we know, we come back here, and, wherever we jump to next, take it from there. Or, if the Physician *is* here on Laurier, we can find him and make him tell us the same way—by keeping him off the ship unless he does."

"I don't know if that will work," I said, "but it's the best idea I've heard so far."

Carrie came back and took her seat.

"Now, wait a minute," said Jamie. "Let me see if I've got this. We break into Rudd's house, take over the place, and keep everyone prisoner until Souci or Justin becomes so scared of missing the boat that one of them tells us how to find the Physician, but we make sure to keep everyone in the house prisoner, in case they can get help somewhere."

"Right," I said.

"If we've managed to do all this, we hope that we can somehow reach the Physician and somehow convince him to talk before the bombs fall. Is that really the plan?"

"Umm, well, put that way it doesn't sound real workable, does it?"

"No, it doesn't," said Jamie.

Libby said, "Do you have any other ideas?"

"Not at the moment."

I said, "We'd better cut the phone lines first, since—"

"Phone lines?" said Christian. "What are those?"

"Oh, right," I said. "Well, we'll have to try to keep them away from their phones. And, Christian, can you get us a car? Rudd's place is a long way out into the country. I ran there once and walked back. It took a long time, and I don't think we'll all fit on Rich's bike, though it would be appropriate."

"Yeah, I know where I can borrow a car. I'll get it this afternoon."

"And remember, if we *do* get the information—"

"When," said Jamie.

"—we have to make sure it gets to Feng's before the bombs fall. Even if that means leaving people behind. Is everyone clear on that?"

Everyone was, except maybe Carrie, who just sat there and shook.

Jamie cleared his throat. "I don't mean to bum everyone out," he said. "But this might—*might*—be the last time we're all together."

"That's true," I said. "What about it?"

"We have some time to kill."

It took me a minute to figure out what he was suggesting, but then I nodded, and Tom and Rose figured it out at the same time.

"Yeah," said Tom.

"I'm up for it," I said.

Rose just nodded as we stood up and went into the back room for our instruments. Tom tuned his mandolin, and I tuned up the banjo. We went into the bar and fired up the sound system. We certainly didn't need it, but why not go all the way?

Christian, Carrie, and Libby were our audience. I played the opening two bars of "The Mermaid," then Jamie and Tom came in, rhythmical drive and elegant taste, followed by Rose, late as usual, missing the beat as usual, but creating harmonies and countermelodies that made the song irrelevant, it was music, and it was her and it was us, we fell into sync and the verse began to sing us right on cue. We rose and fell with it, as if we were playing to assembled millions, for the music was our energy. Rose attacked the lead break like she'd keep the damn ship floating herself, Tom's mandolin giggled around the edges, and I thought I was just frailing along with Jamie's rhythm until I realized that some of those themes the fiddle was playing with were banjo licks.

Jamie launched us into "Peter's Song," before the last notes of "The Mermaid" had died, and that fell headlong into "Botany

Bay." Silly Irish tunes, they were, and a silly Irish band were we, but there was a place we could get to where the songs would play us, and it was there that evening.

Tom sang Sean Phillip's "Ballad of Casey Dies," and by the end I was choked up to where I could hardly sing. Christian joined us on Jamie's twelve-string for "Old Joe Clark," and caught the speed up, and for a while he was with us, too, which broke the mood, because his guitar laughed, and teased the fiddle, and egged me into bigger and bigger chances until it was far too fast to be doing the things we were all doing, and at last it ended and he sat down as if nothing had happened at all.

I was feeling the "end of set" kind of pleasant exhaustion when Jamie started the lopsided almost-rock rhythm of "Blackjack David." Tom's mandolin was barely audible, doing some sort of off-kilter scale that sent shivers down my spine, and the fiddle played the melody by playing everything else, then came back and dropped down as we stumbled into the first verse. Jamie started singing with his usual gusto, but there was a melancholy I couldn't shake, because it seemed to me that this little band of Irish-playing fools actually maybe had something, and I doubted that we would ever have the chance to go—where?

Maybe the future. What could the future hold for four musicians like us? My one wish at that moment was that I would have the chance to find out. I didn't think it likely.

The last verse of "Blackjack David" came, and we all threw in that extra burst of energy that tells us and the audience that we're going to end the set with it. Tom and Jamie and I caught the harmony, and the fiddle screeched and clawed to a terrible high place from which it could never come down, and it didn't, just stopped, and I turned and waved good-bye to verse, song, set, and, maybe, band.

We said nothing to each other as we stepped off the stage. I put my instrument away. Libby caught my eye and gave me a hug that I needed.

There was really nothing else to say.

Intermezzo

The red-haired girl just kept on smiling
"Young man, with you I'll go," she said. . . .
"Red-haired Mary,"
Traditional

The music was loud, the beer strong, the bar crowded. Each was dark, in its own way. She'd been there for half an hour and had already been hit on three times. The first was the guy sitting next to her, a short man with a receding hairline, who seemed nice but dull. The second looked like a musician, and might have been interesting but she wasn't in that sort of mood. The third was a body-building type who looked like he probably couldn't count to eleven without using his toes. The fourth came as she finished her drink, and another bottle of Juliana Dark appeared in front of her. She looked a question at the bartender. He nodded to her left.

Number four was tall and blond, with a square jaw and a good tan, probably acquired out of a bottle or in front of a cancer-lamp. Instead of talking to her, he went up to the guy who was in the next stool and said, "Hey, friend, I'll buy your next two drinks if you'll give me your chair."

There was maybe just a shade of intimidation in how close the big guy stood, but short but dull shrugged and moved. Tall and blond signaled the waiter, paid for two drinks for the guy, and sat down.

"Hi there," he said, showing off his teeth. They weren't bad teeth.

"Hi. Thanks for the drink."

"My pleasure. I'm Jacques."

"Souci."

"You know, you are just about the cutest babe I've ever seen in here."

"Just about?"

He laughed, a big, easygoing laugh that probably turned some girls to jelly. "All right," he said. "*The* cutest." When she didn't respond, he said, "I figure if you're about the best-looking woman, and I'm the best-looking guy, we ought to be sitting together, don't you think?"

She wondered how much of a joke that was supposed to be. She said, "I like this place better when they have live music."

"Yeah, me, too. Wanna go somewhere else?"

"Maybe in a while."

"Sure, whatever you want."

An hour later they were in his car, on the way to her apartment. Fifteen minutes after that, she watched as if from a distance as he undressed her and kissed her nipples and did all the other things that he must have thought made him a magnificent lover.

Then he was on her, then he was in her. She gave him a few perfunctory scratches on his back with her nails and wrapped her legs around his hips until he came. Then, as he lay on top of her, breathless, she came back to herself. She placed her palms against his chest and pushed.

"I didn't come," she said.

"What?"

"I didn't come, you bastard."

"Hey, I'm—"

"You're a horrible lover. Clumsy prick."

"Now, look—"

"Get your smelly body away from me."

He stirred and looked at her, an expression of amazement just beginning to cross his face. "What's wrong?"

"Didn't you hear me? You're terrible. You're the worst lover I've ever had." It had been building for days, and it exploded.

"Ever. Do you understand me, you stupid asshole? Just get out of here. I don't ever want to see you again. If you don't get out of here now, I'm going to call the police."

By now he was kneeling in front of her, staring stupidly. "Get out of here," she screamed.

He scrambled into his clothing and practically crawled out of the apartment, too quickly for her to get all of the bitterness out of her system, but enough for a while. She heard him close the door—quietly, not slamming it. She lay facedown, naked on the bed, and did not cry.

She'd do it again next weekend.

She was seventeen.

CHAPTER
16

I took old Reily by the hair
Shoved his head in a pail of water.
                        "Reily's Daughter,"
                        Traditional

Sunset fell upon New Quebec, the white of Laurier's sun, Chaucer, sending rays dancing off the reflective windows of the Grain Exchange, splashing up the long, narrow corridor of Rue LaVelle, and sending the shadows from the bell tower of the New Hope Reformed Catholic Church to tickle the feet of the tall, Gothic Merchandise Mart.

Now that there is no living man left in the city or upon that world, let it be recorded, lest it be lost as so many things have been, that sunset upon New Quebec was a beautiful thing. I am sorry that New Quebec is no more. I do not believe that I could have prevented the destruction of that city, that world, yet I am sorry. I am sorry for so many, many things, but it is gone, anyway, my sorrow availing nothing. It is gone as are so many of those who were once close to me. Dead by violence personal, as Rich and Fred and the others. Dead by violence impersonal, as those I left behind on Earth, on the Moon, on Mars, and on Laurier. Or dead by violence passive, as are all of those I once knew who did not come with me across this barrier through which I now examine the ghost of sunset past.

What is this quintessence of dust, as the man said, and on bad days I understand why.

We put our instruments away, wondering, I guess, if we'd ever see them again. Jamie came up with a box of shotgun shells. He put several in the pocket of his leather jacket and passed the rest of the box to Christian. Jamie's .357 was under his jacket, and he had two quick-loaders for it in his other pocket. He looked ready.

Christian had his pump-action and an ankle-length leather coat and a long-riders hat and a cigarette dangling from the corner of his mouth. He looked ready.

Libby wore a hot-pink sweater, black pants, and pink leg warmers. She carried her automag, with two spare magazines located, ironically, in her medical kit, which she carried over her shoulder. She looked ready.

Rose had her derringer in the pocket of her jacket, which was an old one of Jamie's. She took a hit off a bottle of Jameson. She looked ready.

Tom's feet were up on the booth across from him. He had three spare magazines in the pocket of his CPO. He looked ready.

I had the commando knife under the arm of my motorcycle jacket. I carried the canister of kerosene with which they'd tried to burn down Feng's. I looked ready, but it was a lie.

"Let's go, troops," I said.

"Just a minute," said Rose. She ran off for a moment and came back with her fiddle case. "I just remembered that I'm the fiddle player."

"Right," I said. "Are you sure you want to take the chance of something happening to it?"

"Nothing will happen to my fiddle," she said.

"All right." We walked out the door. Carrie came with us because we didn't trust her not to warn them if left on her own. She stayed next to Tom and looked frightened but resigned.

Jamie gave Rose Eve's helmet and took Rich's. They wheeled the motorcycle out onto the street. No one noticed us. Jamie started the bike, Rose got behind him, and they waited for the rest of us.

The car was something locally made, solar-powered, and small. Christian drove. The five of us fit in it, but without much to spare. On the other hand, comfort was not our first consideration on that particular ride.

After a mile, the city was behind us and we were definitely in a rural area, and it was another mile before we came in sight of the small horse barn that I remembered near Rudd's house. It hadn't seemed this far away when I was chasing Claude, or during the walk back. On the other hand, I was pleased that, along with a horse, a goat, and a few dairy cows, he did not keep either turkeys or hogs. I know the smell of each, and I'll pass, thanks.

We stopped the car well away from the house and left the kerosene in it. I didn't know if we were going to use it, but I didn't want someone shooting bullets into it in the meantime. Jamie and Rose pulled up behind us and killed the bike.

Jamie and Christian went around to the back. Libby gave them each a grenade, and Tom explained how to use them. "You pull the pin and it's armed," he said. "It'll go off when it hits something. If you want to disarm it, put the pin back in. It doesn't have a timer, just an impact detector."

"Okay," said Libby. "So you, Jamie, go around back and pull it. When you hear the boom from ours, throw yours. You've got the other one in case you miss the door."

"You want to be a good seventy-five feet away," said Tom.

Libby said, "Can you hit that, Jamie?"

He nodded.

"Good. If you don't hear ours go off after about five minutes, disarm the thing and head back for the car, and we'll figure it out from there."

"Got it," said Jamie.

"What about Carrie?" said Tom.

I said, "As soon as we toss the grenade at the front door, she can go."

"How do you know she won't call someone."

I turned to her. "Will you?"

"No." Her voice was very small. I believed her.

"Last chance to back out, everyone," I said.

"Shit," said Christian.

"Let's get to it," said Tom.

Rose said, "I want—"

"Later," said Jamie.

"Right," said Libby. "Meet you in the middle."

" 'Sister Goldenhair,' " said Tom.

"By America," said Christian.

They walked quietly around toward the back. We crept along the wall in front and waited, giving them a good long time to get positioned.

"You know," whispered Libby, "we should have had them throw first, since we're closer."

"Now's a great time to think of that," I whispered back. "Do it."

She stood up and threw and we ducked behind the wall. The sky seemed to brighten and a wind swept overhead. It was almost quiet, compared to the shooting from the day before. Libby took out her pistol. Tom already had his ready. Rose stayed behind me. Carrie ran away. We closed on the house where smoke was clearing to reveal a jagged, but almost round hole where the door had been. The night was lit by another flash, accompanied by a dull boom from the other side of the house.

Tom and Libby fairly leapt through the hole. Rose and I followed more slowly. There were no shots yet, but there was some clattering from a stairway just to our right. Tom walked over and stood at the bottom of the stair, his .45 held in both hands, his elbows bent, while Libby headed for the kitchen. Rose and I waited where we were. Rose was holding her pearl-handled derringer with the ebony dragon's head inlaid.

Rudd came charging down the stair and stopped cold when he saw Tom. There was a small revolver in his hand, but it was at his side. I held my breath. Tom said, "Drop that thing or I'll blow your fucking head off." He said it just like that, and I knew he meant it, and would have done it, and that chilled me, though why it should is a mystery.

Rudd dropped the gun and I breathed again. Tom said, "Get down here."

Libby came back and said, "This must be Monsieur Rudd." There was a heavy note of irony in the way she said "Monsieur."

"That's him," I said.

"Well," she said. "We'll just wait here."

I said, "Rose, you stay with Libby and watch Rudd. Tom and I will go upstairs." We did this thing, creeping up the stairs and bursting into rooms like Starsky and Hutch, except that I didn't have a gun. The first room we burst in on I thought was a bedroom, but eventually realized it was a walk-in closet.

Tom said, "Do you have the map?"

"Map?"

"The floor plan Carrie made."

"Oh. Right." I dug it out of my back pocket and unfolded it, oriented it, and said, "We're here."

"I don't want to look. Just tell me which way."

"Next door on the right is a bathroom."

"I don't have to go."

"*Man*," I said.

The bathroom, or rather, the bathroom suite, could have fitted a king-size bed. Everything was done in ornate brass, and there were frosted bulbs around the mirrors and blue carpeting. Scary.

The first real bedroom was very big, very plush, and had bright yellow curtains, a bright yellow canopy on a big, round bed with a bright yellow bedspread, pale yellow walls, and a comfortable-looking black chair in the middle of the room facing the window.

I shuddered and we moved on. From down the hall, Jamie called, "Billy?"

"Over here," I said.

"Okay. Don't shoot when we come around the corner." Good idea, that warning, if Tom was half as jumpy as I was. Jamie came around a bend in the hall and said, "Christian is downstairs with Libby and Rose. I thought you might be able to use more help."

A splinter of wood hit me in the face and I heard a shot from very close by. Tom knocked me down while Jamie's gun made very loud noises. I stayed where I was while I heard scuffling sounds and "Get out of my way," and "Look out," and more shooting, then stillness.

Tom let me up. I said, "What the fuck—"

"Justin," he said. There was more shooting from the floor below. Tom went over to a window, and his back tensed. "He's getting away," he said. He hit the window with his pistol, but it didn't shatter. He cursed loudly, then turned back to me. "He was sitting up there waiting to nail us. He almost got you, didn't he?"

I touched my cheek where it still stung from the ricochet and I nodded. Tom shook his head. Jamie rejoined us. "He's gone," he said. "I was going to follow him, but he wrecked the bike on his way past it."

"That's another one we owe him," said Tom.

"In any case," said Jamie, "no one's hurt."

"All right," I said. "It could be worse."

We finished exploring that floor, which held two more bedrooms and another bathroom. One of the bedrooms showed signs of being tenanted, but was not currently occupied. There was a phone in the wall, which I took off and destroyed. It took quite a while to explore every nook and cranny of that floor, and I became nervous about Christian and Libby and Rose. Before going up the stairs I called down to them, and Libby called back that they were doing fine. We made our way up the stairs, Tom and Jamie edging in front of me, both of their guns out at waist level. In a large room, actually more like a boudoir, mostly done in red with touches of purple and green, Souci sat, smoking a cigarette and waiting for us. A white Persian cat sat on her lap and shed all over a black turtleneck shirt that was too tight for her. She also wore a pair of corduroys with torn knees, and high black boots, the left had a spur. Her face was still that perfect set of angled planes, her lips still pouted, her eyes were still feline. She looked at me without any expression at all. My throat hurt.

Tom and I escorted her down the stairs without a word being spoken. Libby frisked Souci while I frisked Rudd, then Libby and Christian searched the house again, but there was no one else there. Tom held the prisoners under guard and kept them from speaking with each other while Jamie and I found some wood and hammer and nails and sealed the front door so it would be harder for them to escape. We also made sure the windows wouldn't open.

At last all gathered together in the living room for some private conversation. I was glad that we had the guns.

"Well," I said. "I suppose you're wondering why I've called you here today." Souci rolled her eyes. M. Rudd had the grace to smile. I continued, "There is a particular piece of information that I'm looking for. When I get it, we will leave you alone. Until then, you will all be staying right here. If it takes until the missiles come, then"—I shrugged—"we'll all go together when we go."

"Ah," said Rudd. "You know about the missiles."

"Does that startle you?"

"I suppose not."

"Tell me where Sugar Bear's home planet is. Tell me, and convince me you're not lying, and you can go."

He said, "You tell *me* something. It can't hurt, since we're all to die here together in, what, twelve hours? Twenty-four? Just what was it that you had on me to keep me from killing you here the first time you came in."

I laughed, glad he'd asked. "Nothing. I was bluffing."

He sighed. "I suspected that."

"Good for you."

"Well, not to be melodramatic, but I *am* willing to die for the cause, as it were, and in any case you ought to be aware that only the Physician himself has that sort of information."

"Well, where is the Physician?"

"That is difficult to say, from one moment to the next. This city, another, this planet, another, who can say?"

"I see. Well, we'll give you some time to think about it. All of you, take Souci and Monsieur Rudd away and keep watching them. I'd like them to sweat for a while and contemplate their sins and probable futures. Keep them in separate rooms, though. Jamie, go and get the kerosene from the car, in case we need to keep warm."

They left without a word, and we began to wait. We worked in shifts, changing places every hour. Watching the front and back doors—well, holes, actually—in case Justin chose to return, watching Rudd in the kitchen, or Souci in the sitting room. There was little conversation among us, and our prisoners said nothing at all, except occasional requests to use the facilities or to have water, which we granted.

Each hour moved more slowly than the last, but I didn't start getting nervous until I realized that the sun was coming up. I met Jamie in the hall between the kitchen and the sitting room. He said, "How are you doing, bror?"

"Tired, but still alert. You?"

"About the same. Is Rudd looking at all frightened?"

"No. Souci?"

"Nothing."

"Shit. I don't think we're going to be able to break them this way."

"Let's try a little longer."

"All right."

An hour, two, three, still nothing. The missiles were rushing toward us, we were accomplishing nothing. Should we have told news services? Would they have believed us? Would any good at all have been accomplished if we had? I didn't know, I still don't, but it was something to torture myself with. Three times I went in to talk to Souci, and her only communications to me were the expressions of scorn on her face.

The fourth time I sat facing her it was well after noon. We sat in the same pair of chairs that Rudd and I had occupied earlier, at the same oblique angle. I did not offer her brandy, nor did I offer to light a fire. It seemed that I was more tired than she was. She met my eyes; there was no trace of friendship in hers. It would have been stupid to expect any, under the circumstances.

I said, "You know about the missiles, don't you?"

"What about them?"

"It doesn't bother you that this whole planet is about to be rendered unfit for human life?"

"Should it?"

"There are four major cities on this planet, and a total population of almost a quarter of a million people. It doesn't bother you that these friends of yours are going to kill them *all*?"

"Why should I care? What have they done for me?"

"I can't believe you mean that."

"That's your problem, isn't it?"

I groped for words like a blind man searching for his stick. I could tell her I still loved her and it would be the truth, and she wouldn't care. I could tell her that humanity needed her, and it would be the truth, and she wouldn't care. I looked at her and hurt and tried to keep my feelings off my face. I finally said, "You're going to die, you know. We aren't going to let any of you go until we find out what we need to know."

"What do you mean, need to know?"

"We believe Sugar Bear has a specific home world. We have to find it."

"Why?"

"So that, in the future, we can—"

"No, I mean, why do you *care*?"

"Umm. That seems like a pretty weird question, if you ask me."

"What's so weird about it? Why should you care what happens to people you've never met?"

My mouth opened and closed a few times, then I said, "I don't really know. I guess I was just brought up that way. Why is your friend the Physician working so hard to destroy humanity?"

"To save us from infection by the rest of you."

"Who is 'us'?"

"Those who belong."

"How does someone get to belong?"

"By being born into it, or else selected."

"And all of these people have as a goal—"

"Don't talk about our goals."

"Whatever you want. But tell me, is the Physician crazy to be working so hard for complete strangers?"

"They aren't strangers. They're his people."

"Well, then, the human race, all of us, are *my* people."

"What crap."

"Sorry you feel that way."

"All of humanity except for us, right?"

"Right," I said. "Except for you who are trying to kill the rest of us. You can rot in hell."

At last she said, in a very small voice that reminded me of Eve's, "We're trying to protect ourselves."

"You could look for a cure, instead."

"We're doing that, too, but . . ." Her voice trailed off. She said, "Do you know what I had to go through when they found out I'd made love to an outsider? The tests, the questions, the—"

"Then why the hell did you?"

"I was in love with you."

I don't know what hit me hardest there, the "in love" or the "was." I said, "Why did you stop?"

"You tried to make me tell you about—never mind. It doesn't matter."

"It does, though. That's the whole point. Do you know how hard it was for me to ask you those things? I hated it. But I had to. I—" There came a loud thump down the hall. It sounded like an explosion. I felt a sinking feeling in the pit of my stomach. Tom and Christian came running past me, and soon I heard the distant echo of shots. Then I heard the sound of automatic weapons.

"Well," I said. "It sounds like Justin's come back. With friends." I took her by the wrist. "Let's wait in the kitchen."

"It doesn't matter," she said, standing up.

Christian and Tom came back into the room. "Get moving," said Christian.

"Right," I said, and led Souci faster. Christian came along with us. As I was about to turn down the hall, I took a look behind, and in that moment he emerged—Justin, holding a machine pistol. He ignored the gun that Tom had pointed at him as he leveled the weapon at me and fired.

It sounded like a continuous explosion then, with slight variation in pitch and volume. Just as it began, someone knocked into me from the side and I fell against the wall. Presently I opened my eyes again. Justin had evidently taken several hits from the .45. All of them in the head. It was very ugly. I looked at the floor next to me, and what I saw there was even uglier, perhaps because she was still alive.

I knelt beside her, too stunned to cry or be sick. "Why did you do that?" I said or screamed. "You stupid idiot bitch, why did you do that?" I reached for her hand and encountered a mass of torn flesh. It was almost more than I could stand, but she was too far gone to notice. I didn't know how she could still be alive, with what the machine pistol had done to her.

She said, "Rudd," and coughed up a great deal of blood. There was a wound in her right cheek, and I could see cracked and broken teeth through it.

She said, "Rudd . . . Physician . . ."

"Rudd is the Physician," I said.

She nodded and shuddered. Her left hand reached for me but never made it.

Intermezzo

I know you rider
Gonna miss me when I'm gone.
"I Know You Rider,"
Traditional

Three plain, armless, imitation-oak chairs adorned each side of a plain, armless, imitation-oak table. An identical chair faced the rear of the windowless room. Lighting from an invisible source provided two thousand watts of white light, and distributed it evenly throughout the six hundred square feet of the room. The walls were a pale yellow and twenty feet high; the ceiling was transparent at the moment, and showed the almost starless night sky of Cicero, in the Marko system. The floor was rough with real pebbles, imported from the Coriander Beach on the other side of Cicero, where a small but wild sea chipped away at rock that looked like painted shale, each layer an age, each age a color, to show that, yes, there was some beauty left in the galaxy, after all.

A gentle, warm breeze circulated throughout the room, carrying with it the very faint scent of jasmine. A synthesizer attempted to reconstruct or re-create, or construct or create, as you will, a Bach improvisation in G major. It did a fair job of getting the probable sound of his instrument, but the improvisations were rather lame. The programming realized this eventually and resolved itself into Sonata No. 6.

The door was soundless and efficient, and above it was the only decorative artifact in the room—a symbolic representation of a banana.

The simplicity of the room should not be mistaken for an indication of austerity on the part of the representative cultures, nor on the part of the Grand Banana itself; rather the seven members of the Crisis Committee couldn't agree on any other decor.

Oh, yes: All of the chairs were occupied.

Richard Immanual Feng, of Beauregard around Sestus, who was seated in the middle left chair, had his feet on the table. He was barefooted, but he had washed his feet very carefully before arriving. He dared anyone to say anything. No one did. Across from him sat Nora Delacroix of Sorbonne around Eveleth, glaring and pouting simultaneously. Feng resisted the temptation to bait Delacroix, and resisted the temptation to try to hurry the meeting. He didn't have anything specific in mind to do, he just hated waiting.

At last Carla Weismuller of Broderick around Broderick, in the head position, looked up from the V-tab and said, "We have isolated the time when They began serious operations to within a six-month period."

There was a snort of derision from the far right seat. Feng chose not to look. Byron Santiago of Brine around Neosol said, "Six months? Splendid. We have one functioning Unit, and we need to guess within a six-month—"

"Could you have done better?" rasped old Delilah Corinth of Bangyoulose around Yeats. She was, Feng reflected, rather less obnoxious than most of the others. He wished she would bathe before attending Session, but he was aware that she failed to do so for the same reason that he was barefooted. She twisted in her chair and sent a small feathered dart to make a little hole among several identical holes in the artificial oak next to the door. "We have enough for a gamble."

"We have enough—"

"Kiss my ruddy bum," suggested Corinth. "Feng may be an asshole, but his teams get the job done." Feng smirked and inclined his head at the compliment, but no one noticed. She continued, "We have a chance now. You haven't given us diddly-squat." You must allow a certain freedom in translation here. In any case, Santiago sputtered and went out.

Carla said, "I'd as soon not sit here all day. We need someone to find a team leader to bring a team back through enough nexus points to get the job done without bollixing it up too badly, and do it all without letting Them turn our team into hamburger. Simply stated, the job will be to find out who the enemy is, why he is attacking, and get some idea on how to stop him. It is by definition impossible to stop him in the past, since he exists in the present. On the other hand the past may tell us how to stop him in the future.

"If this sounds like a slim chance, it is. The chance of our fleet defeating their fleet in direct combat is also slim, but we will be attempting that, too, if it comes to it. The chance of one of our human or machine spies learning something useful is also slim, but we will be trying that, too. We will attempt everything that has any reasonable chance, and perhaps one of them will work.

"The backtime will be six hundred and thirty-one years, the starting place will, of course, be Old Earth. Volunteer to find a team leader within twelve hours, or must I pick someone?"

Lois Brockingham of Charity around Biscane, in the near right chair, said, "Why doesn't Feng do it, if he's so bloody smart?"

Normally, reflected Feng, this would have gotten her selected on the spot by the others, but everyone was inclined to give her a break, as her home world had been Reduced a week ago. Her eyes showed no signs of tears, which was a credit to her cosmetician. Feng, who was an historian and research specialist, shrugged and said, "If I thought I was as qualified for field operations as Fredericka, I'd—"

"Forget it," said the representative from Grandview around Zenith. "I'm not—"

"Concerned about the destruction of all human life on thirty planets?" finished Feng nastily.

She paused. "As much as you are."

Feng bit back a reply as he stared into the old, yellow eyes. *A point there*, he thought suddenly.

Carla picked up on it at the same time. "Which of you," she said, "cares more about humanity than his own petty squabbles?"

"Or hers," said Brockingham.

"Betsy's tits and mittens," said Corinth. "*You* stay here and argue semantics. I'll find someone."

"Like hell you will," said Feng.

"Eh?" said Corinth and Carla at the same time.

"You don't have a Reduced chance, old lady. I'm going myself."

She stared at him. "Why?" she said at last.

He shrugged. "To prove that I have as much balls as you, maybe."

"You'll need—"

"An overlay. I know."

Corinth nodded. "Fair enough," she said.

Carla growled, but said nothing. Feng matched stares with her. *She probably planned this all along, the lizard. But then, if she did, it's probably for the best.* Aloud, he said, "I suppose you have the unrefined plans all set to appear before me, eh?"

"And everyone else," agreed Carla, as V-tab holograms sprang up around the room.

"Splendid," said Feng with an ironic bite, blinked the machine to life, and kick-wished the plans to unfold. Just to be contrary, he opaqued the back and sides. After a moment he said, "I suspect it's going to take me at least a week to prepare for the overlay so I don't—"

"We don't have a week," announced Delacroix with a calmness that was effective even if contrived. "Their fleet will be to us in one hundred and twenty to one hundred and thirty hours."

Corinth growled and threw another dart. There was little else to say. Eveleth was the last remaining bastion against Them. If Eveleth fell, it would be only hours before Broderick fell, then Marko, and then . . .

Feng licked his lips. "Nothing like a close finish," he said into the silence. "Very well. I'll schedule an overlay for the day after tomorrow."

"It'll probably improve him," muttered Brockingham.

Carla continued, "We have been out of touch with Old Earth for several hundred years, but we do retain definitive works of their culture from the period in which you will arrive. We have enough that the team le—that is, that you can be effectively prepared. You will speak like a native and think like a native in all of the small things, such as idioms and elements of popular culture, which are the things most likely to give you away. Put another way, you will be a native in every way, including how you think. Be aware that this will subject you to those underlying psychological factors that lead to those cultural elements."

"In other words," said Feng, "I'll talk like a native, but if I'm not careful, I might act like one, too. Got it. What else?"

"We have," said Carla, "military preparedness of a sort. We are ready in other ways. What we need is some means of attack. We have no idea what this might be, save that our indicators say there are nine nexus points where such a thing may be found. And, by the way, if you can help us reestablish contact with Old Earth, that would be a pleasant bonus."

"Got it," said Feng. "Any idea what I should look for in a team?"

Corinth snorted. "A doctor, for one."

"For research?" said Carla. "I would think—"

"No," said Feng. "She means to try to save the rest of the team after They discover we're there. I suspect she's right."

"You'd better find someone who knows the electronics of the era better than you do," said Carla. "We can't send much with you beyond the locators, and that is an area in which our knowledge is quite scanty."

"And," added Corinth, "find someone who can think well enough to tell the banana from the peel, and find the bastards, since I don't think you'd recognize a clue if it bit you. And remember that revealing who you are to *anyone* from the past creates a paradox, negating anything you might accomplish."

Feng nodded, ignoring the cut, and looked back at his V-tab, where clean red and amber lines blocked out his schedule of training in Earth culture and operation of the machine that would allow him, if he was lucky, to stay one step ahead of those who were determined to wipe out humanity, without creating one of those nasty paradoxes that would render the attempt impossible before it began. No problem. He winced.

"What is it?" said Santiago.

"I don't like having my personality overlaid. You'll understand if you ever develop a personality."

Carla tried to hide a chuckle, Corinth laughed aloud, Santiago looked half puzzled and half irate.

Feng sighed. "I might as well get on it. I'll be on my way. If I don't see you gentle souls again, it's either because I decided to stay back in the Light Ages, or because I blew it and you're all radioactive dust. Do the Job."

"Do the Job," echoed Old Lady Corinth, and one by one the others, except for Carla, who said, "Good luck, Richard."

Feng managed a smile. "Take care."

He left the conference chambers and signaled for transport. The pebbles hurt his bare feet, but he didn't let it show.

CHAPTER
17

What will you do
  When it's time to die,
Hey, ho my Johnny?
  "Johnny Is a Roving Blade,"
  Tommy Makem

The sad thing is, when surrounded by death, each one loses some degree of value. Don't hate me because I say it; I'm the reporter, not the agent. Well, perhaps I am the agent, too. But I deny responsibility, whatever. Death loses value, life loses value. Each death is a bit easier to take than the last, and in this is sorrow. Death, where is thy fang? Or Feng, if you wish.

But Souci—

This I had not expected, and were I not at least a little numb by this time, I might have broken. As it was, I waited for the tears, but they failed me.

Someone, I think Rose, got me back into the kitchen while Jamie and Christian held off Justin's friends. Tom and Libby stayed with Rose and me to watch the back door, which was still a large hole. The sounds of gunfire were harder to hear there, but they were present. I looked at Rudd and my mind reeled and spun,

210

and it was all too clear, and too dull, and too much, and too little, and too late.

I took the knife from under my arm and held the point beneath his chin. I said, "Physician, can you heal a cut throat?"

He glared at me. "Go ahead. You'll never find what you—"

"Shut your goddamned face." I brought my temper under control, barely, and walked a few steps away from him.

"Souci told you who I was, didn't she?"

"Yes."

"Is she dead?"

"Yes."

"Did you kill her?"

"In a manner of speaking."

He laughed without humor. "More fool she. I won't help, since no matter what you do, I will not tell you what you want to know. I have devoted my life to curing the human race of you diseased ones, and I will not fail now. It is just as well she died, and I thank you for that, at least."

I closed my eyes. Visions of Souci, lying on the floor, smoke and screams fighting for control of the airwaves, came and sat in the control booth of my mind. Would I ever be free of that memory, or would it always dominate and overwhelm the memories of our shared joys, and rob me of the chance to conquer our shared pain? I didn't know. Perhaps she would have come back to me, and I would never know that, either. But what I did know was that this—this *filth*—would not mock my pain.

I pointed my knife at his stomach, and I would have eviscerated him right then if there hadn't come a thump and a very peculiar sound from down the hall, which stopped me just long enough for another thought to grow. I said, "You'd like me to kill you, wouldn't you? Because you're afraid you'll break. Well, sweat, asshole." To Rose and Libby I said, "Watch him. If he tries anything, shoot him in the kneecap." I went down the hall toward the noise.

Tom was down at the end of the hall, and the noise had been the work he was doing, trying to cover over the doorway so they couldn't come around and get us from that direction. I poked my head out before he had it covered. It was quiet and the sun was setting once more. No one attacked me, or even looked at me, except for a few barnyard animals.

"Tom," I said.

"Yeah?"

"Hold off on that."

"What?"

I told him what I wanted him to do. He looked at me like I was nuts. "Do it," I said.

"If you say so." We went outside. He raised his pistol and shot the goat cleanly through the head. It fell over and flopped, twice. I felt absurdly bad about having killed it. "Now what?" said Tom.

"Help me drag it inside."

"Why?"

"We're going to break Rudd."

Together we dragged it into the kitchen, while occasional gunfire from the other room provided music to drag goats by. When we arrived in the kitchen, Rose said, "What is that?"

"A dead goat," I told her.

"That's what I thought it was."

"Libby, do you have your medical supplies with you?"

She turned her head to the side. "I think it's too late to save the goat."

"If we'd wanted him saved," I said, "we wouldn't have killed him."

"Whatever you say," said Libby. "What do you want?"

"A needle and syringe. Since the Physician here is so worried about Hags disease, I thought maybe we could inspire him by giving him a twenty-five percent case."

He stared. I stared back. "You do know that almost a quarter of all goats carry the Hags virus, don't you? In them, of course, it isn't fatal, but—you didn't know that? My, my. Where could you be from that you don't know that? Well, never mind. Tom, hold his arm still. Libby, draw some blood from the goat. Twenty cc's should do it."

"You're lying," said the Physician.

I shrugged. "If you wish."

Libby drew the blood and brought the needle over. Tom held the Physician's arm tight while I held him in place with an arm around his throat. He began to struggle. Libby stopped. "What is it?" I said. "We can't hold him here forever."

"Just a minute." She went back to her kit, found a cotton wad, and put some alcohol on it. She came back and rubbed this on his forearm. "Now," she said sweetly, "this may sting a little."

"*No!*"

"Tell me what I want to know."

"All right, you bastard. It's Proxima, the fourth—"

"Libby, give him the needle. He's lying."

She took her time approaching him, and I got to watch his face. At first, he had been glaring at me, now he was watching the needle as it got closer and closer, and we had to work harder and harder to keep him pinned. The point of the needle touched his arm. He screamed a scream like Poe must have imagined, which degenerated into unintelligible whimpering. I said, "Where is Sugar Bear's home base? Tell me quickly."

"Oh God . . ."

"*Tell me, you sonofabitch.*"

"Charity," he croaked. "Charity around Biscane."

I blinked, not really believing he'd answered me. "Well, son of a bitch," I said.

Libby said, "How do you know he's telling the truth?"

"I'll explain later."

"If you say so."

I turned to the Physician. "Okay, next question: How can we stop the missiles?" He shook his head. I repeated the question. He just sobbed.

I repeated it once more and he said, "You can't. I can't. They're only an hour or two away, and the transmitting equipment is on the other side of the planet."

"Can anyone else duplicate the transmitting equipment?"

"Not without the codes."

"Where are the codes?"

"With the equipment."

I closed my eyes and took two deep breaths. "All right. Libby, you're a paramedic; you know hospitals."

"Yeah."

"Go get Eve and meet us at Feng's. Be careful. Take a cab. Do you have money?"

"I've got money. But Billy, being a paramedic doesn't have a lot to do with getting someone out of a hospital."

"You'll find a way."

She smiled a bit, then held up her automag. "I'll use finesse," she said. She left out the back.

I said, "I still hear shooting. Rose, you and Tom go find out what's going on with Jamie and Christian. Don't get your head blown off. I have to think."

They walked out of the room. I turned away. I heard the Physician leap from the chair, and my knife was in my hand as I turned, and I stabbed him in the heart as he was reaching for my throat. I think I broke one of his ribs doing it. He grabbed me, his eyes wide and on a level with mine, his breath in my face, his fingers gripping my arms painfully.

"Thanks for doing the expected," I told him.

I owed him that for Rich. And Fred. And Souci. I would have told him that I'd made up all that stuff about the goat, but I didn't think of it. For his part, he didn't say anything. I let him fall, keeping a grip on the knife so it came free in my hand. He lay on the ground, curled up holding his chest. As he rolled over onto his stomach, I stabbed him in the kidney. Then I stabbed him again, and again. I remember my arm rising and falling, and I was detached, thinking this must have been how Libby felt, shooting Claude.

Eventually I became aware of the fact that he was no longer breathing. I chose not to administer CPR.

When I could see once more, Tom and Rose were back, staring at the body. I said, "Well?"

"It's like back at Feng's. There are six of them and we're sort of shooting into each other's general vicinity, and no one is hitting anyone."

"Why haven't they come around the back yet?"

"They're in that living room, completely inside the house, and they can't get back to the entryway without giving Jamie and Christian a good shot at them, so they're pretty well pinned down."

"Six of them," I said. "Let me think for a minute. Can we go around and get them from behind?"

"I'm sure they're watching for it. We'd take some losses, but we could do it—"

"Take some losses. Shit. All right. We'll do something else. Rose, tell Christian and Jamie to be ready to back up, carefully, when they smell smoke. Then get your ass out of here. And bring your fiddle. Tom, go around to the front, get as close as you can without letting them shoot at you, spill kerosene all over the entryway, and light it. Then go outside and shoot anyone who tries to get out the front way."

"What are you going to do?"

"I'll wait here for Christian and Jamie and Rose, in case there's any trouble."

"Take this, then," said Rose, and handed me her derringer. I accepted it. I still doubted I could hit anything, but now I knew I could kill.

Tom went out the back door, Rose headed toward the front. I waited, holding the pistol ready. The Physician's body was facedown, for which I was grateful.

I think it was forever, give or take a few minutes, before Rose returned. Christian and Jamie came backing into the kitchen about thirty seconds later. The cat came dashing out past our legs at about that time.

"Okay," I said. "Let's go."

Rose picked up her fiddle and we headed out the back hallway. I began to smell smoke. Jamie said, "What's to keep them from following us?"

"We'll wait just outside, and nail them as they come out."

"Six of them? That's a wide doorway. If they come out two at a time, shooting, they might get out."

"So, they get out."

"Then they kill us."

The air was cool and smelled of freedom, just as it had the last time I'd found myself fleeing from this house. I said, "Come up with a better idea, asshole."

"I got one," said Jamie. He had the sawed-off shotgun in his left hand, the .357 in his right. He said, "Catch you later," and ran back inside.

I cursed softly. "What the hell does he think he's doing?"

"Keeping them from coming after us," said Christian.

"By himself?"

"The hallway's narrow. He can hold them."

"Sure. For how long?"

"Just until the house collapses. That can't be too much longer."

Rose screamed Jamie's name, and, before we could stop her, followed him into the house. By this time we could see a red glow coming from the windows, and the yard was becoming warm. I heard what I think was a shotgun blast, followed closely by another. I started to follow Rose, but Christian hit me in the back of the head and I went down. I tried to get up and he knocked me down again. I might have tried to shoot him but the derringer went spinning away.

He said, "What do you want, motherfucker? Rose and Jamie, or the mission Feng set out to accomplish?"

"Fuck Feng," I said. "Fuck the future. Fuck humanity. Fuck you."

"Uh-huh."

Another pair of shotgun blasts, this time followed by others. I stayed there on my hands and knees while the house burned, and there was more shooting, until the heat forced us to back away. I heard shots for a while longer, then sirens in the distance, and I will swear as long as I live that I heard the sound of a fiddle playing an Irish reel, just before the roof collapsed, sending sparks high into the air, and leaving only a very large, glowing ember where the house had been.

I must have found Rose's derringer, because I was holding it in my hand when we arrived at Feng's. Carrie let us in. "What happened?" she said.

Neither Christian nor I could answer. Tom said, "Why didn't you go to the ship?"

"I thought I'd rather stay with you," she said.

Tom nodded and sat down, his face empty of all emotion.

Carrie said, "May I?"

Tom looked at me. I shrugged, nodded, and looked away. "Yes," said Tom.

"What happened?" repeated Carrie.

"It doesn't matter."

The door opened then, and Libby came in, escorting Eve. Eve looked tired and drugged, and her eyes were very red, but there were some signs of recognition on her face when she saw us. Libby sat her down in the booth nearest the door.

"How long do we have?" said Libby.

"Maybe a few minutes," said Tom.

Christian came and put his arms around Libby. "I'm glad you made it," he said.

"I'm glad you did. What happened to—no, never mind."

Christian nodded. There was no reason to talk about it. I walked over to the door and opened it. Tom said, "What are you—"

"Shut up," I said, I looked out at the street, which was pretty empty except for a pair of kids, two boys, maybe twelve, who were walking in front of Feng's. I remembered them from the day we'd arrived in New Quebec, parking their bicycles outside of a bakery that was now a mass of bullet holes. I glanced at it, and saw that repair work had been begun on the windows. Pitiful. I said, "Hey, come here a minute."

The kids looked at each other. "*Pardonnez?*" said one.

I gestured toward the inside. They looked suspicious, but, for whatever reason, came inside. As they did, an air-raid siren sounded from not far away. It sounded just like the ones back on

Earth, and the one in Ibrium City, and the one in Jerrysport. They hadn't changed at all. I shut and locked the door.

The two kids looked at each other and made for the door, but it could not be opened from the inside. They stared at us fearfully, but no one had any spare energy to try to reassure them.

I walked over toward the bar to have a drink, but the missile hit just at that moment, knocking me over. It was about as hard as the place had ever been hit, and the picture of Feng fell from its place and landed on the floor next to me. The glass that covered it shattered as the room shook and spun and I went down, and somewhere I heard the whine of a generator and Carrie screaming. I saw Tom holding her. The room tilted and a table or something hit me in the back of the head.

I found I was staring at the Chinese cowboy with the big, drooping mustache and the stupid grin.

I hate your guts, you know, I told it just before everything went dark.

EPILOGUE

So fill to me the parting glass.
Good night, and joy be with you all.
"The Parting Glass,"
Traditional

What can I say?

Two boys ripped from their homes, traumatized, but saved from the flames. They may never believe what happened, will almost certainly never understand, but at least they are alive. That was important to me. If you cannot understand this, I'm sorry.

I stood up amid the dust of the restaurant and looked around at those who were looking around at me and at each other. Libby in particular was watching me closely as she picked herself up. She had good reason. There was a thing called wonder in the air.

My memories seemed sharp and clear, and there was no fuzziness of my senses, after the first seconds of wakefulness. It might have been because we'd arrived at the Unit's home base, which might be significant to whoever wanted to study time travel. Not me. I wanted nothing to do with it, ever again. Jamie, my brother, Rose, my sister, dead now, forever gone, not even dust, not even—

"Anyone hurt?" I said.

No one was. I stepped over to a window, looked out, nodded. I walked back and noticed the broken picture. I ground it into the floor because I felt like it. I went into the bathroom, pulled the d-cleaner out of my wallet, and rubbed it on my face. The rest would wait, but I wanted my face back. When the pink was out, I took the skin-stick off and let my cheeks, eyes, and forehead resume their natural shape. That was enough for now.

When I came out of the bathroom, Libby was sitting at a table drinking from a bottle of Dom Perignon that she'd saved from the Earth. She said, "Would you like a glass, Feng?"

"Call me Billy," I said. "And no, thanks. I don't feel like celebrating just yet."

Tom, Carrie, and Christian stared at me. Libby said, "I thought they were going to figure it out there, when Jamie walked in while you were telling me to get the guns."

I nodded. "Me, too. You did a good job handling those questions about time travel and stuff, although you slipped once."

"I did? When?"

"They were asking about nexus points and you looked at me."

"Oh, sorry."

"Don't worry about it," I said. "One slip in that length of time is nothing. I'm sorry about Fred."

She looked away. "Yeah. Me too."

I studied the floor. Presently she said, "How did you know Rudd would go for that bluff, and that he was telling the truth?"

"It dawned on me that he was my counterpart—that is, he'd been sent from the future to stop me. Well, in my future— here—we've licked Hags disease with carbon-based nano machines which, um, skip it. If they were doing this because they were afraid of Hags disease, then they didn't know much about the disease, so I figured I could fake it. Besides, I'd bluffed him once before. And I knew because I recognized the name of the planet, and that made sense, too."

She nodded and returned to her champagne. "Sissy water," Rich had called it. But Rich was gone, along with Fred, and Rose, and Jamie, who had probably gone the way he would have wanted to, both guns blazing in a last stand.

What a crock.

Eve looked beyond stunned. I think she was. Christian was

beyond interest. Carrie was confused. Tom's mouth still hadn't closed, but I didn't feel like starting any explanations just then.

Libby said, "Was it hard, keeping everyone in the dark about who you were?"

It came to me that she was keeping me talking so I wouldn't dwell on Rose and Jamie. That was like her. I said, "No, I had to."

Tom's mouth finally closed. Then he said, "You mean all this time—"

"I recruited Rich, Libby, Fred, and Eve before the war, then spent all the time in London reading newspapers to find the cause for the thing. After we got here, which was our first breather since London, I gave up and set Eve to the job."

"But what did *you* do?"

"Directed the work, tried to keep us alive while Fred tracked down the saboteurs and Eve and Rich tried to guess who was doing what, and why. It wasn't until something Jamie said that I realized our enemy was likely to be whoever was behind the wars. That was really the first clue. I wish Jamie could know—" I stopped, shook my head, and looked away until I was under control.

"Wow," said Tom.

I laughed.

A few of them lived. Some may regret it now, some later, but they lived.

All of the universe, it seemed, had conspired to beat me into the ground, and yet I lived, and with me were five friends, plus two living reminders of New Quebec. And I had what the Committee wanted, needed. Tragedy is more real than the life that gives it birth, but I laugh in its face because there are two children from New Quebec who will hate me forever.

The door of Feng's opened, and I breathed the sharp, tangy air of Cicero once more. It was at this moment that I felt the sharpest, real sense of loss for New Quebec.

"Welcome back, Richard," said Carla.

"Thanks. Call me Billy."

"Did you—"

"The enemy," I said, "has one home world. It's Charity. Hit them there and it's all over."

"What? Brockingham's home world? But Charity's been Reduced, and—oh. Of course."

"Yes. A spy on the Committee, and move the home world to

easy striking distance of their enemy, then convince everyone the world was Reduced. It makes sense, doesn't it?"

"But how can they move the entire population?" said Carla.

"You'll understand when I give you all the details. The short version is this: The enemy cannot have a stable and large society. If he ever does, he will stop being the enemy. He has a culture based on paranoia, and it requires that he destroy major sections of his own population if there's no one else to destroy."

"I don't understand."

"I don't either, fully. But you'll have to take my word for it. Their entire culture is built on violence caused by fear of infection. The fear that leads to senseless violence is based on ignorance, which in turn leads to more senseless violence. I am certain that they have spent the last few hundred years building up societies and then leveling them, with a chosen few escaping every time. Keep alert for missiles, and attack their home world, and we can either force them to some sort of reasonable terms or destroy them. To be completely frank, I don't give a damn which it is."

Carla stared at me solemnly. "It was very difficult for you, wasn't it, Rich—Billy?"

There was a hard lump in my throat, but I managed to say, "Please, Carla. Charity around Biscane."

"Yes," she said. "We can have a fleet there in a matter of hours. We will decide what to do while the fleet is en route."

"And Brockingham?"

"I will deal with Lois."

"Good."

"Are you going to introduce me to your friends?"

"Perhaps later, Carla. Right now, these children have been taken from a world that is no more, and they need help. And I have bad news about Old Earth, by the way, but that can wait. Also, this is Eve. She needs help. Take them with you. Shut the door on your way out."

Her eyes widened, but she complied.

I cried.

Libby came and put her arms around me, and we held each other. Tom and Carrie had their arms around each other. I badly wanted things to work for them, but I certainly wouldn't make any bets one way or the other. Christian rubbed Libby's neck.

After a moment, I whispered, "I can't believe they're gone."

"I know," she said. "Neither can I. Any of them."

"Look." I held out the derringer that Rose had almost used to shoot down Iverness, the day Fred had died. Pearl-handled, dragon's head inlaid in ebony. "I'm going to keep it," I said. "I've always been the sentimental type."

"I know," said Libby. "But you did the job, anyway."

"Yeah," I said. "I Did The Job."

Tom cleared his throat. "Well, what now?"

"I don't know," I said. "I still have my banjo. You and Christian want to put together a trio?"

"What about me?" said Libby.

"You can be our manager."

Christian shrugged, and half smiled, but wouldn't commit himself to anything. Maybe he knew that there would be a ghost guitarist and a ghost fiddler in any such trio, and maybe that bothered him. Whatever, things would go as they went. Shit happens. I still had my banjo, so how bad could things get?

"Say, Libby?"

"Yeah."

"If I decide to keep the restaurant open, will you tend bar?"

She looked at Christian, who shrugged. She said, "Sure. You're easy to work for, for a pinhead."

"Maybe I'll do that, then. We'll see."

Tom and Carrie still held each other, oblivious. I sat in my favorite booth, and wished there was a band tuning up. Someday, there would be again.

Souci.

Ghosts from the past came to me the night the machine that looked like a bar and grille reappeared on Cicero around Marko, while the others slept. I thought about returning to Sestus, but I was in no hurry. Cicero was fine, and transportation was easy here and now. I badly needed perspective.

I looked back on the events since my arrival upon the soil of mankind's birthplace, and the voice of Rich, my first recruit and the first to die, came to me, soft and ironic, and biting and gentle, *I laughed, I cried, I fell down, it changed my life . . .*

Yeah, Rich. All of that. It changed my life, but didn't end it, and maybe I'd learned some useful skills. Whatever becomes of me now, I am richer, poorer, and carry a sorrow that I will never leave behind.

Souci.

We have the technology in my world to make you go away, or at least the sting of you, but I won't do that. I owe you this much, at least. In my own way, ghost that I love, I lay you to rest and bid you farewell. Maybe I'd write my memoirs, maybe I'd just play banjo.

I went back into the kitchen and, following my own recipe, made a batch of matzo ball soup.

It was good.

The End

Songs Quoted

"The Wild Rover"	Traditional
"The Work of the Weavers"	Traditional
"Jenny Say You're Mine"	Steven Brust
"The Beggarman"	Traditional
"Peggy-O"	Traditional
"Star of the County Down"	Traditional
"Bungle Rye"	Traditional
"Mrs. Rockett's Pub"	Words by Tommy Makem
"Another Time and Place"	Dave Van Ronk
"Move Along"	Ewan McCall
"Been There Before"	Adam Stemple
"Isn't It Grand, Boys?"	Traditional
"When I Was Young"	Traditional
"The Newry Highwayman"	Traditional
"Nancy Whiskey"	Traditional
"Johnson's Motor Car"	Traditional
"I'll Tell Me Ma"	Traditional
"Will Ya Go, Lassie, Go"	Robert Burns
"O'Donnell Abu"	Traditional
"More Thumbscrews"	Stephen Brust
"The Agricultural Irish Girl"	Traditional
"The Rapparee"	McGrath, Brett, O'Brian, English
"The Earl of Morray"	Traditional
"Brennon on the Moor"	Traditional
"Up the Long Ladder"	Traditional
"The Black Velvet Band"	Traditional
"The Wild Colonial Boy"	Traditional
"Red-Haired Mary"	Traditional
"Reily's Daughter"	Traditional
"I Know You Rider"	Traditional
"Johnny Is a Rovin' Blade"	Tommy Makem
"The Parting Glass"	Traditional

Note on Traditional Songs

The more astute among you may notice that many of the above songs are labeled "Traditional," which is supposed to mean they grew out of the ground, as it were, and appeared without the intervention of human beings in their creation. Others have the names of authors, which is supposed to mean that no one else has ever modified a melody note or a word, and that these songs must be performed precisely as transcribed, otherwise they aren't authentic.

Nevertheless, I suspect many of the traditional songs have actually been written by someone, somewhere, sometime. In a number of these cases, the author is known, by someone, somewhere. When I say a song is traditional, I mean that the author isn't listed in my handy-dandy deluxe edition *Folksinger's Wordbook,* by Fred and Irwin Silber (Oak Publications, 1973). Or in my Makem and Clancy songbook, or my *Folksongs of Ireland,* volumes 1 and 2, or any of the others I own or have looked through. This is not proof that no one knows the author. One of my books, for example, lists "Peter's Song" as traditional, while another one points out that Tom Sands wrote it in 1976.

What I'm getting at is: If anyone reading this should happen to know or to come across a source which gives authorship for any of the songs I've labeled "Traditional," I should be pleased to learn of it. Please let me know, in care of:

Ace Books
The Berkley Publishing Group
200 Madison Avenue
New York, NY 10016

I would be most grateful.

—Steven Brust, PJF

CLASSIC SCIENCE FICTION
AND FANTASY

ROBERT A. HEINLEIN
THE MODERN MASTER OF SCIENCE FICTION

___EXPANDED UNIVERSE	0-441-21891-1/$5.50
___FARNHAM'S FREEHOLD	0-441-22834-8/$3.95
___GLORY ROAD	0-441-29401-4/$3.95
___I WILL FEAR NO EVIL	0-441-35917-5/$4.95
___THE MOON IS A HARSH MISTRESS	0-441-53699-9/$3.95
___ORPHANS OF THE SKY	0-441-63913-5/$3.50
___THE PAST THROUGH TOMORROW	0-441-65304-9/$5.50
___PODKAYNE OF MARS	0-441-67402-X/$3.95
___STARSHIP TROOPERS	0-441-78358-9/$4.50
___STRANGER IN A STRANGE LAND	0-441-79034-8/$4.95
___TIME ENOUGH FOR LOVE	0-441-81076-4/$5.50
___THE CAT WHO WALKS THROUGH WALLS	0-441-09499-6/$4.95
___TO SAIL BEYOND THE SUNSET	0-441-74860-0/$4.95